"You won't be able t
to reach the
—Liv Constantine
author of *The Last Mrs. Parrish*

"An irresistible thriller, packed with
treachery and deceit."
—Samantha Downing, internationally bestselling
author of *My Lovely Wife*

"A wicked, clever, and highly entertaining read!"
—Wendy Walker, bestselling author of *All Is Not Forgotten*

"Scheming mean girls, sex and scandal,
secrets and lies, all wrapped up in Buckhead privilege and
opulence—what's not to love?
One of Us Is Dead is wicked, twisty, thrilling
fun from the first page to last."
—Lisa Unger, *New York Times* bestselling author
of *Last Girl Ghosted*

"Scandalous and explosive...
A devilishly fun romp."
—Kimberly Belle, internationally bestselling
author of *My Darling Husband*

ONE

OF US

IS

DEAD

ONE OF US IS DEAD

JENEVA ROSE

BLACK STONE
PUBLISHING

Printed in the United States of America
Originally published in hardcover by Blackstone Publishing in 2022

First paperback edition: 2023
ISBN 979-8-212-18474-8
Fiction / Thrillers / Suspense

Version 2

Blackstone Publishing
31 Mistletoe Rd.
Ashland, OR 97520

www.BlackstonePublishing.com

To my husband,
Drew, who said the first dedication to him didn't count
because my real name wasn't on the cover.
I hope this one counts, my love.

1

JENNY

PRESENT

"I've spent thousands of hours working on these women. I've primped, waxed, cut, painted, spray-tanned, powdered, and massaged them. I know almost every inch of their bodies. But I also know their demons—their deepest, darkest secrets. The things we try to bury beneath the surface so as not to show the world the doppelgänger lurking within us. So, am I surprised something like this happened? Not even in the slightest. I figured it would. It was just a matter of time." I readjust myself, crossing one leg over the other beneath the table.

Across from me sits Detective Frank Sanford, a stern-looking middle-aged man with hard facial features and broad shoulders. He's your classic blue-collar detective. Despite the suit and tie he's wearing, his appearance is anything but polished and put together. His red-rimmed eyes give away the fact that he works far too many hours and gets far too little sleep. We have more in common than he'll ever know.

"How do you know their deepest, darkest secrets, Jenny?

1

I mean, are you their therapist too? I thought you were a hair stylist," Detective Sanford asks, jutting out his chiseled chin covered in stubble. His eyes tighten, staring intently at me as he pauses his note-taking and waits for an answer. We're sitting across from each other in a well-lit interrogation room. The air is stale and cold, and I can't tell if the room is trying to match the aura of the detective or the other way around.

"I'm both, in a way. I don't know how much time you've spent inside salons, Detective Sanford, but women talk." I cross my arms in front of my chest, holding his gaze. "Especially when they're sitting in a salon chair with nothing but time on their hands."

I know this man has never set foot inside a salon, and not just based on his own level of self-care. The truth is, I know more about my clients than I do my own family, especially *this* group of women. I see each of them multiple times a week. They have cash to burn—or at least their husbands do—and they can afford to pour resources into fighting the greatest war of their lives: the one against the effects of time on the human body.

"I see, and you're the owner of Glow Beauty Bar, correct?" He gently taps his pencil on the table.

"The one and only." I nod.

He picks his pencil back up and jots down a couple more notes, careful not to miss anything.

"And how long have you owned the salon?"

My eyes wander for a moment as I recall when I purchased it. "About five years now."

"And have these women been your clients the whole time?" He creases his brow.

"No. They didn't become my clients until around three years ago. Glow wasn't always the salon it is today."

He writes down a couple more notes and circles something

on the paper. I catch a glimpse of the words within the circle: *Glow Past?*

"I see. So, you've known these women for three years, and you're not surprised that any of this happened?" He raises his thick, dark eyebrows.

"No. Don't let them fool you, Detective. Individually, they're genuine and they can be kind . . . but when you put them in a room together, these women are downright toxic."

2
JENNY

THREE WEEKS BEFORE THE MURDER

Olivia plopped her tight, skinny ass in my chair and dropped her oversized Hermes bag on the ground. Her long, lush mahogany hair brushed my face as she tossed it over her shoulder without a care. Thanks to me, it was full of the perfect number of lowlights and highlights. She was dressed in a red jumpsuit that left little to the imagination. Olivia always wore red in some variation, whether it was her whole outfit, a bold lip, or an eye-catching accessory. Red was her power color, her security blanket. And she'd never be caught dead walking in anything other than a pair of red-bottomed Louboutin's.

As I wrapped a freshly cleaned cape around her, Olivia stared at herself in the mirror with pure and utter admiration. She turned her head from side to side observing her perfectly sculpted nose, overinjected plump lips, and high cheekbones. If a brown-haired Barbie doll were blown up to life-size, it would look just like Olivia. I could tell she was pleased with her appearance as she gave herself a slight smirk, revealing veneers so bright they could challenge a hundred-watt light bulb. I'd been her hairstylist, makeup artist, nail technician, waxer, tanner, lash artist, and so much more for years, and as time progressed, I had noticed that her lips kept getting plumper, her cheekbones higher, and her skin smoother. Like tectonic plates, her face was always shifting.

"What are we doing today?" I asked as I gently ran a comb through her soft hair while looking at her in the mirror. I already knew what she wanted, but Customer Service 101 dictates you always let the client tell you what they want. So I waited for her to tell me. She held up her finger at me while she typed vigorously into her phone.

Olivia and I were opposites in every way. While her hair was dark and long, mine was strawberry blond, wavy, and fell right at my shoulders. Her facial features were hard and cutting. Mine were soft and rounded. Her eyes were rich like milk chocolate. Mine were a cool blue. Her face was free of any beauty marks, while mine was speckled with freckles. She set her phone in her lap, briefly looked at me, and then returned her gaze to the single most important thing in Olivia's life: Olivia.

"Roots and trim, and I'll need a wax. Dean is coming home tonight." There was a sparkle in her eye and a bit of giddiness in her voice, like a schoolgirl talking about her first crush. Dean and Olivia Petrov had been married for over a decade, and it surprised me that they still had a flame of passion between them. Then again, toxic relationships are great for extreme highs and lows.

"Well, then, we'll have to make sure you're absolutely perfect for him."

"I'm already perfect for him," Olivia snarked.

I smiled and nodded. I had learned over the years that this was the best way to handle difficult clients, and Olivia held the title of the *most* difficult.

"But you always make me better than perfect," she added.

Olivia had a true talent for complimenting herself before she complimented others. She was the same with kind words and insults. I coined the term "kinsults" thanks to her. It was like she had created a cruel language all her own. You wouldn't even realize she was insulting you, because they were wrapped up like a present, complete with a nice bow.

The best part about my job was making women feel good about themselves. I loved the way their faces lit up after I was finished with them. "Beauty glow" is what I liked to call it, hence the name of my salon, Glow Beauty Bar. Olivia was one of those rare clients that always had that glow, so it wasn't as fun making her over, but she tipped well and her beauty treatments had single-handedly paid off the mortgage on my apartment above the salon.

"What do you and Dean have planned tonight?" I asked.

Olivia looked up from her phone. "A little of this and a little of that." She winked.

She always thought she was so cryptic, but her text messages revealed exactly what she was up to tonight. I nodded and returned to mixing up the dye.

"I love your freckles, Jenny. But have you ever considered wearing a full-coverage foundation?" Olivia's eyes scanned my face.

Kinsult.

"I used to, but freckles are in," I said with a smile. "Women even draw them on now."

She shrugged and returned her eyes to her phone, scrolling through her highly edited Instagram photos. "If you say so."

Although I loved where my business was at now, sometimes I thought it was easier in the old days. I never used to have to deal with high-maintenance clients. I opened Glow Beauty Bar five years ago. It had always been my dream to own a boutique full-service salon, but things weren't as glamorous as I had hoped. I started off with peeling paint and a hodgepodge of used furniture and old salon equipment, and the client list consisted of errant old women that would wander in off the street. I continued to struggle until one day, about three years ago, Olivia came into my salon with a hair emergency. Apparently, her regular hairstylist had up and moved to New York City, so she tried out another salon that completely botched her dye job. I was her saving grace. She got word out to her elite friends about me, and my salon transformed from a barely-making-it-by cheap salon to a full-service beauty bar for the upper-class women of Buckhead. I added two tanning beds, a spray tan machine, a pedicure and manicure area, a waxing room, a makeup bar, a sitting area, and a wine and champagne bar. Basically, anything they wanted, I delivered. There's a waiting list to even become a client here now, and I only accept twenty-five full-time clients. By full-time, I mean my clients agree to have a minimum of eight services a month. If they fail to do so, they're terminated as a client, or at least relegated to the waiting list. It's very exclusive and very expensive.

"Are you adding facials anytime soon?" Olivia pulled at her skin. It didn't move. Her face never moved, thanks to her frequent Botox sessions.

"I hadn't considered it," I said.

"This is exactly why you need me. Someone to think about the bigger picture. You should hire an aesthetician. Some of your clients are going to be in serious need of antiaging treatments soon, like Shannon." Olivia attempted to raise an eyebrow, but instead, her eyes half squinted.

I gave her a small smile and directed my focus back to her hair. Olivia thought she was the sole owner of Glow. Unfortunately, she was an angel investor, but I hoped that within three years I'd buy her share out. She was far too demanding. I was grateful she had saved the salon, but in a way, she had used it to propel her social status. This place had become my clients' personal hangout, their home away from their mansions. Olivia and her friends treated it like their own living room, hosting book clubs, wine nights, hangouts for gossip, and committee meetings.

Her phone vibrated, and she picked it back up, typing vigorously. I read texts here and there as I began applying the dye to her roots. If my clients weren't talking to me, they were making calls or texting. Always fearful of missing out on the next hot piece of gossip. It was hard not to pay attention, not to put things together, not to figure out what was happening among these women.

"So, where has Dean been?" I asked.

The second-best part of my job was chatting with my clients. They told me everything—sometimes not intentionally, but they did. Their hopes, dreams, failures, worries, problems, insecurities . . . everything. I really enjoyed getting to know them. I liked feeling like I was a part of their lives, even if I wasn't. It made work feel less like work and more like I was just hanging out every day. I was good at asking questions, and I was great at listening. I hated any attention on me, so it was a good match, because my clients loved to talk, especially about themselves.

"Oh . . . ummm . . . actually, I'm not sure," she said. "He's like a stray dog sometimes. Can't keep track of him," she added with a laugh.

Olivia and Dean were two of the most influential and powerful people in Buckhead, so for them, it was all about keeping up appearances. Even though I had known her for three years, I didn't have a clue what Dean did for a living, and I don't think she did either. As long as she kept getting her allowance,

I don't think she cared. Rumor had it that he was into some sort of shady smuggling business, but if you asked him, he'd tell you it's supply chain.

"Speaking of stray dogs, are there any in *your* life?" She smiled.

I continued to paint her roots with the rich dye, which smelled like ammonia. It wasn't a smell most people liked, but I did. It was comforting.

"No, none for me. This salon is my life." I glanced around, taking it all in.

Five years from its inception, Glow is now clean and modern with hardwood floors throughout, exceptional track lighting, and the newest and most expensive salon equipment. There are black velvet floor-to-ceiling curtains separating the reception area from the rest of the salon. No one gets past those curtains unless you're a client or an employee. Nonclients speak of this place like it's the throne room at Buckingham Palace.

"Oh, sweetie. You can't make a building your whole life," she said with a chuckle. "And that says a lot, coming from me. I'd sell my soul for a Crocodile Birkin. Oh, you probably don't even know what that is, which is for the best. You have simpler things to focus on."

Kinsult.

I gave a tight-lipped smile and began trimming her ends. She had just had a trim last week, so it was quite unnecessary, but she was the one with the Black AmEx. Her phone buzzed again, and I glanced down, seeing it was a text from someone named *Bryce's Midlife Crisis.*

"Sorry, Jenny. I completely forgot I have to grab lunch with the ladies today. How long is this going to take?" She bounced her foot quickly.

"Thirty minutes for the hair, but waxing will take another thirty."

"Well, we'll have to skip the wax for now. Gotta make nice with the new wife." Her voice was laced with sarcasm.

"New wife?"

"Crystal Madison, new wife of Bryce—and if you ask me, a major upgrade from Shannon." She smirked.

"Yeah, I heard Bryce left Shannon for a younger woman. They just married, right?"

Bryce was a US congressman, and he served on a committee for trade. There were rumors swirling of infidelity two months before his reelection campaign ended. He barely got reelected. Right after he was voted back in, he left Shannon and married Crystal, spinning the whole thing with the press as though he was stuck in a loveless marriage and finally found true love. I assumed he planned it out nicely to give himself enough time to repair his image before the next election.

"Have you met Crystal yet?" She shot me a quick glance in the mirror.

"Nope, haven't had the pleasure." I shook my head.

"You probably won't, she's real country," she said putting a little twang in it. Olivia always tried to hide the slow drawl of her thick Georgia accent under some odd combination veneer of Upper West Side Manhattan meets Midwestern news anchor, but once in a while her country would come out, to her great dismay.

"Not into the glitz and glam of Buckhead?" I brushed out the ends of Olivia's hair and checked the time on the dye.

Buckhead is a wealthy uptown district of Atlanta. It doesn't sound all that nice with a hard name like Buckhead, but to give you an idea, the average home costs well over $800,000. It's known as "the Beverly Hills of the East."

"Not at all. Don't get me wrong. She's beautiful, a real Jessica Simpson look-alike. But I don't think she'll be a regular of yours.

Too all-natural and fresh-faced for my taste, and she's young, like twenty-five." Olivia rolled her eyes. Olivia didn't like young, because she wasn't anymore. She would never be one of those women that aged gracefully. She would fight it tooth and nail.

"Much younger than Bryce," I noted.

"Oh, yes. Shannon was probably most mad about that. You know, her husband trading her in for a younger woman. But Bryce is all about trade," Olivia said pointedly with a chuckle.

"I bet that hasn't been easy for her. How's she holding up?" I gestured Olivia to a sink. She sat down and leaned her head back as I gently rinsed out her hair.

"Don't know. Don't care," she said flippantly.

"Well, you two are friends," I said a little louder to speak over the sound of the water and because I was also shocked to hear Olivia hadn't checked up on Shannon after everything she had been through.

"Correction: *were* friends. I have to distance myself from *that*. Shannon is a sinking ship in this town. Sure, she has alimony, but Bryce has all the influence and power."

My eyes grew wide as I processed what she had said. Olivia and Shannon had been close, and to learn they weren't any longer because her husband left her was a shock. At that moment, I knew something wasn't right. The balance in the group wasn't the same. It was like when all the wind stops and the sky turns bright, right before the storm explodes.

I hadn't seen Shannon this month yet, and she was close to getting terminated as a client. She had seven days to come in for eight treatments, and I had intended to give her a little wiggle room, but it was clear Olivia wanted her out. I made a mental note to call Shannon that afternoon to remind her.

"That's a shame to hear. I feel bad for her," I said.

"Don't! Shannon was never that nice a person anyway. She

was awful to me, and I had to practically force her to become a client of yours. She thought this place was beneath her . . ." Olivia twisted up her nose.

A slight frown spread across my face as I patted Olivia's hair dry with a towel.

"Oh. Don't let it bother you too much. Shannon's just a bitch every day." Olivia waved her hand dismissively.

"I'm not bothered by it. She's been through a lot." I walked Olivia back to the hair station.

"Well, she's a has-been, and it won't look good for business to have her here. She's just a reminder of how far the mighty can fall. It's sad, really." Olivia pulled out her phone and began scrolling through her thousands of selfies while I blow-dried her hair.

I had loyalty to all my clients, even the worst of them. I never minded listening to the drama between the women. I understood that people needed to vent and not everyone got along all the time, but I never wanted to be pulled into the middle of it. I'd listen, but I refused to participate. However, that's the thing about drama: participation isn't always required.

Olivia typed up a text to a group named Buckhead Women's Foundation. I read the words as her bony fingers pecked at the keys. Things were about to get bad.

The front door chimed just as I finished fluffing Olivia's hair with my fingers. It was perfect. The volume and shine made it look like she just walked out of a shampoo commercial.

"Go on back," Mary, the salon's receptionist, said from the front.

Olivia stood up and admired herself once more in the mirror, puckering her lips and ensuring every strand of hair was in place.

Karen Richardson emerged from behind the curtains. She had a shoulder-length bob of red hair that looked like the glowing warmth of fresh coals on the bottom of a campfire. She was a loyal client, a luxury real estate lawyer, and a close friend of Olivia's—well, as close as one can get in Buckhead. She was thin and wispy, without an ounce of fat on her. With her concave cheeks, flat wide jaw, and large toothy smile, she looked more like a runway model than a mother or a Realtor.

Karen directed her attention to Olivia. "Did you just call an emergency committee meeting?"

Olivia turned and faced Karen, her hair whooshing over her shoulder dramatically. "Yes. Don't worry, it won't take long."

"And why is it at the café instead of here?"

"I figured it'd be easier since we're meeting Bryce's midlife crisis afterward for lunch." Olivia gave a small smile.

Karen sighed and hesitated for a moment like she was trying to read Olivia.

"What's the meeting about?" she said, putting a hand on her hip.

"You'll find out when you arrive."

Olivia turned toward me. "Thanks so much, Jenny. You're the best!" She planted two light kisses on either side of my face, grabbed her bag from the floor, handed me a one-hundred-dollar bill as a tip, and walked out glowing, my specialty.

"She's too much sometimes." Karen shook her head and watched Olivia strut out of the salon.

"But not all the time," I said with a smile. Peacekeeping was also a part of my job, and it seemed one of my biggest responsibilities going forward.

"Shall we?" I gestured with my hand toward the back, and we walked to the spray tan room.

Karen stripped down naked quickly. There was no awkwardness as I had spray-tanned her over a hundred times before and by now it was all routine. I knew her body better than I knew my own. Every freckle. Every scar.

"Big day for you. Emergency committee meeting and lunch with the ladies."

"God. Don't remind me." Karen let out a huff of annoyance. I grinned.

Karen smiled as I continued to spray her milky white skin a light bronze color. "I'm not sure what Olivia is up to, but I'm sure it's no good. And you've heard about Crystal, right?"

I nodded.

"I haven't met her in person yet. But I feel like I'm betraying Shannon by being welcoming to her."

"Have you talked to Shannon about it?"

"Yes, but not about Crystal. Shannon's been a mess, and I didn't even mention that I was getting lunch with her and Olivia." Karen turned to the side just as I finished spraying the front of her.

"Maybe you should talk to her about it. Shannon, that is."

"I should, but if she has an issue with it, there's not a lot I can do." Karen turned and I sprayed her back. "I have a business that I have to run, and I run it professionally. You understand that?"

I nodded because I understood better than anyone. Karen wasn't like the other wives. She had a young son, and she didn't depend on her husband for money. Although, as a plastic surgeon, he brought in plenty. But Karen had built a real estate empire from the ground up, and she'd become so successful that she had an entire team behind her, so all she had to do was sweep in and close the deals.

"And then obviously, we have to welcome Crystal into our circle, since she's married to Bryce, and in this town it's all about who you know, what you wear, how you look, and how much money and power you have." Karen sighed.

"You don't have to remind me." I laughed.

"Oh stop." She patted my shoulder. "You are the 'it girl' of this town."

"Just no one knows it," I gave a crooked smile and handed her a towel.

"Oh, honey, but they will."

3
OLIVIA

"Perfect. Everyone is here." I glanced at each of the women sitting around a table in a private room of a nice café. A large smile was plastered across my face. I couldn't help it. I had waited years for this. We were the board of the Buckhead Women's Foundation. We were the elite because we planned the hottest events for some charity or other. Everyone wanted to be us.

Karen raised an eyebrow at me. "Shannon isn't here."

"That's right. Because this is about her," I said, lifting my chin.

Sophie, the secretary, sat to the left of me, writing down everything I said like I was Shakespeare himself. She was a nice person to have in line behind me, but she'd never be a part of my inner circle. Sure, Sophie was wealthy, but aside from that, the only thing she had to offer was note-taking. Plus, she was as bland as a box of unsalted saltine crackers. Her appearance matched her personality . . . boring.

Tina, the treasurer, flipped through her ledger. Each flip of the page blew a whiff of that musky, disgusting perfume she always wore. Even though she was rich, she smelled poor. If Tina weren't so hard to look at, we'd certainly be close. But she had started her plastic surgery journey before it was perfected and with a surgeon that was less than skilled. As a result, it looked as though her skin would slide right off her face into her lap. My eyes could only take so much.

"Tina, your skin is glowing," I complimented. "I can barely notice the lack of elasticity today."

"Olivia, you're too kind," she said with a smile.

"And Sophie, your outfit is so you. I could never pull that off."

Sophie looked down at her plain white tee. "I'm sure you could, Olivia. Everything looks good on you."

"You're right. Shall we get started?"

Tina and Sophie nodded. Karen leaned back in her chair and tilted her head. I didn't have to get her on board for this decision. I just needed two votes, and I had them.

"Buckhead Women's Foundation emergency committee meeting is now in session," Sophie said.

"Great. So, the reason I called you all here today is out of concern. We all know Shannon has been going through an extremely tough time. My heart hurts for her." I placed my hand against my chest and made my face sympathetic. It was my least favorite facial expression.

Tina and Sophie nodded again. Karen sat forward in her seat.

"I'm calling a motion for Shannon to step down as chairwoman. All in favor?"

Sophie and Tina started to put their hands up.

"Hold on! This isn't right," Karen practically yelled. *So unladylike.*

Sophie and Tina quickly put their hands down. *Cowards.*

"No, Karen. What isn't right is our events and charities suffering like Shannon is." I kept my voice calm.

"How are they suffering?" Karen's eyes went wide.

"Sophie, please read out those that were missing from the last two meetings," I instructed.

She nodded and flipped through her notes. "Shannon."

"I rest my case," I said with a tight smile.

"But she's been planning the upcoming gala just fine. I've relayed everything she had to say at those meetings," Karen argued.

"A leader leads, Karen. She doesn't relay through the PR chair." I shook my head.

"Olivia's right," Tina cut in. "I don't even have the finances updated because she hasn't gotten them to me."

"And it's not fair that I have to mark her absent. I get enough hand cramps as it is with all the note-taking," Sophie added.

I nearly rolled my eyes. Her argument was weak and boring like herself. We had rehearsed this.

"I don't want to be the bad guy here." *Yes, I do.* "But according to our bylaws, two or more meetings missed by a board member without a proper reason is grounds for dismissal from their position," I said. That was what Sophie was supposed to say.

"Yes, that's right." Sophie flipped through her folder and pushed a piece of paper in front of Karen.

Karen quickly read it over and looked back at me. "Isn't divorce a proper reason?"

"No. It's not in the bylaws," I said.

"We didn't include it because it's so common these days," Tina said. "Some of our regular members are on divorce number three, but members get more leeway than the board."

Karen let out a groan. "Can't we make an exception?"

In unison, I and my two minions shook our heads. "It's a slippery slope, Karen. So, motion to remove Shannon as chairwoman?"

Tina, Sophie, and I raised our hands.

"All opposed?" Karen raised her hand.

"Okay, it's settled. Shannon Madison is no longer chairwoman of the Buckhead Women's Foundation. Don't worry, Karen. She is still a member, and she can always run again at the next election," I said with a smile.

Sophie quickly wrote it all down in the meeting notes.

"I'd like to make a motion," Tina said.

Good girl.

"Motion to make Olivia Petrov chairwoman. All in favor."

I shot up my hand so fast I nearly dislocated my shoulder. Tina and Sophie followed suit. Karen let out a deep breath.

"All opposed," Tina said.

Karen didn't even raise her hand. *Defeated.*

"This is bullshit," Karen said.

"No, it's business, which is basically the same thing," I said with a lighthearted laugh. "How about this? We're only a week away from the gala, and Shannon has worked so hard on the event. It should be her last event as chairwoman. We'll make the announcement to the rest of the members at the following meeting. How does that sound?" I cocked my head and upped my smile a few notches, not too big, not too small.

Karen pulled her lips in and thought for a moment. It was a nice offer. Actually, it was rather kind of me. I was playing the long game. You had to sprinkle some kindness in there.

"Okay. That gala means a lot to her, so that's fair," she said, pushing out her full lips.

"I'm glad you feel the same way. We do have a vice-chairwoman position to fill, so we'll take nominations at the next meeting and vote the meeting after. Everyone good with that?" I asked.

Nods all around.

"Here you are," the server said. "Four cucumber mint detox drinks." She placed one in front of each of us.

I held mine up for a cheers to myself, of course. "I figured we needed to cleanse ourselves too," I said with a laugh.

Tina and Sophie chuckled too, as they should.

"Cheers to the end of suffrage and to a new beginning with a new leader." I clinked my glass against Tina and Sophie's. Karen just brought hers to her lips and sucked the whole thing down, clearly unhappy with the decisions made. But she'd get over it. After all, she wasn't like me. She was a forgive-and-forget kind of person. I, on the other hand, always believed there was another option on the table. Forgive, forget, or fucking never let it go.

4
KAREN

I left the private room of the café in a huff. Shannon would be furious, maybe with me too. But there wasn't much I could do with Olivia blindsiding me, while Tina and Sophie lacked the backbone and brains to stand up to her. Had she been planning this all along? Technically, Olivia was right. Bylaws were bylaws, and Shannon had been absent at the past two meetings. But still. The whole thing didn't sit right with me.

I walked through the café and found Crystal already seated at a table waiting for Olivia and me. I'd seen photos of her on social media from doing a little stalking with Shannon while deep into a few bottles of wine, but she was much prettier in person. She sat with her legs crossed, wearing a floral summer dress, at a round table adorned with expensive glassware, fresh tulips, and a white linen cloth. Her long blond hair had natural waves throughout and she was tan—not like me, a tan from being outside. She had a different glow to her. She was fresh-faced and beautiful in an effortless way. I could see what Bryce saw in her.

I approached the table, and she seemed uncertain as to who I was. She clearly hadn't done her research.

"Crystal?"

"Yeah, that's me." She smiled. Her voice was full of Texas.

I held out my hand. "I'm Karen Richardson. It's great to meet you."

She stood from the table and gave me a hug instead. I expected her to be giddy, but she had a calm demureness to her. She was pleasant. I wanted to hate her for Shannon's sake, but I couldn't—at least not yet.

I took a seat at the table, setting my bag on the chair beside me and ordering a Chardonnay from the server. I didn't normally drink on a weekday at lunch, but after that committee meeting, I needed something stronger than celery juice.

"So, how's Buckhead treating you?" I asked, knowing she had only been in the area for a couple of months and was just now putting herself out there in the community. She'd been a recluse while she settled in. I didn't blame her. Most of the women immediately didn't like her, since she had stolen Shannon's husband.

"Fine so far, just trying to get a feel and understanding of the town." She fidgeted with her napkin, wringing it up and then flattening it out.

"Oh, honey, I've lived here for over a decade and I still don't feel like I understand this town," I said with a laugh.

She laughed too. "Got any advice?"

"Just be patient. People will come around." I took a sip of my wine. I could see her loosen up a little. She was clearly nervous and didn't want to be here. I assumed Bryce had pushed her into making nice with us. He was all about fixing his reputation after leaving Shannon.

"So, what do ya do?" Crystal asked.

"I drink." I took a sip of my wine.

Her eyes went wide for a moment.

"I'm kidding."

She took a gulp out of her pint glass. It was a beer. I hadn't even noticed she was drinking beer. I knew then that I liked her. The women around here drank blended vegetables, champagne, wine, or vodka. They never drank beer.

"Seriously, though." I set my drink down. "I run my own luxury real estate firm, and I have a five-year-old son named Riley." I grabbed my phone and showed her a couple pics of my wild little man, a lanky boy who looked like a perfect cross between Mark and me. He had my eyes and nose but Mark's hair and height.

"He's precious," Crystal gushed.

"Yeah, he's my world." I put my phone back in my purse. "Do you have any kids?" I knew she didn't, but I wanted to gauge if she wanted them—if she and Bryce had talked about having any. I don't know if I was asking for myself or for Shannon.

"Gosh no. I'd love to have a few someday, but not for a while. Don't think I'm ready for that."

"I'm sure Bryce is more than ready." I didn't know why I said it. It was a dig, a small one for Shannon. It would be my last, I told myself. Crystal was nice. There was no reason I should hate her. She let out a small awkward cough.

"And you run your own real estate business. That's impressive," she said, sounding truly genuine.

"Thanks. I built it from the ground up when I first moved here. I wanted to have something of my own, and it's gotten so successful that it doesn't take up as much of my time anymore. I'm more the face of it now. I make the appearances and close the deals." I smiled at her.

"I'd love to do that someday . . . ya know, have something of my own." She took a small drink of her beer.

I sipped my wine, and at that moment, I spotted Olivia walking across the restaurant. She was late as usual, which made no sense because she was already at the café. But that was Olivia. And she had changed since our meeting. She was now dressed in a tight, scarlet dress that was the perfect mix of classy and sexy. Olivia had mastered "clexy," as she coined it.

"So sorry I'm late." Olivia took a seat at the table. "Hi, I'm Olivia Petrov."

She and Crystal hugged and introduced themselves. Olivia ordered a Chardonnay and a salad. I ordered a salad as well, and Crystal ordered a burger with fries. Olivia squinted her eyes at her order, clearly judging her and hating her at the same time. Crystal was twenty-five. She could get away with eating whatever she wanted. Olivia and I were in our midthirties; we had to save our calories for our wine.

As Olivia and I nibbled our salads and sipped our glasses of wine, Crystal took large mouthfuls of beer and massive bites of her burger. Olivia watched her as if she were watching a caged animal at the zoo, a curious yet pitiful creature.

Crystal let out a small burp. "Excuse me."

She dabbed the corners of her lips and then continued eating. She was at least trying to fit in, but a Texas girl can't just throw out her cowboy boots and lasso. She tried to sit up straight, copying the way Olivia was sitting, but every minute or so her shoulders would slouch, and she'd have to reposition herself. We sat in silence, focusing on the food in front of us and exchanging quick glances and small smiles. I didn't know what to say. It was awkward. Not my idea of a fun afternoon. It was Olivia who finally broke the silence.

"So, you and Bryce . . . How did you two meet?"

Of course, Olivia was going to go there. Straight to the

gossip. I would have said it was inappropriate, but I was curious myself. How did a girl like Crystal meet a man like Bryce?

Crystal set down her burger and wiped her mouth with a napkin. She cleared her throat. "At a bar in Texas I was working at. He was in town for some business thing, and we hit it off." There was a twinkle in her eye, not in a malicious way but in a loving way. She clearly cared for Bryce.

"Did you know he was married?" Olivia smirked. "I'm not judging you," she added, as if that made her question less inappropriate.

Crystal darted her eyes at both of us while she bit at her lower lip. She chugged the rest of her beer and set the pint glass down with force. "I'm just going to lay this out there because I don't want it to be a thing any longer. I didn't at first. He didn't tell me right away, and when he did, I had already fallen in love with him. I'm not that type of woman, but I guess in a way, I am. And I feel bad for Shannon. I never intended this to happen, but it did. I met a man, and I fell in love with him. I'm not sorry for that, and I don't think I should be." She said it all in one breath as if she had practiced it countless times before. Crystal looked at each of us for our approval.

"No need to be sorry," Olivia said, giving Crystal the support she was seeking. It was obvious Olivia didn't mean it. "When you know, you know," she added.

Olivia winked at me. I wasn't sure why she was winking at me, but I gave her a smile anyway. Buckhead was all about smiles. You smiled when you were pissed, and you smiled when you were pleased.

"I just want to lay this out there too. I'm friends with Shannon, but I want to be cordial with you as well. I hope that you can understand, and I hope Shannon can too." I felt entirely guilty for being there. My loyalty was and should've been with Shannon.

"I understand." Crystal nodded. "And I respect that."

I smiled at her, a pleased smile that is.

Olivia tossed down her napkin and drank the rest of her wine. "I don't. I'm done with Shannon, and you should be too."

I tilted my head and furrowed my brow. "Was taking her position as chairwoman not enough?"

"No. Do you not remember the way she used to treat me when I first arrived in Buckhead?" Olivia lifted her chin. She took a sip of her freshly poured glass of wine.

"No, and besides, that was a long time ago." I rolled my eyes.

"The bully forgets they're a bully. The victim never does. Besides, she's a has-been now. Divorced from her husband and her committee position. I don't need any deadweight in my life, and I can't deal with that sort of negativity." Olivia pursed her lips.

I threw my napkin down on the table. Yes, there was a time that Shannon and Olivia did not get along, but I don't remember it being that bad. It was like five years ago, right around the time I had Riley. Things got a little ugly, I think. I don't really recall. I had my hands full with a newborn and running my business. But who holds on to something for this long? Olivia does.

I was about to storm out but had resisted because I hadn't paid my check and because Crystal didn't deserve that . . . just yet. I knew there was more going on here than Olivia and Shannon's history that was causing Olivia to be upset. It was obvious. Shannon wasn't much older than Olivia and her husband traded her in for a newer model. Her hatred toward her was laced with insecurity and fear. Olivia was clearly trying to ostracize Shannon because she feared becoming her. Fear makes people crazy. Insecurity makes them crazier.

"I don't want to cause any problems." Crystal looked at me. "I admire that you want to maintain your loyalty to Shannon and be sociable with me too." She looked at Olivia. "And please don't feel like you need to cut Shannon out because of me."

"I'm not cutting Shannon out because of you. I'm cutting Shannon out because she fucking deserves it." Olivia stood up with force. The chair fell behind her. She threw a one-hundred-dollar bill on the table (her specialty) and stormed out of the restaurant without looking back. She was always one for dramatics. This was Olivia's insane way of showing Crystal two things: one, that you don't mess with her, and two, that she'd do well to keep her close. Delusion is a powerful force. I rolled my eyes, finished the wine in my glass, then drank the rest of Olivia's too.

Crystal crinkled her nose, dabbed her chin with a napkin, and took intermittent sips of water.

"You'll have to get used to her," I said with a laugh. It was true. Olivia grew on people . . . like cancer. She was never a person you'd like immediately, unless she wanted you to like her, and the only way that happened was if you could offer her something. I mean she was my friend, but I remember not liking her, and even then I often felt as though I was just tolerating her. Such was Buckhead.

My phone buzzed and so did Crystal's. A message appeared in a group text from Olivia.

> I'm sorry for my outburst. I'm under a lot of pressure with my new position as chairwoman, and what Shannon did to me five years ago is still so raw. Please forgive me. I've covered the bill. Xoxo, Olivia.

"You'll have to really get used to her," I said, shaking my head.

"Yeah . . ." Crystal trailed off. The server asked us if we wanted anything else. I ordered two shots of tequila. They came with the wheels—lime, salt, and Olivia's tantrum. We licked the salt, and before we took the shot, I gave us a toast.

"Cheers to Buckhead! I hope you make it out alive." We tipped back the shots, sucked the lime, and laughed.

5
CRYSTAL

I left the café feeling good, buzzed and better than when I arrived, thanks to Karen. She was a breath of fresh air, like Texas on an October morning. She reminded me of home—her honesty and how down-to-earth she was. Olivia was a different story. She was a bit of a loose cannon. Her flippancy toward Shannon surprised me. I wondered what Shannon could have possibly done to Olivia to upset her so much. There was a mention of some sort of past wrongdoing, but I was unclear as to what happened. To me, Shannon was the victim in all of this. I didn't like that, and I know I helped cause it. I didn't know Shannon, but I didn't need to in order to know that I was wrong to take her husband from her.

Bryce's campaign building looked like a mini White House. It was here before I arrived, but he had told me he had designed it himself and paid for the construction out of his own pocket. Apparently, a regular office building wouldn't do him justice. I walked into the building, greeted his secretary, and waltzed straight into his office, carrying a sandwich and chips from a nearby café. I figured he'd be hungry and would want to know how it went with the women. It was he, after all, who encouraged me to meet with them. He was determined to fix his image and rise within politics, and he needed me and my cooperation to achieve that.

"Hey, hon," I said.

He turned around from his window that overlooked a small green lawn and pressed a finger to his lips as he continued to chatter away on his phone. I sighed, unwrapped his sandwich and chips, and placed them in front of his chair. Taking a seat on the other side of his desk, I admired him as he paced back and forth. He was my ticket out of Texas, out of bartending, out of my past, and out of living a life I wasn't proud of. I wanted more, and some of us aren't capable of more without hitching a ride, like a tick burrowing its way deep within the warm skin of an unsuspecting carrier. But don't get me wrong. I fell for Bryce. And I fell hard.

It was his perfectly dimpled chin, tall athletic build, and piercing blue eyes that drew me to him when we first met. Bryce had it all: looks, brains, money, and power. A local group of mothers even coined the unofficial tagline of his last campaign: "Bryce Madison, a smile so nice you'd vote it into office twice." It never really took off, but I think it helped him win his reelection.

"I don't care. Do not give those trucks any hassle," he said, ending the call abruptly. He tossed the phone on his desk, and his face lit up when his eyes met mine.

"I brought you lunch." I smiled as he made his way around the desk. He returned my smile with a passionate kiss. His hands pressed on my lower back, sliding down, grabbing at my butt, making their way under my sundress. I gave a laugh and kissed him harder. He pulled back, straightening himself and returning to his side of the desk.

"No other woman makes me lose control like you, Crystal."

He winked at me and took a seat, diving into his sandwich. He was famished. Always focused on the job.

"I'm glad I have that effect on you, Mr. Madison." I blushed.

He pressed a button on his desk phone. "Bring me a water," Bryce commanded to his secretary. Moments later she entered with two bottles of water, one for me and one for Bryce. I thanked her. Bryce didn't. I reminded myself to give him grief later. I understood he was busy, stressed, and tired, but I was raised to know there was no such thing as being too busy, too tired, or too stressed for manners.

"How did it go with the ladies, Mrs. Madison?" He raised an eyebrow.

"Fine." I wanted to leave it at that, but I knew he'd press for more. Bryce was that type of man—he always wanted more. He needed so badly for me to get along and fit in with them. It was all about repairing his image and enhancing mine. I understood, I guess. It was the life I chose. I knew there'd be sacrifices.

"And . . . ?"

"I like Karen," I said.

"Good. She and her husband contribute a modest amount to the campaign, and she's a good person to know. Her luxury real estate firm helped make this here office a reality. What about Olivia?"

"She's . . . fine."

He tossed his sandwich on the desk. "Please be straight with me."

"I didn't get much of a chance to really know her, I suppose. She stormed off in the middle of lunch after getting in a tiff with Karen about Shannon. And then she sent an apology text like two minutes later, which was rather odd. So, if I had to give you an opinion right now, I'd say I'm not a fan." I crossed my arms over my chest.

"You have to give her a chance. Her husband is a huge contributor, and Olivia has a lot of influence in this town. I heard she's the new chairwoman of the Buckhead Women's Foundation. You'd do well to keep her close."

"Would *I* do well, or would *you* do well?" I cocked my head.

"*We'd* do well," Bryce said, getting up from his chair. He walked over to me and raised my chin with his hand, locking eyes with me. In one fell swoop, he picked me up and put me on the desk, parting my knees with his waist. He kissed me hard—so hard that I didn't even notice his pants were undone and my panties were pushed aside. Bryce was a passionate man in everything he did, including me. I knew what got him off: control, power, dominance. I knew it the moment he walked into my bar. It looked as though he had a hanger in his suit jacket, that's how high his shoulders were raised. He had flashed that smile of his, not in a courteous way, but like it was a mini advertisement for himself, the five-second ad before a YouTube video. And when he took a seat at the bar, it was as if he had bowed rather than sat down. The hundred-dollar bill he set on the bar was strategic. The Macallan Rare Cask single malt scotch whiskey he ordered wasn't one he had a taste for. It was one he ordered to show that life had a taste for him. We tend to gravitate toward people like Bryce, people that seem untouchable, like nothing bad could ever happen to them. Like the world exists because they're in it, and not the other way around.

"I'm going to make you scream," Bryce panted as he entered me. We're both inside each other now but in different ways. I swallowed my screams and became breathless, while Bryce rocked fiercely, back and forth. I let him do me fast and hard because Bryce liked everything that way: sex, business, life itself. I knew what he wanted, what he needed, and I gave it to him. People that get their way think they're the ones in control. But the ones that give are the ones that rule. It's not the politician in office, but the donor behind the check that wields the sword.

After he was done, he circled back to the conversation I wasn't keen on having. He zipped up his pants and pulled me into a sitting position. "So, you'll give them a chance?"

I resituated my panties, hopped off the desk, and pulled down my dress. "I guess." I shrugged my shoulders.

Bryce brought his fingers to his temples and rubbed them as if I had suddenly caused a headache. He was always so dramatic about getting his way. It was why he had fared well in politics.

"I will," I said. "I'll make nice. I'll fit in. I'll be their best goddamn friend if that's what you want."

His hands fell to his side. His headache was magically cured. He walked to me and kissed me on the cheek. "Perfect. You'll want to join that committee. Perhaps, run for vice-chair too. And that salon they all go to on Peach Street. You'll want to become a client. They're there all the time, and it's the perfect way to bond and fit in quickly." He smiled.

"I'll never get into that salon. Karen said there's a waiting list." I put my hands on my hips. I was relieved, too, when Karen told me there was a wait list. I'd rather spend my time outdoors or reading—not gossiping in a salon with women I barely knew. Like I said, I knew there'd be sacrifices with my life with Bryce, but I didn't think socializing with catty, middle-aged women would be one of them. This world wasn't one I was familiar with, but it was one I knew I could learn to live in and live in well.

Bryce picked up his phone. "Stephanie, call that salon on Peach Street. You know the one." He looked up and smiled at me, "With me, babe, there is no wait list."

I smiled back, but inside I was screaming. I knew it would be a mistake.

6

OLIVIA

The front door opened and closed quickly. I knew he was here, and I was waiting for him in the upstairs bedroom, draped in a red leather corset with matching thong, black fishnet tights, and red-bottomed heels. My hair was slicked back, my lips were a deep red, my eyes were smoky, and my patience was thin. He was late. I'd punish him for that. I stood with one hand on my hip, waiting for him to enter the room and then me . . . when I'd allow him of course. I ran the flogger up the outside of my thigh, slapping it against my toned leg. It stung, but I didn't wince. I was just testing out how hard I'd hit him with it—enough for it to hurt, but not so much that he wouldn't want to come crawling back to me. That was the name of the game. Just enough, not too much.

He entered the room with a smile, and it quickly diminished when he saw the stern and annoyed look on my face. He was six two and looked like a yuppie from New England, completely out of place down in the South, but he still carried himself with a tremendous amount of confidence.

"You're late." I slapped the flogger on the gold sheets of the California king bed.

"I know, I know." He flicked off his shoes, removed his pants and shirt, and put his hands up as if he were surrendering to me. "I got caught up with a patient."

"No excuses. Kneel," I commanded, and he did. "On all fours." He listened well because I had trained him well. I walked to him and whipped his shoulders, back, butt, and thighs—until he used our safe word, or should I say words.

"Karen's a bitch," he yelped.

I stopped immediately and smiled. I had texted him earlier our new safe phrases for tonight. His body was covered in splotches of red, and his face was flushed from holding his breath to counteract the pain signals. I typically never went this hard right away, but he pissed me off with his tardiness and Karen pissed me off at lunch.

"What do you want to do to me?" I propped the flogger beneath his chin, pulling his head up.

"Whatever you'll allow me to do, Mrs. Petrov."

"I'm in a giving mood tonight." I raised an eyebrow. "Stand up!"

He stood before me, his body fully erect. His penis followed suit. I knew exactly how to push his buttons. I knew what he wanted, and I knew how to get what *I* wanted.

"I'd like my allowance first." I smirked, sticking out my hand for payment. He grabbed his wallet from his pants and placed the money from it into my hand. I didn't have to count it to know it was well over $2,000. I threw the money on the bed and turned back to him as he waited for my next command.

I pointed to the money that was strewn about on my silk bedding. "That money."

"Yes," he nodded.

"I want you to fuck me on it."

No other words were spoken. He picked me up and flung me onto the bed, ripping off my corset, fishnets, and thong. He left the heels on, and I kept the flogger in my hand. He liked to be in control, but only for small periods of time. I let him kiss and lick me from my neck to my vag, and then I slapped him. It was always about teasing. Never let him have too much at once, or he'd walk away forever. It was how I controlled him, how I made him mine.

I forced him to lay on his back, and I flogged his chest and stomach until he used another one of our safe phrases.

"Chairwoman Olivia Petrov," he yelled.

"Good boy." I kissed his chest, his stomach, and made my way down. I looked up at him like the girls do in porn films. He smiled, and then I consumed him. His eyes went wide. His body tensed up. His legs jerked. Before he could relieve himself, I sunk my teeth into him, waiting for another safe phrase.

"Shannon's reign is over," he cried out.

Opening my mouth a little wider, I pulled away. I thought my safe sentences were going to be too much for him to remember, but he was a smart boy. He exhaled heavily, a combination of pain and pleasure. I crawled back up to him and whispered in his ear, "I want you inside of me."

Two seconds later he was inside, and thirty seconds after that, he was lying beside me, panting like an overweight English bulldog and telling me how great I was.

I got out of bed and wrapped a little black silk robe around myself. He was still gasping as if they were his last breaths. I was entirely composed.

"Goddamn, Olivia. You're a damn goddess."

"I know. I'm going to shower. Stack up my bills after you catch your breath." Before I left the room, he was already collecting my money, his breath still ragged. *Dogs are so easy to train, especially the stray ones.*

Dropping my robe to the tiled floor, I stepped into the shower. The warm water splashed and slithered on my skin. I leaned my head back into the stream of hot liquid and closed my eyes. My mind was practically blank. Wealth will do that to you. Make you not worry. I know this. I learned this. Because there was a time when I didn't have the security of cash. But there was also a time before that when I did. They say it is better to have loved and lost than to never have loved at all . . . the same is not true for money.

As a child, my family was rich . . . like Oprah rich, but not the legal way. Apparently, there's a difference. But try explaining that to a fourteen-year-old. Try telling a teenager they have to sell all their stuff, that their father's going to prison, that they'll have to transfer to a public school, that their friends would no longer be their friends, that everything they've ever known would come crashing down around them and be nothing more than a cruel memory, a dream just short of reach.

When I grew up, I made sure my life was exactly what I wanted it to be—a life of privilege. Just as it should have been all along, had my screwup of a father not derailed everything. But I suppose I do have to thank him, in a way. Without him, I wouldn't have this hunger inside me, this need to never return to the humiliating poverty of my childhood. The truth is, I'd rather be dead than poor, and the easiest way to stay rich is to stay powerful.

7
JENNY

The sun had yet to fully rise as I unlocked the back door of the salon. I flicked on the lights and ventured in. This time was always special to me. I liked to open Glow earlier than needed so that I could enjoy a quiet sense of peace before the day truly began. Plus, my best friend, Keisha, always came in early to mentally prepare before a day of hair and makeup, and before the inevitable drama would begin.

It wasn't long later that I heard Mary (our front desk receptionist) come in through the front door. She called out, "Good morning," and got right to work. The desk chair slid across the floor, and the computer chimed. Keisha came strolling in, full of confidence and with two cups of Starbucks, one in each hand. Her father was White and her mother Black, creating this gorgeous woman with icy-blue eyes, full lips, and long, voluptuous, naturally curly brown hair (that, I may add, I never had to do any work on—it was that perfect).

"Jenny, coffee's here," she said handing me my cup.

"You're a lifesaver." I grabbed it and immediately pressed it to my mouth.

"What's on the docket today?" Keisha took a seat at one of the beauty stations, swiveling around in the chair as she sipped at her coffee.

"Shannon will be here essentially all day. She has to get in all of her treatments before the end of the month."

"Oh yes, she's single . . . ready to mingle?" Keisha waggled her eyebrows.

"I'd assume not. The divorce was out of nowhere, I heard, and I think Shannon really loved Bryce."

Keisha took another drink. "Or was it the money and power she loved?"

"With these women, you never know." I finished up my coffee and dropped the Starbucks cup into a garbage can.

"Speaking of love, when are you going to let me set you up on a date?" Keisha winked.

"Never," I said as I walked around the salon ensuring everything was perfectly clean and in place. This salon was my baby, my relationship, my everything. It was important to me that it was pristine.

"Oh, come on. Let's get you back on the horse. What's your type?" she asked.

"I don't have a type." I raised an eyebrow.

"Yes, you actually do. It's sterile and can't return any feelings or affection." Keisha gestured in a swooping motion.

I took a seat in the salon chair beside her. "Ha ha, very funny."

"This salon can't love you back."

"I know that, but I just don't have the time to date." I turned my chair toward the mirror and applied some light makeup, ensuring I didn't conceal the spackle of freckles that covered my nose and cheeks. Olivia was wrong about those. They were beautiful. There were no wrinkles or lines to be found, aside from my deep dimples. I straightened my white flowy blouse. I wasn't sure if it was right for my small frame when I bought it, but it grew on me because it was plain and didn't draw any attention.

"Make the time. Hire another person to work the salon." Keisha got up from her seat and stood behind me. She placed her hands on my shoulders and looked at me in the mirror. "You're not getting any younger."

"I'm only thirty-one," I challenged.

"And soon you'll be forty."

"That's an awful thing to say!" I laughed.

Keisha shrugged her shoulders. "I only speak the truth." I spun my chair around and rolled my eyes at her playfully.

She was right. Time didn't stop or slow down for anyone. And it seemed the busier you were, the faster it passed by. I hadn't been on a date since before I opened Glow, and I knew deep down that I needed something more, something outside of these four walls, outside of the wealthy women I served. I had been living vicariously through them, but that's just a fancy way of saying I hadn't been living at all.

"So, how are we going to deal with the whole Shannon situation? Can we stagger everyone else's appointments?" Keisha picked up the salon planner.

"I think that's what we're going to have to do."

"It's pretty ridiculous, you know. I thought this was a salon, not a day care for middle-aged women," Keisha teased.

"Well, that's where you're wrong. These women have it all, and they still find something to complain about or fight over."

"Can we raise their membership fees, since we added babysitting to our services?"

Our laugh was cut short as the front door chimed.

"Go on through, Ms. Block. Jenny is ready for you," Mary said.

"It's Mrs. Madison," Shannon corrected.

Oh, good God. She was keeping Bryce's name, holding on to the possibility she'd regain her fortune, power, and husband. That poor woman.

Shannon emerged from behind the black curtains dramatically, as if she were entering the stage of a sold-out Broadway show. All that was missing was a spotlight and the applause. Her long golden-blond hair was faded, as she hadn't had it touched up in a while. I'd take care of that today. Her perfectly carved nose looked as if it had been created by an artist, and it was. That artist's name was Dr. Richardson, Karen's husband. Her skin was as smooth as marble in a way that only Botox can do. Also thanks to Dr. Richardson. She wore only the fashion greats—Armani, Gucci, Prada, Chanel, Versace—and on this day, she was dressed in a hodgepodge of them all. White Versace linen pants, Prada sling-back heels, Armani blouse, and Chanel sunglasses with a Gucci bag. She was thin and curvy in the way only a forty-year-old can be, which requires copious amounts of time in the gym, extreme dieting, and regular trips to the physician. Unlike women much younger than her, she looked like she put a lot of effort into achieving her appearance. *Effortless* was never a word you'd put in the same sentence with Shannon.

She whipped off her sunglasses and smiled at Keisha and me. Her makeup was heavy. She was overcompensating for the loss of her marriage—that much was obvious. My heart broke for her. Shannon was a housewife. It was how she had introduced herself the first day we had met just over three years ago. "I'm Mrs. Shannon Madison, wife of Congressman Bryce Madison," she had said. It was her identity—until it wasn't. Now, another woman held that title. As humans, we define ourselves by the things we are most proud of—being a mother, a salon owner, a free spirit. But what happens when you lose that? Who do you become?

"Hi, Shannon. We're so glad you could make it in." I walked to her and kissed both her cheeks.

She hugged me a little harder than she usually did. I knew she needed it, so I hugged her tightly, rubbing her back with one of my hands. We released one another when she was ready, and I smiled and nodded at her. She nodded back. Her eyes moistened. She took a deep breath, and her eyes lost their glisten almost instantly. She had been practicing composure. Keisha and Shannon hugged and exchanged pleasantries.

"What can we do for you today?" I asked.

"First, champagne. Then, the works. Head to toe. Every treatment and service you have, I want it. I want to leave here drunk and beautiful." She laughed, but she was very serious.

In the time I had known Shannon, she had always been so put together. She wasn't a big drinker, and she rarely lost control. She did juice cleanses and every fad diet under the sun. She took care of herself. *This* Shannon wasn't one I was familiar with, but I understood she was hurting and clearly trying to numb the pain.

Keisha grabbed a bottle of champagne and popped it. She poured a glass and set the bottle beside her, while Shannon took a seat in the salon chair.

"Beauty is my specialty," I said as I wrapped a cape around her.

"And booze is mine," Keisha added.

"Then I'm in good hands," Shannon laughed and looked at both of us. She raised her glass and drank the whole thing in one big gulp.

8

SHANNON

My hair was dyed, cut, and styled. My body had been exfoliated, waxed, massaged, and spray-tanned. My lashes were full, and my eyebrows were tinted. My makeup was perfectly done, lighter than I had asked for, but I trusted Jenny's advice to go for a subtler daytime look. My fingernails were drying, Keisha was working on my pedicure, and I had switched from champagne to white wine. I was thoroughly buzzed and feeling extremely beautiful and confident, something I hadn't felt in a while.

Jenny and Keisha delivered as usual, and by midafternoon we were talking about the divorce. I never intended to, but there's something about salons and booze that bring out the truth in you. Mix them together and you'll spill your guts. They were both understanding and supportive, asking all the right questions and dishing out all the right compliments and all the much-needed man-bashing remarks.

"Now that you're single, has anyone caught your eye?" Keisha pried.

"A lady never tells," I said with a laugh and a hiccup.

"Oh, girl!" Keisha fluttered her eyelashes and switched to painting my other set of toes.

"It's nothing like that," I said, flicking my wrist. "I still love Bryce, and I have hope that we'll get back together one day."

Keisha and Jenny looked at one another and drew their brows together. I knew they thought I was crazy to say that, but even with everything Bryce had put me through, I still loved him. We were good together. He was just having a midlife crisis, a very long midlife crisis. Jenny leaned against her salon station. Her forehead wrinkled. I knew she wanted to ask me something, but Jenny was always so careful, never wanting to offend anyone.

"Oh, just say it, Jenny," I said with a huff. She walked over to me and topped off my wineglass with more Chardonnay. Between the champagne and the wine, I was nearly two bottles deep. My words were coming out freely with a southern drawl on the end.

"Do you really think Bryce will come back to you? He remarried," she said.

"He divorced once before. He can do it again," I said matter-of-factly.

Keisha and Jenny nodded. I know they didn't agree and probably thought I was delusional. But they'd see. They would all see. Bryce hadn't been interested in me when I first pursued him fourteen years ago. He was too focused on his career. But I changed his mind, and I could do it again. Throughout our marriage, I had always warned him that I'd be the worst ex-wife he'd ever have, because I never forget and I never let things go, including ex-husbands.

"They say if you love someone, let them go, and if they don't come back, go and get that asshole yourself." I chuckled.

Keisha laughed, and Jenny gave me a look of pity but quickly turned it into a small smile.

"Got any plans for the evening?" Jenny changed the subject.

"I have to finish prepping for the gala next week, turn in some expense reports and whatnot. I missed a couple of committee meetings, but regardless, this event is going to be incredible. It has to be. I haven't been able to get ahold of any of the board members today to finalize some details. Speaking of them, has Olivia been in here?"

She had been dodging my calls for months now. I didn't quite understand it, but I hadn't been able to wrangle her in to figure out what her deal was.

"She was in yesterday," Jenny said.

"Did she mention me?"

"Nope," Jenny answered quickly as she tidied up around the salon.

I had the feeling she wasn't telling the truth, but I didn't press her. Jenny thought it was her job to keep the peace, and I understood where she was coming from. It must be hard to be at the center of all of Buckhead's gossip. Before the divorce, I had always thought I was the most powerful woman in this town, but deep down I knew it was Jenny. Knowledge was power, and Jenny had all of it. I took another sip of wine.

"You know? I almost canceled my membership here," I confessed.

Jenny's eyes went a little wide before she turned her customer service face on, neutral with a small smile. "Really? Well, I guess I'd understand with the divorce and all."

"Oh, no. Not because of money. The alimony is strong." My lip perked up. "I wasn't sure if the new wife would be a client of yours as well."

Jenny opened her mouth and then closed it, hesitating for a moment. "Well, Bryce did give me a call yesterday. So, full disclosure, I accepted her as a client, but I'll make sure to stagger your appointments."

"Very good." I nodded.

"Besides, I don't think we'll see her for a while. From what Olivia has told me, Crystal isn't into the whole beauty thing," Jenny explained, but not in a judgmental way, just like she was reading from a teleprompter.

I raised my eyebrows and took another sip. *A woman who isn't into keeping up appearances.* I let out a laugh. Bryce surely wouldn't keep her around for long. He needed someone like me beside him, not some down-on-the-farm little country girl. Knowing that gave me hope that Bryce and I would reunite again.

"All finished." Keisha propped both my feet up. My toenails were all perfectly polished a midnight-blue shade. "Give them ten minutes to dry."

"Thank you both! I feel beautiful and buzzed." I raised my glass. "What a perfect day!"

It was perfect because it was the first day in a long time where I didn't feel the pain of my life falling apart, the loneliness of a divorcée, and the embarrassment of losing my husband to a younger woman. But that was probably just the effects of the alcohol.

The front door chimed. "Hello," a meek, country voice from the front said.

"Do you have someone?" Keisha asked Jenny. She shook her head.

"Mary's on lunch. I'll take care of it." Jenny disappeared behind the black curtains.

I heard faint whispers. "Can you come back in ten minutes?"

"Who is it?" I called out.

Jenny peeked her head through the curtains. "It's Crystal."

"Oh, lovely. Don't let me be a bother. Go right ahead, Have her come on back," I said, trying to keep my speech intact, but I ended up slurring every other word.

Jenny disappeared behind the curtain again. More whispering ensued.

I took another drink and held out my glass. Keisha immediately refilled it, and then she took a big gulp from the bottle herself. Clearly, she was not looking forward to being a part of this meet and greet.

"What's taking so long?" I called out. More whispers. I could hear Jenny asking Crystal to come back. I got up from my chair and balanced myself.

"Your toenails are still wet," Keisha warned.

I waved a hand at her dismissively. I raised my toes in their oversize pedicure flip-flops and took one big step and then another and then another, trying to keep myself upright with my arms outstretched for balance. The foam flip-flops slapped hard with each labored step.

When I reached the curtain, I tugged hard to open it in a dramatic fashion, "Come on back, Crystal. I'm dying to meet you." The alcohol seemed to have numbed my legs too, because I lost my balance. I pulled down one side of the curtain, tumbling to the ground, wrapping and entangling myself in it.

"Shhhit," I called out from inside the velvet cocoon. This was not how I had intended to meet the woman who stole my husband. I had imagined it'd be more like when a commoner (Crystal) meets the Queen of England (me). Crystal would bend the knee, and I'd whack her head off with a sword. The royal treatment! Okay, perhaps not that graphic. But my fantasy did not look like *this*.

"Oh my God," Keisha shrieked as she ran toward me. She unwrapped me and helped me up. I immediately shuffled back to my pedicure chair, avoiding eye contact with Crystal. Keisha and Jenny hung the curtain back up and Crystal stayed on the other side of it. I quickly fixed myself, caught my breath, tapered my embarrassment, and smoothed out my hair. Holding the champagne glass between my fingertips as elegantly as possible, I waited for Crystal to walk in. I looked down at my toes and saw they were covered in nail polish. Damn it.

There were more whispers.

Keisha entered. She gave me a look of solidarity, then went to work on fixing my toenails without saying a word. Keisha was always so good to me.

Jenny pushed open the curtains and walked through with Crystal following behind her quietly. I'd seen thousands of photos of her online, and I hated to admit it, she was beautiful in person. She glanced over at me and then back at the ground and then at her phone. She wanted to be anywhere else in the world right now. I wanted to be right here. She was uncomfortable. And I was drunk.

"You can have a seat right here." Jenny motioned to a salon chair. I heard Crystal say she was looking for a trim and then a basic manicure and pedicure. Jenny wrapped a cape around her and began combing through her long blond wavy hair.

"So, how are you getting along in Buckhead?" Jenny asked.

"Just fine." Crystal's voice was soft, almost too soft. It was difficult to hear her, and she kept glancing in the mirror back at me.

"All fixed," Keisha said as she stood up and gave me a smile. "Ten minutes and they'll be dry. Ten minutes." She held up all her fingers. I nodded, mouthed, "Sorry," and returned my focus to Crystal.

"That's great to hear," Jenny said. I could tell she felt awkward as well. "Would you like something to drink?"

"Yes, please," Crystal said sheepishly. "Make it strong."

Jenny nodded. Keisha poured a vodka soda and handed it to her.

"Thank you." She brought the straw to her lips and didn't stop sucking until it made the slurping noise. Keisha immediately refilled it. I continued to sip at my drink and stare at Crystal.

"I don't think we've had the pleasure." I got up from my chair, toes up, and carefully walked over to Crystal, holding out my hand. "I'm Shannon Madison," I said. Jenny fidgeted with her comb, and Keisha's face crinkled up. They exchanged worried looks. I didn't care.

Crystal got her hand free out of the cape and shook mine. "I'm Crystal." Her eyes met mine for mere seconds before darting away. *Weak people can't hold eye contact.*

"Crystal what?"

"Crystal Madison," she coughed.

"Madison, huh? Well, we must be related or something," I cackled as I stumbled back to my seat with Keisha's assistance.

"Toes up," she said as I took several large steps.

Crystal grabbed her drink and sucked hard on the straw. *That's probably how she got my husband.*

"How is Bryce, by the way?" I raised an eyebrow and gave a smirk. I wanted to make her feel uncomfortable. I had been uncomfortable for months. I wanted her to feel the way I felt.

She set her empty glass down. "Bryce is fine." Her eyes bounced around the room, trying to find something to focus on. She finally settled on pulling out her phone. My toenails were dry, and I could have left then, but I didn't want to. Crystal was like a unicorn to me. She didn't seem real, yet she was sitting right in front of me. When Bryce told me he was leaving me, I didn't believe it. When he told me there was someone else, I didn't believe it. When he handed me the divorce papers, I didn't believe it. Even when the moving truck arrived, I didn't believe it. When I moved into an apartment, I didn't believe it. Now, I was sitting in front of the woman who had caused all of it, and I still couldn't fucking believe it.

"So, did you know Bryce was married when you fucked him?" I spat venomously.

Crystal's eyes widened. Jenny's mouth fell open. Keisha didn't know where to look. I smiled. Crystal let out an awkward cough and then looked directly in the mirror at my reflection. Her eyes locked on me. There was hurt in her eyes just as there was hurt in mine. I wasn't sure what her hurt was from, but I saw it.

"No," she said firmly. She turned toward me. Jenny stepped aside. I crossed one leg over the other and bounced it, waiting for an explanation.

"I'm sorry he left you. I truly am," she said. "I did not know he was married until after I fell in love with him. So, rest assured. He didn't fall out of love with you because of me. He fell out of love with you because of you." She turned back around.

My mouth fell open. *Where did she get off talking to me like that? What does she know about love? She's twenty-five. She's a child.* My words were stuck in my throat, and just when I was finally going to speak, the front door chimed.

"Hello! I have a nail emergency," Olivia called from the front. She waltzed into the back and stopped dead in her tracks when she saw me. She glanced over at Crystal and then back at me.

"What the hell are you doing here?" she asked. It took me a moment to realize she was talking to me and not Crystal.

"What do you mean, what am I doing here? I'm a client," I said, raising my slurred voice.

"Jenny, I thought Shannon's membership was going to be canceled," Olivia pressed.

My eyes went wide as they bounced from Jenny to Olivia and then back to Jenny again.

"I never said that, Olivia. She completed all her monthly treatments and she's all paid up."

I stood from my chair and slid on my sling-back heels. "Why's it any of your business, Olivia?" I yelled.

"Shannon, just stop." Olivia dismissed me, putting her hand on her hip.

"Excuse me! No one tells me to stop, especially a woman who looks like a blow-up doll!" I struggled to stand up straight. I was pissed. Olivia was my friend and suddenly, because I didn't have a husband anymore, she was acting as if I were a nobody, like I didn't exist.

"At least I'm not old!" Olivia screamed. She spat a little as she spoke, and her voice came out twangy. I was only a few years older than her.

"You both need to stop right now," Jenny said sternly.

"She started it." Olivia pointed at me.

"Screw you, Olivia!"

"Enough, or I'm revoking both of your memberships," Jenny crossed her arms over her chest.

I immediately closed my mouth.

Olivia stamped her foot. "Can you fix my nail or what?"

"Keisha can fix it quickly," Jenny said.

Keisha nodded and walked Olivia over to a nail station.

"I'd hope so. It was I that made you, Jenny. Let us not forget that," Olivia said over her shoulder. Her eyes shot daggers.

Jenny stopped, turned toward Olivia, and walked right up to her. Olivia took a step back. She was afraid, probably of losing her coveted membership. I hoped Jenny would kick her out right then and there. Olivia may have helped make Jenny's salon what it was, but it was *Jenny's* salon. It was her talent and her personality that kept it going strong. People loved Jenny. She was a breath of fresh air in a town full of greed, lies, and ugliness.

"Actually, you can see Mary at the front to make an appointment. We're all booked up today."

"I wouldn't do that if I were you," Olivia huffed.

"Well, you're not me." Jenny turned away and refocused her attention on Crystal's hair.

"And thank God for that!" Olivia turned on her heel and stormed out of the salon.

I appreciated Jenny standing up for me, but challenging Olivia would be a mistake. She was like the Grim Reaper of Buckhead. When your time was up, she would get you, one way or another.

9
JENNY

Detective Frank Sanford leans back in his chair and taps his pen on the table. Each tap is a second apart, and it's rather annoying. It's ten taps before he stops abruptly.

"And that was your first time meeting Crystal?"

I take a sip of stale coffee from a Styrofoam cup. "Yes."

"That fight at the salon was the beginning of the end for this group of women?"

"I think there was no going back after that." I fiddle with the elastic ponytail holder on my wrist, the one that promises to leave no indentation in the hair. Lie. We all leave some imprint of ourselves behind, even plastic ponytail holders.

"You were mad at Olivia?"

"If I were truly mad at Olivia, I would have terminated her membership right then and there. I knew Olivia was having issues of her own, so I let it slide," I say, returning my gaze to the detective.

"There was a lot of tension within that group of women. Would you agree with that?" He raises his chin.

"I think *tension* is putting it lightly." I lean forward, placing my elbows on the table.

"How would you put it?"

"Well, one of them ended up dead." I crinkle up my face.

"And who do you think did it?" He leans forward, matching my posture.

"The way these women treated each other, I think it could have been any one of them."

His forehead rises, creating a row of deep parallel ridges. "Any one of them? It seemed some of them were getting along."

"Are any of us ever truly getting along, Detective Sanford?"

"Aren't *we*?" He raises an eyebrow, cocking his head slightly to the left as though he were offended.

"Surface level, yes, of course. But I don't know what's going on in your head and you don't know what's going on in mine."

"So, you're saying that some of these women were pretending to get along?"

"I think these women were pretending to be a lot of things."

Detective Frank Sanford pauses for a moment before jotting down a few more notes. "Did you know about the affair?" he asks.

I let out a laugh. "Which one?"

10
KAREN

After closing on a multimillion-dollar home, I decided to go for a run through town. Exercise was the only healthy way to rid myself of that rush that came with achieving something exceptional. Most people would turn to indulgence in alcohol, food, an expensive gift, but I liked to run it off. It kept me going, in motion. It made sure I didn't stagnante.

Buckhead is what you'd expect out of a wealthy town. The streets were lined with expensive boutiques and designer stores. There were splashes of greenery everywhere—trees, bushes, flower beds. You can tell when you're in a wealthy city . . . look for the green. It's expensive to maintain when everything around it is concrete. People were quick to move to the side as I ran the sidewalk on Peach Street. This was the South, after all—still a place of chivalry and good manners, if only on the surface. I was on mile four when I spotted Olivia up ahead. She swayed her hips and walked with purpose. Her face was pinched together, so even from a block away, I could tell she was mad. I knew she wouldn't move aside, and I almost crossed the street to avoid her. When she spotted me, I watched her face soften, but she had a new look . . . determination. I didn't want to deal with her. I was still upset about what she had done to Shannon. Unseating her was cruel. We hadn't told Shannon yet. I wanted to, but not before the gala. She needed to focus on that. We had all agreed we would tell her at the meeting following the gala. So far, Olivia and the rest of the committee had kept their word.

I stopped right in front of her, pulled out one of my AirPods, and immediately began stretching my quads and calves.

"Do you know what just happened?" she practically shouted.

I shook my head.

"I just got into a huge fight with Shannon at the salon, and Jenny took her side. Oh, and Crystal was there too." She folded her arms in front of her chest and tapped her foot quickly on the ground as if she were impatiently waiting for me to come to her aid.

"Did you tell Shannon about her chairwoman position?"

"Of course not. I'm a woman of my word," she said, lifting her chin.

"Then what happened?" I feigned interest.

I didn't care about the Shannon and Olivia fight. I knew Olivia had it out for her. I was happy to hear Jenny shut that drama down. Good for her. I was only curious about the interaction between Shannon and Crystal. Shannon was my friend, and I could see Crystal being my friend too, and I thought maybe there was a chance they could one day get along, maybe even be pals—but then again, this was Buckhead.

"Shannon was being a total b-i-t-c-h to Crystal." She literally spelled out the word. "I called her out, and then Jenny had the audacity to kick me out. Who the hell does she think she is?"

"Well, it is her salon," I said. Olivia could be pretty

unreasonable and if it got to the point that Jenny had to kick her out, then I assumed Olivia was being a monster. I took some deep breaths, regaining control from the run.

"I don't give a damn if it's her salon. Without me, she'd be nothing. You know that, Karen. I made her."

I had never seen her this mad before. Olivia wasn't used to people standing up to her, and I don't think she'd ever been kicked out of anywhere her entire privileged life. I tilted my head. It was more like a half nod. Olivia liked to pretend she was God in that salon, but she had been an angel investor and she did bring a lot of clients to the salon, including myself. But that was years ago, and Jenny had made it what it is now.

"I have half a nerve to cancel my membership and get everyone else to cancel too," she said with a huff.

Before I could say anything, Olivia spoke again.

"Obviously, I won't do that." She waved her hand in a dismissive way. "But I expect an apology out of her."

Once again, I said nothing. I just stood there stretching out my arms and checking the time and stats on my Apple Watch. Olivia was the type of person that could have an entire conversation with herself and not even notice you hadn't spoken.

"Well, I just wanted to warn you how wicked Shannon is being. You'd do well not to associate yourself with her."

"Thanks for the heads-up. I have to get going." I put my AirPod back in. "Mark will be home soon," I said as I jogged away.

"Oh yes. Tell him I said hi." She smiled and waved her fingers at me as she continued strutting down the street.

I ran up the driveway of our oversized redbrick Tudor home. It was homey yet large, yet relatively modest compared to our second home in Miami, where Mark's other plastic surgery office was located. He left Sunday nights and returned typically on Wednesdays, so he could do three days in the Miami office and two in Atlanta. Although, this week he was back Thursday afternoon due to more appointments in Miami than Atlanta.

I walked right through the front door and found him sleeping on the couch. Mark and I had been married for over a decade but together for nineteen years. We fell in love in college, and I accompanied him when he got into medical school at Johns Hopkins. His feet were hanging off the couch thanks to his six-two stature. His light-brown hair was out of place, and the bags under his eyes were heavy. He worked too hard. I had hoped when we moved down south he'd live life at a slower pace, but he was still that overworked yuppie from New England. We were both still those people. I had my real estate company, and he had his plastic surgery offices. I knew we both needed to slow down. I leaned down and kissed his forehead. His eyes instantly shot open.

"Sorry, babe, I didn't mean to wake you."

He pulled me into him and kissed my lips.

"No need to apologize," he said. Mark and I hadn't been intimate in a while, so the kiss was a nice surprise. I didn't know what was wrong with me. I loved Mark, but lately, I never wanted to make love to him. I assumed my hormones were out of whack or I was too stressed for sex. I had reminded myself again to go to the doctor. I pulled him up from the couch.

"How did it go today?" he asked.

"I closed on that house on Foxcroft," I said with a smile.

"That's amazing, Karen. Congrats!" He gave me another peck on the lips. "Where's Riley?" he added.

"He's doing an overnight sleepover with some of the neighbor kids."

I thought Mark was asking where Riley was because he wanted to make love to celebrate. The thought of it made me nervous, and I had no idea why.

"On a Thursday?"

"I know, but he begged me and gave me that cute little pouty face." I smiled.

I wrapped my arms around Mark, and he winced.

"What's wrong?" I asked.

"Think I pulled something at the gym. I'm going to take a hot shower."

"Want me to massage you?" I raised an eyebrow and bit my lower lip. I was trying . . . trying to seduce my husband, just to make sure there was nothing wrong with us or me. But deep down, I knew there was.

"No, babe. That's all right. But I am hungry though," he said, walking toward the hallway.

"Sure. I'll make dinner."

As he left the room, I noticed red marks on the back of his calves and neck. Poor guy. He worked too hard at the office and at the gym, and I'm sure those commutes from Atlanta to Miami and back every week were taking a toll on him. I made a mental note to urge him to take a vacation. After this recent closing, I could get away. I had more than earned it. He, Riley, and I could go someplace nice for a week or two, just the three of us.

Before pulling out the ingredients for an avocado-and-chicken salad, I poured myself a glass of red wine from a previously opened bottle. I took a long, slow sip, and as the red liquid made its way inside me, I thought of the last time Mark was also inside me—over six months ago. It was after a dinner party. We had the house to ourselves, and we were both rather intoxicated. As soon as we entered the house, he pushed me against the wall, wrapping my legs around his waist before thrusting into me. We tore into each other. It was intimate yet animalistic. I wanted him and he wanted me. These days, I'm not sure what either of us wants. I set the wineglass down and tossed the chicken breasts into a frying pan. I'm not the woman I was when he married me, and I'm not the woman I was even six months ago. I no longer know who I am, because sometimes we become strangers to even ourselves.

11
SHANNON

I took a seat at a high-top table and ordered two vodka martinis from the server. I had asked Karen to meet me for a drink to discuss what had happened yesterday at the salon and to get her take on the whole thing. She was the one person I could count on to be honest with me. And while part of me wanted her honesty, that didn't necessarily mean I was going to listen to any of it. I was dead set on winning Bryce back, and not even Karen or her pragmatism could stop me.

"Hey, hon," Karen said as she set her tote down and pulled me in for a hug, squeezing me a little tighter than usual. She took a seat across from me and gave me a wide smile. She was definitely hiding something behind her perfect veneer.

"I ordered you a vodka martini," I said just as the server placed one in front of both of us.

"Perfect. Thank you." Karen brought the glass to her lips and took a small sip. "Now, what happened at the salon yesterday?"

"How did you know something happened?" I raised an eyebrow.

"Olivia."

"Of course." I rolled my eyes. "Well, I was pretty drunk, so my recollection of events is blurry at best, but all I know is that Olivia is a bitch."

Karen laughed. "She said you were being rude to Crystal, and she was just defending her."

"We all know Olivia doesn't defend anyone but herself."

She nodded.

"But was I being rude to the woman who stole my husband? Abso-fucking-lutely. And she deserved it." I raised my chin.

Karen let out a sigh. "Can you really be mad at her? Bryce is the one that did this to you."

"I still love Bryce," I confessed.

Karen shook her head. "No, you don't."

"I do, and he loves me too." I took a long sip of my martini.

"No, you don't, and he definitely does not love you. If he loved you, he wouldn't have done what he did. That's not love." She pressed her lips firmly together to make her point.

I resituated myself in my seat and sat up a little taller. "He's just confused."

"No, he's just an asshole," Karen quipped. She reached out and grabbed my hand, looking directly into my eyes. "And you can do so much better."

I stared at her hand, deciding if I wanted to push it away or not. The weight of it felt right though. Like a small security blanket that I didn't know I needed. "But I don't want to do better. I want Bryce." My bottom lip quivered.

Karen rubbed my hand. "That's a temporary feeling, I'm sure. He's not a good man, and to be honest, I have never liked Bryce."

My mouth fell open. "Really? Never?"

"Never."

My eyes darted around the room. How could she never have liked my husband without me knowing? All the dinner dates, events, and even vacations we've all taken together over the past decade . . . Karen sure can act. If she's pretended to like Bryce all these years, what else is she pretending? I took a long drink of my martini and then returned my attention to her. "Well, regardless of your opinion, I'm still going to try to make our marriage work."

Karen plucked the skewer from her empty glass and bit down on it, sliding two olives into her mouth. "That's your decision in the end. But hell, if it's any consolation, I'll probably be joining your club soon."

"What club?" I tilted my head.

"The ex-wives club." She tossed the skewer back in the glass and pushed it away from her.

My eyes widened. "Are you and Mark getting a divorce?" I couldn't believe it. They had always been such a solid couple. Then again, I thought Bryce and I were too.

"I'm not sure. We haven't had sex in six months, which is both of our faults, but he just seems generally uninterested in me, and not just sexually." Karen shrugged as if she didn't care, but I know she did, she really did.

The server collected our empty glasses and we ordered sparkling water. "What are you going to do?" I asked.

"I don't know. Figure out what's wrong with me, what's wrong with us. It's not just him either. I have no interest in having sex with him."

"Well, you *are* getting older." I snickered.

Karen laughed. "Thanks for your sympathies."

"I'm sure it's nothing. Just a lull. All relationships have those." I placed my hand on top of Karen's.

"I hope so," she said. "Anyway, let's talk about something else, instead of the fact that we're both becoming wrinkled-up old hags." Karen smiled.

The server carefully poured two glasses from a bottle of San Pellegrino and placed them in front of both of us. He nodded and set the bottle in the center of the table before backing away.

"Have you met Crystal yet?" I asked.

I knew Karen was hiding something from me, and I was sure it had to do with the girls. Perhaps she knew why Olivia was being such a bitch to me, or she had interacted with Bryce's new wife.

"Yes. I'm sorry I didn't tell you. But I had lunch with her and Olivia the other day."

I swirled my drink. *Bingo. That's it.*

"And?" I raised my chin.

"And she was nice. But it didn't go well. Olivia did what she always does: made a scene, stormed off, and apologized two minutes later." Karen rolled her eyes.

"Over what?"

"You. She was adamant about not socializing with you anymore."

I took another sip. I knew Olivia had it in for me after the incident at the salon, but I wasn't sure why.

"What is her fucking deal?" I crossed my arms.

"Honestly, I think she's insecure and she's scared. And in Olivia's twisted-up mind, I think she thinks divorce is contagious and she'll end up in the same situation."

"Oh, that's ridiculous." I waved my hand dismissively.

"She also mentioned something about you mistreating her years ago," Karen said, raising an eyebrow.

I squinted my eyes, trying to recall this apparent

mistreatment, but nothing came to mind. "I don't know what she's talking about, and you know how dramatic Olivia can be."

Karen let out a small laugh. "You can say that again." She took a sip of her water. "Anyway, how's the gala coming along?"

"Pretty well. But I haven't been able to get ahold of Tina about the budget, and Olivia hasn't helped at all." I gripped my water glass a little too tightly.

"That's odd." Karen pulled her lips in. "Anything I can do to help?"

"You've done your fair share. You secured the location, and the whole town knows about it, thanks to you as well," I said with a smile.

Karen nodded.

"And . . ." I hesitated. "I'm still going to go through with introducing Bryce for his award."

Karen raised an eyebrow. "Are you sure that's a good idea?"

"Yes. I want to appear strong like I was before this whole divorce. If I chicken out, people will talk. Besides, I'll be fine as long as you're there with me, and you just make sure I don't do anything stupid," I said with a nod.

"Of course. I'll be by your side the entire evening."

"And also, don't be nice to Crystal."

"I will try," Karen said with a half smile.

I looked down at my hands, which were adorned with half a dozen rings, and then back at Karen. "I hope to God this event goes well," I confessed. "Because if it doesn't, I don't think I'll survive this town."

Karen gave me an encouraging smile. "It'll go perfectly. I promise."

12
OLIVIA

It was the night of the gala, one of the many events that were put on for the elite of Buckhead. It was highly exclusive, and it recognized those that went above and beyond for our community, basically those that were successful in everything from politics to business to art and more. Although it was about honoring members of our community and raising money for some charity (I was never sure what charity it was for), deep down it was truly about honoring ourselves. The women dressed up in their most expensive gowns, trying to outdo one another. The men wrote large checks to compensate for other areas in which they were lacking. And this was the last event Shannon would ever lead. It was important that it *not* go well.

A week had passed since my tiff with Jenny and Shannon, and I hadn't spoken to either of them. I had every intention of patching things up with Jenny, but time slipped away from me, and personally, I didn't care, but now I was stuck doing my own hair and makeup. I needed to look my absolute best.

After all, it would be I who was head of the Women's Foundation from this point on.

"Goddamn it!" I raked my eyelashes with mascara, slipping up and getting some on my eyelid.

"Fuck!"

I threw down the mascara wand and stared at myself in the mirror. My hair was straightened, but it looked as if *I* did it. It wasn't the blowout I was going for, and my makeup was half done. I had spent the day watching YouTube videos, the likes of Jaclyn Hill and Jeffree Star, trying to perfect a smoky eye and sky-high lashes, but no such luck. How the hell did they make it look so easy?

"You almost ready?" Dean asked, entering the bedroom wearing a tuxedo. I turned from my vanity to look at him. He was rugged in a very Bond-villain kind of way with a permanent five o'clock salt-and-pepper shadow that never seemed to shrink or grow. It perfectly complimented his defined jawline and strong cheekbones. Even though he was wearing a tux that covered his body full of tattoos, you could see how ripped he was underneath. He cleaned up very nicely.

"Does it look like I'm almost ready?" Sarcasm enveloped my question. I was still in my robe, and I looked average . . . like Karen.

"Where's Jenny? I thought she was doing your hair and makeup." He walked to me, placing his hands on my shoulders.

I turned back, looking in the mirror at myself and then at him. I narrowed my eyes and pursed my lips. "I told you we got into a fight."

"That was a week ago. You haven't apologized yet?" He took a seat on the bed behind me.

"Why should I have to apologize? She was wrong. Not me!" I jerked my head in his direction and scowled.

"Babe. You went into that salon, her place of business, and started a fight with Shannon. It sounds like you should be the one who apologizes. And look, we still have an hour before we have to leave. If you call her now, maybe she can swing by and do your hair and makeup."

"I don't want to," I huffed. He was right. Despite being such a hothead about his own issues, Dean could be pretty rational when it came to mine.

"Yeah, so? I do lots of things I don't want to do. It's called being an adult, Olivia."

I gave him a nasty look and folded my arms in front of my chest.

"How are you getting along with Bryce's new wife, Crystal?" he asked, changing the subject.

I stood from the vanity and paced back and forth. "I don't know."

"What do you mean, you don't know?"

I started pulling out a couple of dresses from the large walk-in closet and laying them on our California king bed. It was adorned in the richest silk sheets and an oversized comforter that was stuffed with goose feathers. "I mean both interactions I've had with her haven't been great. But it wasn't my fault. Karen worked me up the first time I met her. And Shannon and Jenny worked me up this last time. Plus, I'm under a lot of stress with my new position."

"Oh, come on." Dean stood up and grabbed my wrists, pulling me into him. "You need to make nice with those women. Stop with the drama or you're going to end up ostracized like Shannon. Is that what you want?" He pulled my chin up, looking me in the eyes.

"No," I said, hanging my head. His question was clearly rhetorical, but Dean liked to pretend he was intelligent by asking dumb questions that required no answer. He knew that being considered of less value than others was my one and only fear. I didn't fear death. I feared being nothing.

"Good. Well, you can start by calling Jenny and apologizing to her. Then, tonight, please no drama. Just be pleasant. Are you capable of being pleasant?" He pulled my chin back up, so our eyes met again. Dean knew me inside and out. He knew I was capable of being something I'm not. Another dumb rhetorical question.

"I can try," I said, rolling my eyes.

"Good girl." He kissed me on the forehead and stepped away. "I'll be downstairs. I have some calls to make."

I let out a huff. I only put up with his patronizing because I knew it made him feel better about himself, which made him perform his job better, which afforded me anything and everything I could ever want. It was the circle of life—or better yet, wealth—and I was willing to play the game . . . for now.

I walked to the vanity and examined myself in the mirror. This night was so important to me. I needed the women of Buckhead to love me no matter what. If they had to love me out of fear, I was fine with that too. I needed them to fall back in line . . . right behind me. My social circle was coming apart, and I had to put it back together—minus Shannon, of course. She was dead to me—had been for years. Crystal would take her place. This was my evening. I picked up my cell phone, took a deep breath, and repeated to myself in the mirror, "Don't be a bitch. Don't be a bitch." I smiled a devilish grin and dialed Jenny.

13
CRYSTAL

I was anxious about the upcoming evening as I sat beside Bryce in the limo. I didn't want to go, but Bryce was being honored at the gala, and he would make a speech. This night was very important to him. A long green dress with a high slit from some designer I had never heard of hugged my body, a little too tightly if you asked me. My hair was pulled into a gorgeous updo, and my makeup was bronzed and glowy, thanks to Jenny. Bryce slid his hand toward me and grabbed mine. I looked over at him. He was dressed in a fitted tux. He smiled that million-dollar smile, and I returned a much smaller one.

"Where's your gold bag? The one I just bought you?" he asked. Bryce always noticed trivial things like that.

I glanced down at my silver purse. "I accidentally left it at the salon earlier today. I was in such a hurry to get back and change, so we wouldn't be late," I said with a smile. "I know this is important to you."

He smiled back. "Just don't lose it. It's very expensive."

I gave a slight nod.

"How are you feeling about this evening?" he asked.

I was unhappy with how I was being treated in the community, and honestly, I blamed him for that. If he had been truthful with me from the beginning, I would never have started a relationship with him until he ended the one he was in. Now, in the town of Buckhead, I was labeled a gold digger and a home-wrecker. That wasn't who I was. I knew that, but no one else did. But it was too late to change the past, and I knew my role. I had to win them over. I had to be the nice, beautiful girl from Texas that Bryce just couldn't help falling in love with. I'd have to enchant them like I did the poor, unsuspecting married politician who would have been faithful if he hadn't been under my spell. Sounds a bit ridiculous, but people love fairy tales, and whether I liked it or not, this was now my narrative.

After what happened at the salon, I was worried about seeing Shannon again. It was obvious she really hated me. I don't even think there's a strong enough word for how she felt about me. Then there was Olivia. She made me uneasy because she was so hot and cold. She was too much for me, but I guess I'd have to learn how to deal with her. Sacrifices.

"A little nervous," I finally landed on.

"Don't be. They're going to love you, just as I did." Bryce rubbed my hand.

This event was our coming-out party. It was the first time he and I would be seen together out in Buckhead as a couple. I had avoided doing date nights or really being seen with Bryce at all up until this point, but I couldn't put it off any longer.

"But they don't. The women in Buckhead don't like me at all," I confessed. My voice cracked at the end. I didn't mean for it to, but every hard exterior has a soft spot.

"Sweetheart. That's not true."

"Yes, it is. These women hate me because I broke up you and Shannon." I turned away from him, looking out the window.

"You didn't break up Shannon and me. We were already done when you and I started dating." He grabbed my hand again.

"Did she know that?" I looked back at him, tightening my eyes.

He put both his hands on my shoulders and shifted toward me. "I'm going to clear all of this up tonight. I'll make sure people know the real story." He planted a kiss on my cheek.

"The real story or the politician's story?" I jabbed.

"The real one. I promise," he said, kissing me again.

"I'm not sure this is the right place to do this. This is Shannon's event." My eyes searched his. I hoped he'd call it off, that we'd try this another night. It didn't feel right. None of it felt right.

"This is my event. After all, I am the one being honored." He flashed a toothy grin that was neither reassuring nor encouraging. Bryce's arrogance was unmatched, and there was no point in arguing with him. I gave him a small smile and turned my face toward the window. A feeling settled in the pit of my stomach . . . a bad one.

14
KAREN

Mark and I walked up the red-carpeted stairs of the art museum where the gala was being held. There were photographers snapping photos. Bulbs flashed. Cameras flicked. It was all quite disorienting. The building was an architectural masterpiece with large stone pillars, marble flooring, and forty-foot ceilings. It was truly the most beautiful building in all of Buckhead, and I was thrilled I was able to secure it for the gala.

Entering the front door of the museum was like walking onto the set of a big-budget Hollywood film. The place was adorned with *Rosa laevigata*, Georgia's state flower. They had large soft white petals, a yellow center, and a fragrance that filled the entire space. The centerpieces at each round table were vases filled with the flower and the ripest, plumpest peaches Georgia had to offer. It was truly a nice touch, and it was obvious that Shannon had put in a great deal of effort. This was her way of showing everyone that divorce had not affected her and that she could lead on her own. A pang of guilt rushed over me, knowing this was her last gala as chairwoman. Everything brought in for the event screamed opulence—gold tableware, crisp white tablecloths, high-back chairs, white candle lanterns hung throughout, and a string quartet playing soft classical music in the corner. A DJ was set up off the dance floor, ready to take over after dinner. The servers were dressed in white button-downs and black pants, and each of them carried a tray of wine, champagne, or hors d'oeuvres. At least Shannon was going out with a bang. Olivia would have massive shoes to fill, and I was sure she wouldn't even come close.

Mark immediately walked to the bar, leaving me trailing behind him as quickly as I could in my heels. He kept his head down while I exchanged pleasantries with members of the community, most of which were clients of mine. I asked how their homes were. I exchanged hugs and compliments and smiles. Charm was a part of my job.

As I made my way through the crowd, I heard whispers about Shannon.

"I can't believe she's here. How sad."

"Is she really going to introduce Bryce?"

"That poor woman. What is she going to do now?"

"I'm not surprised how beautiful this event is; Shannon doesn't have a man to tend to."

I couldn't help myself overhearing that last remark from a woman named Carol, who was dating a man twice her age.

"I totally agree, Carol. It's so amazing how much time Shannon has to plan incredible events like this. I'm sure you wouldn't have enough hours in the day, what with you caring for your grandfather, Richard. Bless your heart," I said with a Buckhead smile.

"Richard is my boyfriend!" Her lips pursed together and her eyes tightened. She opened her mouth for a moment, but then snapped it closed.

"My mistake." I placed my hand gently on her shoulder as I walked past her. Even my insults were charming. If you passed it off as a misunderstanding, the other person couldn't really get mad at you. I felt I needed to protect Shannon this evening . . . no matter what. She was beyond fragile.

I finally caught up with Mark at the bar. He was already working on his second glass of scotch and chatting with Bryce. Crystal stood on the other side of them, sipping at a flute of champagne, completely zoned out. I grabbed a glass of white wine and walked over to her. It was clear she needed someone.

"Hey, hon. How are you?" I leaned in for a hug. She immediately snapped out of her daze and hugged me back. I know I had promised Shannon I wouldn't be nice to her tonight, but I felt bad for Crystal. I mean, all she had in this town was Bryce.

"Oh my God. I'm so glad you're here," she whispered in my ear. "I'm bored to tears."

I released the hug. "You know how I get through these events?"

Crystal perked up. "How?"

I held up my glass. "A whole hell of a lot of this."

She giggled, downed her drink, and grabbed two more from a waiter's serving tray as he walked by. She downed a second one and set it on the bar, then clinked her third glass with mine.

I overheard Bryce and Mark chatting about Mark's plastic surgery business and Bryce's plans to run for president one day. I let out a small chuckle at the thought. A few years ago, I'd say he never had a chance, but now it's clear anyone can be president, including that insincere asshole.

"Have you seen Olivia?" Crystal asked.

"Not yet. She usually likes to arrive a little late to make a grand entrance." I rolled my eyes.

I could see Crystal was nervous about seeing the

women—especially Shannon and Olivia, given their last inter-action. "Listen, don't worry about Olivia. She's all bark and no bite. And Shannon, she'll come around. She's just bitter, as I'm sure you can understand."

Crystal nodded. "I know. I know. It's weird. I want them to like me even though I don't really even like them."

"I think you might just be starting to understand Buck-head." I winked at her.

She smiled and took another sip of her champagne. "Look, there's Jenny and Keisha." Crystal pointed across the room.

My eyes followed her finger. Jenny and Keisha walked in side by side. Jenny was in a gorgeous long black lace dress with a deep V-neck. It hugged her body in all the right places and accentuated her strawberry-blond hair, which had an old Holly-wood look to it tonight. Keisha was wearing a strappy gold sequin dress. It was long and tight, highlighting her perfect curves. Her naturally curly hair was even more glorious than usual. Her full lips were painted red, and her icy-blue eyes were heightened with shades of purple eye shadow and full sets of fake eyelashes, a new service recently added to Glow. As they walked toward us, heads turned.

"They come here?" Crystal asked.

"Yes. Jenny owns a highly successful business in the area, and she always brings Keisha as her date. Plus, they do touch-ups on their clients throughout the night. Jenny's never not working."

Crystal nodded. As Keisha and Jenny approached us, they both grabbed a glass of champagne from a server walking by, almost in unison. I had known Jenny very well, but as much as I saw Keisha, I didn't know her like I knew Jenny. Our conver-sations had always been limited, small talk here and there and exchanges of pleasantries. But Keisha fascinated me. She was truly the most beautiful woman in all of Buckhead. She always struck me as talented, driven, and genuine, yet she was under-appreciated and underestimated in our community. She knew it, but it didn't seem to faze her. She was unapologetically herself, and she didn't care who liked her and who didn't. In a town full of insecure women and arrogant men, I found such quiet confidence mesmerizing. I had a feeling Keisha was going to achieve great things in life. It was just a matter of time.

"Hello, ladies," Jenny said as she stopped right in front of us. Keisha stood beside her with one hand on her hip. "Hey, girls." We all exchanged hugs and pleasantries.

"I heard about what happened last week with Olivia. I'm sorry," I said.

I hadn't been to the salon all week, because I had been preoccupied with doctor and therapist appointments as well as house showings. The doctor said there was nothing wrong with my hormones and referred me to a therapist to try to help uncover what was happening with my libido. So far, we were just scratching the surface, as my $500-an-hour therapist put it.

"You don't have to apologize for Olivia. She actually called me up earlier tonight and did that herself." Jenny took a drink.

My eyes widened. "Olivia apologized?"

Olivia's apologies were always immediate. If more than an hour had passed, you'd never get an apology out of her. And you'd also know she'd always have it in for you. I swear she kept a hit list of some sort, of all those that had wronged her.

Jenny nodded.

"It seems hell has frozen over." I laughed.

Keisha cracked a smile, forcing her pearly white teeth to make an appearance. She took a sip of her champagne, and there was a twinkle in her eye. I assumed she didn't typically have fun at these events.

"So, everything's good between you two?" Crystal asked.

"For now. Listen, I hope you know it's not typically like that. Times are tense and stressful right now. It'll calm down," Jenny said.

I wasn't too sure of that. Once Shannon found out that Olivia had removed her as chairwoman, all hell would break loose.

Crystal nodded. We clinked glasses, finished our drinks, and then grabbed another.

"Speak of the devil. There she is." Keisha pointed across the room at Olivia. She was dressed in a lacy red halter dress with a train. The back was so low, you could almost see her ass crack. Her hair and makeup were beautifully done, so I assume she apologized to get Jenny to come over and fix her up for this event, because we all knew Olivia couldn't do anything for herself.

"Be nice." Jenny playfully swatted at Keisha. They exchanged tight-lipped smiles as if they had some sort of understanding as to how they were going to get through this evening. I wished I was in on it. I never enjoyed these types of extravagant soirees, but Olivia thrived on them. They reminded me of staging a home. It was all a façade. When you sold the house and removed everything from it, it was empty. That's how these events felt, entirely vacant. Olivia acted as if they were specially put on for her and not for the people we were honoring or the charity we were raising money for. She waved and smiled at people as if she were the queen of England.

"Olivia sure loves the spotlight," Crystal commented.

"She thinks she *is* the spotlight," Keisha quipped.

Olivia and Dean made their way through the crowd. Dean walked straight up to Bryce and Mark, who were still bellied up to the bar. They shook hands and ordered more scotch. Olivia waltzed up to us and said hello. She planted small pecks on our cheeks as she gave us these awkward half hugs. She was trying to make nice . . . or pretending to make nice. I couldn't tell.

"I wanted to thank you again, Jenny, for coming over last minute. I have never felt more beautiful," Olivia gushed, and I rolled my eyes. Olivia was the queen of handing out compliments to herself.

"It was no problem." Jenny nodded.

"And I want to apologize to you too, Crystal, for my outburst earlier this week. There's no excuse for my behavior, but I had just gotten my period and I thought Shannon was attacking you. I'll always stand up for the weaker person. I'm sorry." Olivia placed her hand on Crystal's arm.

Olivia was also the queen of not actually taking responsibility for her own actions and adding a dig to everything.

"It's fine." Crystal took a large gulp of her drink.

"And Karen, I heard you closed on that mansion over on Foxcroft. Congratulations! You know I don't work, but that sounds like it's probably an amazing accomplishment," she said with a toothy grin and a chuckle.

Another dig. But at least she tried.

"It is." I took a sip of my drink.

"So, ladies, who are we saving this week?" Olivia laughed.

Jenny and Keisha exchanged looks. They slightly shook their heads and closed their eyes for a moment.

"The gala is to benefit at-risk youth throughout Atlanta," I said. As vice-chair, she should know this, and as the new chairwoman, I worried for the future of the Buckhead Women's Foundation.

"At-risk youth? They have their whole lives ahead of them. What are they at risk of? Being young?" Olivia laughed . . . at her own joke.

Crystal gave her a small smile. She was learning how to live in Buckhead. I downed my drink.

Olivia looked around the room and then at each of us, up

and down, the way an art appraiser looks at a painting, searching for defects.

"You can tell the divorce had a negative effect on Shannon. This gala definitely suffered. I'm glad we made the tough decision we made. You know, end the suffering." Olivia said, shaking her head.

Keisha, Jenny, and Crystal exchanged confused glances.

I tightened my eyes and then relaxed them. "I think she did a wonderful job. This is the most beautiful event I've ever attended."

Olivia raised her chin. "Well, your taste has always been ordinary, Karen. And I mean that in the most endearing way."

Keisha raised her chin to match Olivia's. "I think it's incredible."

I placed my empty glass on a passing tray and grabbed two more. I handed one to Keisha. We nodded at one another, exchanging small smiles.

"I need one of those." Olivia pointed at my drink, ignoring Keisha's comment. "Excuse me for a moment." She backed up to tap Dean on the shoulder but bumped into my husband.

"I didn't see you there, Mark." Her lips curved into a devilish expression.

"Oh . . . hey, Olivia," Mark stammered. She brushed her arm past his chest, grabbing a vodka soda from the bar top, and bringing the straw to her lips. She sucked and made a satisfied sound when she finished. Tiny beads of sweat formed at Mark's hairline. I wasn't sure what was going on between them, but it was odd. His eyes were locked on her lips. She took the lime from her drink and bit into it, sucking up all the juice.

"Hey." Keisha tapped me on the shoulder, leaning into me. "Thanks for this," she held up the drink.

"No worries. Sorry about Olivia. She's—"

"A bitch," Keisha interrupted.

I laughed and nodded.

We locked eyes as we extinguished our laughter with sips of champagne. There was something in the way Keisha looked at me that made me feel as though I'd known her forever. I felt so at ease in her company, as though I could drop the façade and actually be myself. It was a strange and unaccustomed feeling. But I liked it.

Just past Keisha, I spotted Shannon making the rounds. She was trying to show how strong she was and that a broken marriage wouldn't break her. I admired her for her strength, and I couldn't imagine what she was going through. Her marriage fell apart so publicly, and then she had to watch her husband remarry a much younger woman just months later. I sat with her so many nights as she lounged around her home, dressed in over-sized sweatpants, eating ice cream straight from the container, and crying about how her life was over. But tonight, she was a whole other woman, and she looked like a million bucks. Her sparkly silver Versace dress outshone Olivia's. Her heels were high. Her golden hair draped down, softly curling along the ends, and her makeup was full of exquisite effort. Clearly Jenny's work.

I waved her over. She resisted for a moment with a slight shake of her head. I waved again and smiled, mouthing, "Come here."

She slumped her shoulders in defeat but then raised them again and strutted over to the group. I knew it might be awkward with Olivia and Crystal—and Bryce, for that matter. But Olivia was preoccupied with my husband, talking about God knows what. She was a patient of his, so maybe that was it. I made a mental note to ask him about it later. Bryce was deep in whispered conversations with Dean, and Crystal meant no harm. This was Shannon's event. She had planned the whole damn thing, and she deserved to feel comfortable, to socialize with whomever she wanted, and to enjoy herself.

"Hi, honey," Shannon said, giving me a hug, careful not to spill the drink she picked up on the way over. She hugged Jenny and Keisha. Shannon looked at Crystal and said through tight lips, "Hello, Crystal."

Crystal did this awkward nod mixed with a slight curtsy. She was clearly tipsy. "Hi, Shannon."

"This event is so beautiful. You did a wonderful job." I motioned around the room. Jenny, Keisha, and even Crystal gushed their compliments as well.

Shannon blushed. "Thank you. I'm thrilled it came together so well. At least I have this and the Buckhead Women's Foundation," she said with a laugh.

The guilt sat heavy in my stomach.

Olivia turned from Mark and reentered the circle of women.

Shannon raised her chin at her. "Hello, Olivia." Her greeting was curt.

"Hello, Shannon." Olivia held out two shots of a clear liquid. She extended one to Shannon. "I want to commend you on this event. It came together. Cheers," she said with a smile.

Shannon appeared a bit apprehensive, but her face relaxed as she clinked the shot glass against Olivia's. They tossed them back and gave each other looks of approval.

"Thanks, Olivia. I'm glad we can make amends and get back on track." Shannon nodded.

"As am I," Olivia said with a grin.

It looked like the two were getting along again, and maybe this night wouldn't be a disaster after all. Jenny and Crystal were quietly chatting about the purse she had left at the salon. I turned to Keisha. She was zoned out with a hundred-mile stare. Her slender fingers held the stem of an empty champagne glass.

"Want to grab a drink at the bar with me?" I asked.

Keisha looked at me with a twinkle in her eye. She nodded an enthusiastic yes.

15
SHANNON

Olivia handed me another drink. I thanked her and took a sip. It was heavy on the vodka, light on the soda. I couldn't believe she was being so nice to me. It was like how it was before Bryce and I divorced. It gave me hope that I could have a bright future with or without him.

"I'm sorry I haven't checked in on you, Shannon. I've just been stressed and not feeling like myself. How have you been?" Olivia asked. She took a small sip from her drink, and her face turned sympathetic.

Before I could open my mouth, a middle-aged woman named Bethany filled in the gap in the circle beside me. She was thin and dressed in all black.

She leaned in, "So sorry to hear about your husband." Bethany placed her hand on my shoulder and gave me a look of pity.

I blinked several times, trying my hardest not to roll my eyes. "What? Did he die?"

She squeezed my shoulder, "You're so strong. I wouldn't be able to show my face if I were you."

"Where is your husband, Bethany?" Olivia cut in. She dramatically glanced around the room, pretending to look for him. Everyone knew full well he was not there.

Bethany let out a small cough. "He's with his niece."

Olivia tightened her eyes. "Is that what you call his mistress?"

Bethany gave her a harsh look, raised her shoulders, and stormed off without another word.

I looked to Olivia, surprised because she had come to my defense. "Thank you."

"Of course. Besides, the only difference between you and her is that your husband left you, while Bethany's is still having his cake and fucking it too," Olivia spat.

She let on a hearty laugh, and I chuckled too.

"What was that about?" Jenny asked.

"More condolences." I rolled my eyes and looked down at my Cartier watch.

"Some people are just vile." Olivia shook her head.

She glanced down at her watch too and turned toward the bar. When she turned back, Olivia had another shot in her hand. This time it had a yellowish tint. "Here, Shannon. Your big moment is almost here. Tequila will help."

I hesitated for a moment, but then took it from her and tossed it back. I checked the time once more. I had less than five minutes before I had to be onstage to introduce Bryce. I had almost backed out, but I wanted to show everyone that I was strong and capable, with or without a husband. I wanted Bryce back, but sometimes, I found myself wanting *me* back more—the me I was before him. Tonight made me feel like I could have that.

"Let me walk you to the stage," Olivia said, grabbing my hand.

I looked down at her hand and then at her face. She gave an encouraging smile.

"Okay," I said.

The first step I took was wobbly. Those drinks had hit me quickly. My vision was a little blurry, but I felt beyond confident—like I could take on the world. I smiled at people as Olivia led me through the crowd. They threw compliments at me, and I thanked them. This was where I was supposed to be. I was Shannon Madison with or without Bryce. We stopped off to the side of the stage.

Olivia placed her hands on my shoulders and looked me in the eye . . . only I was seeing two Olivias.

"Shannon, you're going to do great. Bryce will be up here shortly, so you can introduce him," she said.

I nodded or at least I think I did.

"I just want to say congratulations on your last event as chairwoman. You did a wonderful job, but I'll be taking the reins from this point on." She smiled . . . twice, or maybe once. I closed my eyes for a moment and shook my head slightly, trying to make sense of her words.

"Wait, what? What do you mean, last event?" I stammered.

"The board voted last week for you to step down as chairwoman. Your divorce got in the way of your ability to lead. We were afraid our charities and events would suffer under your leadership. I'm sorry. I wanted to tell you sooner. It's been weighing so heavy on my heart, keeping this from you. But it was unanimous." Olivia pulled her lips in.

My eyes went wide and I felt them get glossy. "No, this can't be right."

"It was a tough decision, but it was the right one," Olivia said, tilting her head.

"Are you ready?" Bryce said, standing beside me.

His head was held high, and his shoulders were pinned back. I looked up at him, realizing I had lost everything. All because he left me.

Olivia removed her hands from my shoulders and smiled. She looked at Bryce. "She's ready," she said and then disappeared into the crowd.

His politician grin was plastered across his face now, signaling he was ready to be introduced. I knew now that if I wanted my life back, I needed Bryce in it.

"I'm glad you decided to go through with this," Bryce spoke through his large beaming smile, never letting it falter.

I tried to say, "Me too," but my voice cracked, so I nodded instead.

He glanced down at me, "Perhaps we can work things out if this goes well."

My heart swelled, my pulse raced, and it felt like I had a swarm of butterflies inside my stomach. Bryce leaned down and kissed me on the cheek. It felt warm against my skin. "You look beautiful," he whispered.

I felt my cheeks flush. Bryce and I were getting back together. He said so himself. The rest of my life would fall back into place. Chairwoman of the Buckhead Women's Foundation. My social status. My marriage. Everything. I walked up the stairs to the stage with my head held high—ready to reintroduce Bryce and me to the world.

16
CRYSTAL

I watched Bryce kiss Shannon on the cheek. I felt a bit uneasy, but I knew he was just trying to make nice. He didn't need his ex-wife making a scene, and he knew Shannon was like a China dish, fragile and prone to breaking into a million pieces.

"Is Shannon trying to steal her man back?" Olivia said with a laugh.

"She's just being professional," Karen said.

"As is Bryce," I added.

"The only thing worse than hope is false hope." Olivia sipped her champagne. "I'm going to go get a better view. This is for sure going to be a train wreck." She tried to grab Dean's hand, but he grabbed her arm with force.

"Stop," he warned in a low growl.

"Stop what?" Olivia tried to pull her arm away.

"With the drama." He tightened his eyes.

"Ow. I'm just having fun."

This time when she pulled, her arm came free. It was covered in red marks from where his fingers had been. She rubbed her arm with her hand, trying to soothe it.

"That hurt, you asshole. Cool it on the drinks." She pushed him back, turned on her foot, and disappeared into the crowd.

When I glanced around at the other girls, it seemed none of them had noticed what happened. I had seen this type of toxic relationship before, and I knew firsthand that it could be deadly.

"Are you guys still having the monthly book club at the salon tomorrow morning?" Jenny asked.

Karen laughed. "If you can even call it that, thanks to Olivia's pick."

"What book did she choose?" Keisha asked.

"*Vogue*."

The girls laughed, but I didn't. I was still thinking about what had just happened between Olivia and Dean. Was this a common occurrence? Was Dean abusive? The room suddenly quieted as the spotlight lit up Shannon onstage. As much as she and I were at odds, I hoped this would go well. Shannon needed to show Buckhead that she had moved on, even if she hadn't yet.

She grabbed the mic and cleared her throat. "Good evening, ladies and gentlemen. As you all know, I'm Shannon Madison," she began.

Whispers ensued throughout the audience, followed by shushing. Karen, Jenny, and Keisha helped quiet the crowd. I shook my head slightly. She should have said Shannon Block. She was no longer Shannon Madison.

She smiled and continued, thanking everyone for their generous contributions and talking about the charity and what the money would be used for. She thanked those that had volunteered. She thanked the members of the Buckhead Women's Foundation, and then it was time for her to introduce Bryce. He was being honored for the work he had done to secure a building and the finances needed to open a recreation center in Atlanta for at-risk youth.

"And now, it is my pleasure to introduce the man of honor," Shannon began.

Karen clasped her hands together as if she were praying.

"You all know him as your congressman, but I know him very differently as he was once my husband. Bryce and I met fifteen years ago. We fell madly in love, and together we built a beautiful life. Yes, I know you've all heard about our temporary separation."

Whispers ensued.

"This is so painful," Keisha said to Jenny.

"Should we stop her?" Karen asked.

"That'll make it worse." Jenny leaned in.

"Nothing can be worse than this," Keisha said.

Shannon held her smile through all the whispering and continued. "Love like the love Bryce and I had, excuse me, have . . . never dies. It just changes, morphs like clay, but it can always get back to its original shape."

"She's drunk, right?" Keisha asked.

"Has to be," Jenny said. She looked over at me and gave me an encouraging smile. I wasn't the one that needed the reassurance though. Shannon needed all the strength in the room at this moment.

Shannon paced back and forth on the stage. The mic slipped from her hand and hit the floor with a thud. She bent down, nearly falling over, and picked it up.

"Oopsie daisy," she said. "Now, where was I? Oh, yes. Bryce and I are getting back together."

People whispered and looked around the room. Eyes were on me. Eyes were on Bryce and eyes were on Shannon. Bryce started quickly up the stairs of the stage.

"They say if you love someone, let them go, and if they come back, then it's meant to be. So, Bryce . . . here you are." Shannon motioned to Bryce right as he got onstage. It had looked as though the whole thing had been planned, but Bryce's face told the truth as it was red with anger and embarrassment.

"Come to me, my friend, my lover, my everything, my—" Bryce grabbed the mic from Shannon. She tried to lean in for a kiss, but he stepped aside, and she tumbled over.

"It would appear someone's had a little too much to drink this evening," Bryce said with a smile. He looked at Shannon, who was still trying to get her footing. Her face was wrinkled up in confusion, as if she had no idea what just happened. The crowd exploded with laughter.

"Oh, Shannon. You sure know how to put the *ex* in ex-wife." He laughed.

Shannon's eyes moistened as she searched the faces in the crowd. My heart broke for her.

"In all seriousness, you did a wonderful job here tonight putting on this event. So, thank you for the handoff, but I'll take it from here. You certainly deserve our gratitude and a night of relaxation, minus the alcohol," Bryce said, winking to the crowd and then looking at Shannon. Her eyes grew wide like she was just starting to understand what was going on. He returned his gaze to the crowd. "Give it up for my ex-wife, Shannon, everyone." Applause ensued as she slowly walked offstage.

"But as the great Taylor Swift once said, 'We are never, ever, ever getting back together.'" The crowd roared with laughter as Bryce slapped his own knee and the DJ quickly threw on the track.

Shannon's eyes filled with tears. Karen, Keisha, and Jenny scurried toward her, while everyone sang along to Swift's catchy lyrics. Bryce found my face in the crowd as he led the sing-along, and he winked at me. My eyes narrowed. My lips remained pressed firmly together. How could he have done this to Shannon? How could he have embarrassed her like this? He loved her once. She had been his wife. If he could do this to her, what would he do to me?

17
KAREN

"Shannon, it's not the end of the world," I said, holding her against me. Hugging her was like trying to hold on to Jell-O as she was falling apart in my arms. We were seated in the back of an Uber Black SUV on our way to Shannon's apartment. I needed to make sure she made it home okay.

"Yes, it is." She pulled away. Her makeup was smeared, and she now looked like a Picasso painting. "I don't know what the hell happened. One minute, everything was fine. And the next, everyone is laughing at me, and I'm being escorted offstage."

"It wasn't that bad," I said. But I knew it was bad. I have no idea why she decided to do that. When I saw her earlier in the night, she was put together and seemed to have everything under control.

"They booed me offstage! And my ex sang, 'We're never ever getting back together.'" She cried harder.

The driver looked at us in the rearview mirror and raised his thick eyebrows.

"Eyes on the road," I said. Shannon had had enough people judging her for the night. His eyes snapped ahead as he turned onto her street.

"Shannon, what came over you? Why did you do that?" I asked.

She sat up straight and rubbed her temple. The car pulled up to the curb and parked. Shannon looked at me and then down at her lap. "I'm . . . not sure. Olivia was feeding me shots and being really nice to me, and she walked me to the stage and she said . . ." Shannon rubbed her temple again, willing the memory to come back.

"What did she say to you?" I asked.

"Bryce said there was a possibility we could get together if all went well." Shannon snapped her head up and look at me.

I rolled my eyes. "He's just toying with you because you were about to introduce him to all of Buckhead."

"Maybe he wasn't. Maybe he meant it." Her eyes went wide.

"Shannon, don't fall for that bullshit. He embarrassed you right after, in front of everyone. So, that was why you talked about reuniting when you were onstage—because he led you on." I took her hand and held it.

She looked down at my hand. "But Olivia."

"What about her?" I asked.

The driver got out of the car and opened Shannon's door. She didn't get out. Instead, she stared at her lap. And then a light bulb went on. Her head snapped up and her eyes went wide. She pulled her hand away and shuffled away from me.

"Olivia said you all voted to remove me as chairwoman. That the gala was my last event. She said it was because of my divorce. Is that true?" Shannon narrowed her eyes.

My mouth dropped open. "You were removed as chair-woman, but—"

"When? When the hell did this happen?" she interjected.

I tilted my head. "A little over a week ago, but . . ."

Shannon stepped out of the vehicle with the help of the driver. "How could you, Karen? You were supposed to be my friend." Her face was a mixture of anger and sadness. "You and I are done."

"Shannon, wait. It's not what you think. I—" The door closed with a slam, and she stormed off toward her apartment building without looking back. As the car pulled away from the curb, a tear escaped from my eye and ran down my cheek.

18

JENNY

I placed an assortment of lipsticks back in the slots of an acrylic organizer along with a few eye shadow palettes and a couple of bronzers and highlighters. I had considered going right to bed after the gala, but my brain was buzzing, and I figured I may as well clean up the salon since Keisha and I didn't have time earlier. My fingers pressed a switch on the wall, shutting off all the lights in the salon. Grabbing a handful of dirty makeup brushes, I made my way to the bathroom in the back. I pulled the sink drain closed, plopped a rubber cleansing mat in it, and ran the water. The makeup brushes sunk to the bottom as soon as I tossed them in, a rainbow of colors bleeding off of them, staining the water like a tepid bath bomb.

A crash in the salon made me instantly turn off the water. It was the sound of breaking glass. My breath quickened, and I was frozen in place while my brain vacillated between fight or flight. Another crash, and then there was the chime from the front door. The alarm didn't sound as I hadn't set it yet. The panel was next to the back door, and it was the last thing I did before leaving at the end of each day.

There were whispers, but I couldn't make out what they were saying. The crunch of glass told me someone was walking farther into the salon. I slid off my heels quietly and tiptoed toward the bathroom door, my pulse pounding in my ears. The metal curtain rings screeched across the rod. I peeked my head down the hallway toward the back door. I could make my way out and run upstairs to my apartment, but my cell phone was in my purse on the front counter. There was a loud crash. The sound of something being knocked over and the spilling of various items. I assumed one of the vanities.

"Cool it," one voice said.

"Just having a little fun," another voice said.

I heard the sound of glass smashing against the floor, a mirror perhaps. They were destroying what I had built, piece by piece. Finally, before I could convince myself it was a bad idea, I started moving swiftly across the floor. I picked up one of the candleholders from on top of the vanity cabinet. It was colored like marble and extremely heavy. After a couple of deep breaths, I made my way out of the bathroom, down the hallway, and into the back of the salon. It was dark. I could see the outline of a man dressed all in black. He was ransacking the place. The register beeped, so I knew the other person was on the other side of the curtains. The one closest to where I was had his back to me. He was bent over, looking through the cabinet where we kept extra bottles of alcohol.

"Veuve Clicquot. Nice," he said, pulling one out and ripping off the seal.

The other man yelled, "I can't get this stupid thing open!"

"It doesn't matter," the man closest to me said while fiddling with the bottle. Something small hit the floor. I assumed the wire cage. The cork popped off and he chuckled, immediately bringing the bottle to his lips. Champagne went everywhere.

"What the hell are you doing back there?" the man up front yelled.

Before he could answer, the candleholder came crashing down on his head. He yelped and fell forward.

The curtains flew open, and the other man stood there, taking in the scene. All I could see were the whites of his eyes beneath his ski mask.

"Oh, shit."

I took my eyes off of the guy on the floor for too long because all of a sudden, I was falling to the ground. My head hit the tile with a thud, and my vision blurred. The candleholder flew from my hand. The man with the ski mask was on top of me. His hands around my neck, squeezing harder and harder. I tried to reach for something around me but there was nothing.

"Stupid bitch," he seethed. Spit gathered at his lips and his eyes were red with fury. I tried to reach for his ski mask to remove it, but couldn't.

"Dude, stop. You're going to kill her," the other man begged.

It was getting harder and harder for me to breathe. More pressure on my neck, my windpipe caving in against the pressure.

"You wanna play rough?" he teased.

My voice croaked. "Yeah . . ." I sent a knee right into his groin.

He winced, and I shuffled out from under him. Before I could get away, he grabbed my ankle and pulled me back. His fist connected with my face, twice. First, the eye. I saw stars dancing across my vision, everything else going black. Then, the mouth. The taste of warm, thick iron coating the back of my tongue. I heard the other guy yell. Then footsteps, running from me rather than toward me. The glass crunched under his shoes. He had left, and I was pinned beneath the other man once again, fighting for every breath.

19
CRYSTAL

A long walk was what I needed after how the gala had ended. Bryce said he had business to tend to and celebratory cigars to puff with the boys. I was grateful for a reprieve from him because I was so angry and disappointed with how he had treated Shannon. She didn't deserve that. He had completely humiliated her in front of all of Buckhead. I had told him I was going for a walk and would Uber home from the salon. Earlier I told Jenny that I had left my purse there, and she said she'd wait up for me so I could grab it. But it was late. Honestly, I just wanted a walk to clear my head, so it didn't matter if Jenny was still up. A cool breeze made the humidity bearable and the walk from the gala to Glow on Peach Street pleasant. I had never seen Buckhead so quiet and peaceful. Not a person or car in sight. The only sound I heard was the click of my heels along the sidewalk. I turned onto Peach Street and saw the sign for Glow up ahead on the left. From where I was, it looked dark inside, so I assumed Jenny had gone to bed. I considered calling an Uber right there, but my feet kept moving forward.

A large man dressed in black shorts and a hoodie suddenly darted out from one of the businesses, and I was sure it was Glow when I saw a shimmery gold bag in his hands. That was *my* bag. He was just ten yards away, rifling through it.

I quickened my pace and called out, "Hey!"

He snapped his head in my direction. The ski mask covered most of his face except his wide eyes and partially open mouth.

"Goddamn it. I didn't sign up for this," he said as he turned on his foot and ran in the opposite direction.

A large inky tattoo covered the back of his pale calf. It looked as though it hadn't been done by a professional because it was unclear. I considered chasing him down but stopped in front of Glow when I saw the broken glass and the open door. I dialed 911 and placed the phone back in my bag. I was about to yell out, but I heard rustling inside followed by a scream.

My hand went back into my bag and emerged holding a Ruger .380 ACP pocket pistol. It had a chrome finish and a hot-pink grip.

"Better safe than sorry," I recalled my stepfather saying when he gifted me the gun all those years back. "Treat it like a cell phone and always have it with you." I was grateful for his advice now. Taking a deep breath, I quickly decided between running in, guns blazing, or making a careful entrance. The man I just saw clearly didn't have a weapon. The odds were if anyone else was in there, they wouldn't have one either.

Running through the door, I threw open the velvet curtain and found a man dressed in black, pinning Jenny to the ground. I fired a warning shot. The man quickly scrambled off her and ran down the hallway, crashing into a cabinet as he furtively fled for what I'm sure he thought were his last moments. I flipped the light switch as Jenny sat up. Her eye was already blossoming into what would be a massive bruise. Her mouth was bloody. And vicious red marks covered her neck. She gasped for air, sucking deep, painful breaths that brought tears to her eyes.

"Oh my God, Jenny," I said, running to her side.

20
JENNY

Detective Sanford enters the room carrying two cups of coffee. This time, instead of the Styrofoam cups full of essentially stale brown water, it's Starbucks. He places one in front of me. He's gotten more accommodating as the hours have passed, or perhaps he's taken a liking to me.

"Thank you," I say, bringing the cup to my lips.

He nods. "I appreciate your cooperation and you coming forward." Detective Sanford pulls out a chair and takes his seat. "So, the gala didn't go well?"

"It was a disaster."

He takes a sip of his coffee. "Shannon must have been very upset after that."

"Obviously. Bryce embarrassed her in front of everyone who was anyone in Buckhead."

"And there was tension between Shannon and Olivia?" He raises an eyebrow.

"I think there was tension between everyone," I say matter-of-factly.

"I found a police report that indicates that Glow was broken into the night of the gala, and you were injured that evening." He gives me a sympathetic look.

My hand runs along my neck, rubbing it. Sometimes I can still feel my windpipe being crushed. I simply nod. I'm not sure what else he wants me to say. He clearly read the report, my statement, and Crystal's statement. There's nothing more for me to add.

"They never caught the people responsible?"

"No, the police never caught the people responsible." I take another sip of my coffee.

"Had anything like that ever happened before?" He tilts his head.

"No, never."

"According to the report, only a gold purse was stolen?"

"That's correct. They couldn't get the register open." I swivel the Starbucks cup slightly.

"Do you think it was random?" Detective Sanford raises an eyebrow again.

I lean forward a little in my seat. "I don't think anything that happened in Buckhead was random."

21
OLIVIA

I had to wear my long-sleeved red Valentino dress today thanks to Dean grabbing my arm so aggressively last night. I don't know what the hell got into him. I mean I get it; he doesn't want me stirring up trouble, but still, it was unnecessary, and I left this morning without speaking a word to him. I'm sure I'll come back home to a new designer bag and a few dozen red roses. I was off to Glow Salon for our monthly book club, and I was excited to discuss *Vogue* and, of course, Shannon. I assumed she wouldn't even attend after her embarrassing episode at the gala. Ugh! Glow's left window was boarded up and there was duct tape holding together the glass on the door. This place was going downhill fast.

"Why does this place look abandoned?" I called out as I threw open the velvet curtains, making my way into the salon. "I almost didn't come in, in case someone saw me. What would they say? But it's my pick this month, so I had to be here." I turned up my nose and slid off my sunglasses. The place did look a little dingier, not as clean as usual. A makeup vanity was missing.

"Jenny should really get a maid in here. This place needs a lot of work."

Crystal and Karen were seated on a couch, while Keisha was filling glasses with mimosas and finishing setting up. The coffee table was covered in platters of fresh-cut fruit, croissants, and sliced cheese. Crystal looked rough. Dark circles sat under her eyes, and she was dressed in Lululemon leggings and a white T-shirt. Karen looked average as well. Had these women just given up? I rolled my eyes.

"Glow was broken into last night." Karen looked at me.

"What? That's terrible."

"And Jenny was hurt pretty bad," Crystal said. Her eyes were glossy and her lip trembled.

"What?" My hand flew to my mouth. "Where is she?"

Before any of them could answer, Jenny walked in from the back. Her right eye was black and blue. Her lip was swollen and bruises covered her neck.

"Oh my God, Jenny. Are you okay?" I ran to her.

"I'm fine. It's not as bad as it looks," she said, beelining for the vanity. She applied some powder onto her neck, trying to cover it up, but the injuries were too dark.

"Can I get you anything? I have Vicodin," I offered.

"Oh, no. I just want to enjoy this book club meeting and not talk about it, if that's all right." She forced a small smile, but winced a little, bringing her finger to her lip.

There were nods all around.

"You know I can handle everything here, if you want to go upstairs and lie down." Keisha offered.

"Nonsense, I'm fine."

I took a seat on the couch. "Well, this is absolutely appalling, and I'll be bringing this up at the next committee meeting for a potential charity event," I said.

"Olivia, it's fine. Insurance is covering everything. The windows are getting replaced today," Jenny said, pouring herself a glass of orange juice.

"But your face. It's hideous."

"Olivia!" Karen scolded.

"I mean that in the best way possible of course," I said with a smile.

"It'll heal," Jenny said, taking a sip.

I shifted uncomfortably in my seat. "Karen, you should really get Mark in here to look at her. She'll probably need reconstructive surgery," I said.

Karen rolled her eyes. Apparently, she didn't care about Jenny like I did.

Jenny clapped her hands together. "Let's begin book club."

"Actually, this month it's a *Vogue* club." I pulled out my fresh copy of *Vogue* from my bag. "Top five worst outfits, go," I said, pointing at Crystal. She looked as though she was going to cry, and I didn't know why.

"Are you okay, Crystal?" I asked.

She nodded. "Yeah. But shouldn't we wait for Shannon?" Crystal looked around at the rest of us for approval.

"Is she even going to show up? I mean after last night . . ." I grabbed a mimosa and brought it to my lips to extinguish the impending laughter.

"It wasn't that bad," Karen piped in and took a mimosa of her own.

I pulled out my phone. "You're kidding, right? I got it all on video. It's hilarious." I pushed Play. "I'm thinking about submitting it to WorldStar."

Karen scowled at me. "Turn that off, Olivia."

"What? It's just a joke. Lighten up. Keisha, you're probably the only one who knows what WorldStar is anyway." I winked at her.

Keisha furrowed her brow. "You are something else," she said, shaking her head.

"Thank you." I smiled wide.

Karen downed her whole glass and refilled it with just champagne. "Why the hell did you tell Shannon that she wasn't chairwoman anymore, Olivia?" she asked, narrowing her eyes.

"I did?" I placed my hands against my chest. "It just slipped out. I'm so sorry. I know we agreed to wait. I must have had a little too much to drink." The lies came extremely naturally. They just rolled off the tongue one by one.

Karen exhaled deeply and then took a drink of her champagne. "She's pissed now. She's not even talking to me."

I shook my head. "That's awful, but you know how she can be. I'm sure she'll get over it. You two are friends," I said with a small smile.

Crystal leaned forward and filled a plate with cheese and two croissants. She stuffed the bread with cheese and ate it like a sandwich. How repulsive. What did Bryce see in her?

"I didn't get a chance to apologize to Shannon for Bryce's behavior last night, so hopefully she comes," Crystal said with a mouth full of food. *Uncultured swine.*

"His behavior was appalling," Karen confirmed.

Crystal's eyes moistened. "I still can't believe how he acted." Her voice cracked at the end.

Little Miss Country sure put the *pathetic* in *sympathetic.* How dare she not stand behind her man? Bryce did nothing wrong. It's not his fault Shannon is like a case of herpes: hard to treat and never truly goes away. The only way he'll ever get rid of Shannon is via a death certificate.

"I agree with you both. Bryce was out of line last night," I said, biting my tongue.

Crystal gave me a pleased smile. Keisha's eyes widened and then relaxed when she made eye contact with Jenny. Probably because it was hard to look at her. It was as though someone had taken a mallet to her face. It really put Glow in a bad light.

"Are you sure you're okay to be here, Jenny?" I tilted my head.

"Yeah, I'm fine." She took another sip of her orange juice as her eyes bounced around the room and then back on me.

"Well, anyway. I think Bryce owes Shannon an apology." I piled the bullshit on thick.

"I agree," Karen and Keisha said in unison.

Jenny gave a slight nod and then rubbed her bruised neck. She should be wearing a turtleneck.

"I'm going to make sure he does apologize," Crystal reassured.

"I'm so glad we're all getting along again," I said with a smile as wide as a six-lane highway.

"Not everyone. Like I said, Shannon hates me," Karen said while sipping her champagne.

"You two will work it out," Jenny said. Her voice was soft and raspy.

There's a wedge I could push in further. "It's not your fault that Shannon got drunk and made a fool of herself. And it's not your fault that I accidentally spilled the beans on the whole chairwoman thing," I said with so much conviction in my voice.

"And how Bryce treated her isn't your fault either," Crystal added. I smiled at her.

"Hate to say it, but I agree with Olivia." Keisha gave me a curt smile.

"I appreciate that, Keisha." I smiled back.

The front door chimed, and through the curtains walked Shannon, dressed head-to-toe in designer clothing. Her face was puffy, probably due to the alcohol she drank in excess the night before. Aside from that, she looked rather pulled together. That's probably why she was late, trying to make herself appear strong when we all knew she was like a compact of pressed powder: ready to fall apart.

"Sorry, I'm late. What are you hens talking about?" Shannon waltzed in and grabbed a bottle of champagne. She poured herself a drink and took a seat. Her voice was light and forced.

"You," I said.

"What happened to the window?" Shannon asked, ignoring my comment.

"Break-in," Jenny said.

Shannon looked to Jenny. "Oh my God! Are you okay?" Her eyes and mouth went wide.

"She doesn't want to talk about it," Keisha said, placing a hand on Jenny's shoulder.

"Yeah, let's just focus on the book club." Jenny's voice was quiet.

Shannon closed her mouth and nodded. "Okay, sure."

"How are you doing this morning, Shannon?" I asked.

It took a moment for Shannon to look away from Jenny. She immediately looked back at her. "Are you sure, Jenny?" she asked again.

Jenny nodded.

"Shannon, I asked you a question," I said, swirling my mimosa.

She shot daggers at me. "I've got some things I need to take care of now, thanks to a recent betrayal." Her eyes flickered at Karen.

Jenny and Keisha exchanged worried glances. Usually I

never noticed those two, but I knew I needed to be observant of everyone if I intended to gain power over this group of women. Shannon's reign was over. All hail Queen Olivia.

"Shannon, if you have something to say, just say it," Karen said.

"Is someone talking?" Shannon held her hand to her ear. "Sounds like an ex, backstabbing friend."

Karen rolled her eyes and took a sip of her champagne.

"Listen, Shannon," Crystal turned her body toward her. "I want to apologize for Bryce's behavior last night. I'm truly appalled by it, and I, too, am upset with him. You planned a wonderful gala, and people are only going to remember how incredible your event was." Crystal smiled.

Shannon nodded slightly but then raised her chin. "There's no need to apologize for Bryce. He and I are having dinner tonight to discuss what happened between us."

Crystal leaned back. "Oh, I didn't realize he had arranged that." She took a gulp of her mimosa, finishing the rest of it.

"Do you really think that's a good idea?" Karen asked.

Shannon grabbed a few grapes and popped them in her mouth. "Not sure who's talking, but yes."

This exchange between Shannon and Karen reminded me of how Shannon used to treat me when I first arrived in Buckhead. At first she pretended like I didn't exist, and then she bullied and ridiculed me. It was nice to see it happening to someone else for a change.

"It's inappropriate to go out to dinner with another woman's husband, Shannon," I said, knowing full well that I, the pot, had just met the kettle.

"He was my husband first," Shannon shouted. She took a deep breath and pretended to straighten her jewelry.

"So, which outfit did you guys like most?" Keisha asked,

holding up her copy of *Vogue* and trying desperately to change the subject. She was being the peacekeeper since Jenny surely couldn't handle it now.

"Page fifty-three," I said, throwing poor Keisha a bone. She quickly flipped through the pages.

"I don't mind that you and Bryce are going out to dinner. We're happily married," Crystal said meekly.

Keisha took a swig straight from the champagne bottle. Karen bounced her foot faster. Jenny took the magazine from Keisha and flipped through it with so much vigor, she was ripping every other page. I was at the edge of my seat. The only thing that would make this more perfect was a small bag of SkinnyPop popcorn.

"SO. WERE. WE," Shannon said in the most dramatic way possible.

Crystal's eyes tightened, and I thought for sure she was going to jump down Shannon's throat, but instead, tears came slithering out the corners. How pathetic.

"Shannon, come on!" Karen shook her head.

"What? Did you all forget? She stole my husband." Shannon threw her hands up.

"No, she didn't. One in two marriages end in divorce, Shannon. It's not that big of a deal," I said calmly.

"Oh, eat it, Olivia." Shannon waved a hand at me dismissively.

I dropped my mouth open, acting as though I was appalled by her words, but really, I was rather enjoying myself. I thought I'd have to do so much more to get Shannon out of our group, but here she was, committing social suicide.

"I think you should leave," Karen said.

"Crystal, you should leave." Shannon smiled.

"No, you, Shannon." Karen raised her chin.

Shannon whipped her head in Karen's direction. She scowled at her and stood up from her seat with force. "Fine. I don't want to be here anyway, especially around a fake friend like you, Karen." She looked at each of us. "*Vogue* isn't even a book, Olivia, you half-wit. And Crystal, I'll tell *my* husband his whore said hi."

Shannon turned on her foot but stopped and looked back at Jenny. "I'm so sorry. I'll call to check on you later." She gave a sympathetic look and then turned back and stormed out.

We all took intermittent sips of our drinks and glanced at one another.

Keisha refilled her glass. "Well, that was interesting."

"Can we revoke her membership now?" I raised an eyebrow.

"No, she's just having a hard time," Jenny said.

"Yeah, she was doing so well. I guess the mixture of what Bryce did and losing the chairwoman position just made her freak out." Karen glared at me and shook her head.

"I feel bad for her." Crystal wiped her eyes with a napkin and took a bite of her cheesy stuffed croissant.

Karen bounced her foot. "We all do."

I nodded along, my body doing the opposite of what my mind was thinking.

22
SHANNON

"Right this way," the hostess said as she escorted me to a corner table set for two. She pulled out my chair and told me she'd send the server over when my other guest arrived. "I'll have a bottle of Dom Pérignon right away," I said. She nodded.

I was dressed in my tightest designer dress and my highest heels, waiting eagerly for Bryce to arrive. I had asked him to dinner so we could discuss what happened and how we'd move forward (as a couple). He had agreed; however, he was unaware of my true intentions. Sure, Bryce had embarrassed me in front of the whole town, but I backed him into a corner, and he couldn't just outright declare his love for me. He had his career to think about. Now that we'd be alone, he could disclose his true feelings like he did just before the mishap onstage. I knew I sounded delusional, but this was how it had always been with Bryce. I had to convince him to love me the first time, all those years ago, and I knew I'd have to do it again. He was the type of man that made decisions with both his heads. The heart never played a part. Bryce was like an ice sculpture, cold and inflexible, so I just had to chip away at him carefully. Either he'd be sculpted into the man that once loved me, or he'd be destroyed in the process.

A moment later, two servers arrived with two glasses and the bottle of champagne in a bucket of ice. One popped the champagne and poured it, while the other straightened the table and placed the bottle back into the bucket. I gave them a pleased smile and thanked them. I took a sip of the champagne; the cool, crisp bubbles made my tongue tingle.

I glanced down at my watch. Bryce was five minutes late. Of course, he'd make me wait just a little longer. I quickly pulled out a compact and ensured my makeup was perfectly set. Just as I placed it back in my purse, I spotted Bryce across the room. I waved and smiled. His lips were pressed firmly together as he gave a small nod and headed in my direction. I stood from my chair and went in for a hug, even though he was already half seated.

"Thank you so much for coming," I said.

He patted my back and sat down. I made my way to my side of the table and took a seat across from him. I couldn't help but smile. He grabbed his glass of champagne.

"Oh, a toast. Perfect," I held my glass up. He pulled his from his lips.

"To us," I said, and I clinked mine to his.

"Shannon, what are you doing?" He set the glass back down, raising an eyebrow. He leaned back in his chair, looking me up and down. It was clear he liked what he saw.

"Just greeting my husband." I winked.

"Ex," he corrected.

I shrugged my shoulders. "Potato, potahto," I giggled.

"Have you been drinking?" he asked. "Because I don't want

to have this conversation with you if you've been drinking." He put his elbows on the table and leaned toward me. "I mean it, Shannon. I don't want another episode like last night."

"Of course not. This is my first glass. Promise," I lied. I had had a small cocktail—or four—at home.

He nodded. "Now, what did you want to discuss exactly? You mentioned living in Buckhead amicably."

"First, let's order food. I'm famished." I picked the menu up and pretended to read it. I just wanted more time with him. I needed more time to explain why it would be in his best interest to get back together with me. He needed to see how good we were as a couple.

"Fine," he said just as the server arrived.

"Can I start you off with some appetizers?" she asked.

Bryce shook his head.

"Yes, we'll have one of each to start," I blurted out. She nodded and walked away.

"I don't have all night. I have some things I'm working on."

"I know, babe. I understand more than anyone else how important your work is to you. Just relax and enjoy yourself."

Bryce took a deep breath and grabbed his glass of champagne, taking a large gulp of it. The server returned with bread and some of the cold appetizers.

"So, how was work today?" I served myself steak tartar and a piece of bread.

"Busy," he said while slurping up an oyster. Oh, it was like we hadn't even missed a beat. Everything was just as it had always been.

I knew the girls were pissed at me for my behavior earlier, but I was just as pissed at them. None of them believed in Bryce and me. None of them had my back at the gala. But I knew that after we got back together, they'd all come around. They'd have to.

"Did you hear about the break-in at Glow? It's such a shame. Jenny did not look well," I said. Despite my own problems, I was absolutely gutted to have seen Jenny in that state earlier.

He nodded. "Yeah, Crystal was there when it happened. She's shaken up, and I should be with her right now."

I gasped. "Crystal was there? I didn't know that."

He let out a deep breath. "She wanted to go for a walk after everything that happened and had left her purse at Glow. When she got there, one of the men ran off, and the other was strangling Jenny. She shot her gun, and he ran off too."

I brought a hand to my mouth. "She has a gun?" My eyes went wide.

Bryce didn't answer. He just took a sip of his champagne.

I had no idea Crystal had basically saved Jenny, and now I felt a little guilty that I had arranged this meeting. But Bryce was mine first, and I needed him back if I was going to get my life back, so I charged onward.

Another set of appetizers arrived, and we placed our entrée orders. Bryce even asked for a second bottle of Dom Pérignon. It seemed he definitely wanted to be here . . . with me.

"Everything is so lovely." I gestured to the food.

He nodded. "It is. This is my favorite restaurant in town."

I patted my lips with a napkin. "I know."

He gave me a sly smile. "It appears we can get along?"

"I think we can do way more than that." I took a long, slow sip of my champagne while Bryce devoured another oyster.

"Right, I did want to apologize for my behavior last night," he started.

"Oh, enough about that. It was all just a misunderstanding," I interrupted while flicking my hand.

"No." He put his hand up. "My behavior was out of line, and I apologize for embarrassing you. That was never my intention." Bryce glanced around the room and then back at me. "I hope that we can move past it together," he said with a smile.

I nodded and smiled back. "Of course."

"Good." He tossed a piece of fried calamari into his mouth. "Glad to hear it."

Just as we finished with our appetizers, our plates were cleared and our entrées arrived.

"Looks yummy," I said as I dug my fork into my honey-glazed salmon.

Bryce busied himself eating his filet mignon and fingerling potatoes.

I took a few deep breaths, readying myself for what I was going to do next. This was my moment. I had thought about it all day, and after the argument at the salon, I knew this was what I needed. It was going to make everything all better. I set my fork down on my plate and took a sip of my champagne. Bryce hadn't noticed that I had stopped eating. He hadn't noticed that my eyes were on him as I reached into my purse and pulled it out.

I stood from the table, with one hand behind my back, shielding his eyes from what I was holding. "Bryce."

He looked up at me, our eyes meeting, confusion setting in on his face, composure already set in on mine.

"What are you doing? Do you have to use the bathroom or something?" he asked.

"It's over."

"What's over?" He looked me up and down.

"You and Crystal."

He glanced around the restaurant uneasily and then back at me. "Shannon, don't do anything crazy."

Collapsing onto one knee, I gazed up at him, a smile wide

on my face, and pulled the object from behind my back—a small box with his old wedding ring in it. I opened it, and Bryce's eyes grew wide. He was clearly surprised, but it was a good surprise. His face became red. He was blushing. His eyes tightened. He was trying to hold back tears.

"Get up. Get the fuck up," he harshly whispered.

"Bryce, you are my beginning and my end. I know we got lost in the middle, but let's not waste any more time apart. Will you be my husband again?" Tears rolled down my cheeks, and my voice cracked, which caught the attention of the other patrons in the restaurant. Whispers ensued. All the attention was on Bryce and me. There were lights shining on us from cell phones. People were capturing our special moment together.

"Get up," he whispered through a clenched jaw.

"I'll stand if you say yes," I whispered back.

He nodded.

I stood up quickly, announcing to the restaurant, "He said yes." People cheered and clapped. Immediately, the server brought us a plate of chocolate-covered strawberries. (I had arranged for that earlier.) I leaned in for a hug and attempted to plant a kiss on his lips, but he pushed me off.

"Enough, Shannon!" The restaurant immediately went silent. "What do I have to do to get it through your head that our marriage is over? This is pathetic. *You* are pathetic."

My joyful tears turned to sorrowing sobs almost instantly. "But I love you, Bryce. We're good together. You said it yourself at the gala. It's kind of a blur. I swear I was drugged, but I remember you said maybe we could work something out. You called me beautiful."

"I only said that so you would do a good job of introducing me. I don't love you. I *loathe* you. We are not good together,

Shannon." He shook his head and rubbed his temples. "Sometimes, I think divorcing you wasn't enough."

"What is that supposed to mean?"

Bryce looked at me, his eyes darkening. He threw his napkin down and chugged the rest of his champagne. "Trust me. You don't want to find out. Just stay out of my life," he said, pointing a finger at me.

I threw my hands on my hips. "Is that a threat?"

"I'm a man of my word." He leaned into me. "And as much as me being a widower would drum up sympathy votes next election, let's not have it come to that," he whispered.

My mouth fell open. He leaned back, placed a hand on my shoulder, and smiled at me.

"Sorry about that, folks. Just an honest misunderstanding and my ex-wife here is off her meds," he said in his politician voice as he turned toward the other patrons. "How about a round of drinks on me?" Bryce flashed a toothy smile. The crowd clapped and cheered. I stood there stunned, unable to move, unable to speak. My eyes erupted with tears again.

"She'll be fine," he assured the server.

I grabbed my purse and bolted out of the restaurant. Everything around me was spinning. I could barely walk straight.

How could I let him do this to me? Do it once, shame on you. Do it twice, shame on me. Do it three times, and I am truly a fucking idiot.

23
CRYSTAL

I finished applying my ChapStick and gave myself a once-over in the mirror. I was dressed in a black romper, flats, and a jean jacket. I'm sure Olivia would balk at my choice of outfit, but we were just meeting for drinks—my idea. I had decided to give Olivia another chance at becoming, at the very least, acquaintances. After witnessing Dean put his hands on her at the gala, I understood that she was going through more than meets the eye, and I wanted to be there for her. Plus, anything to occupy my time and my mind was welcomed. Sometimes when I closed my eyes, I saw Jenny on the floor of the salon, bloodied and bruised. Who could do something like that to another person? And for what . . . a purse? That was all they got away with. Police said the robbers clearly didn't expect anyone to be there, which is why it went south fast and why the other guy fled. So far, they had no leads. All they could go off of was the blotchy tattoo on the back of the man's calf who ran away. But his voice. If I heard it again, I'd know it in an instant. *Goddamn it, I didn't sign up for this.* His words, but sometimes they felt like mine too.

I heard the front door open and close. Bryce was home from his dinner with Shannon. He had phoned me earlier to let me know that he had agreed to a dinner with his ex-wife in order to smooth everything over and apologize for his behavior. I appreciated the effort, minus the fact that the dinner and the apology wasn't his idea. His footsteps were loud as he made his way up the stairs to the master bedroom. I fluffed my hair with my fingers and threw a purse over my shoulder just as he entered the room. He pulled loose his tie and took off his jacket, tossing it on the bed.

"How'd it go?" I asked.

Bryce unbuttoned his white shirt. "Well enough."

"Did you apologize?"

"I did."

His answers were short. I knew he wasn't telling me the full truth.

"Are you two on good terms then?" I raised an eyebrow.

He pulled his shirt and pants off and stood there in a white T-shirt and boxers for a moment before walking over to me. Bryce lifted my chin with his hand. "She's not going to bother us anymore," he said, planting a kiss on my forehead and then on my lips. "I'm going to shower. Want to join me?"

"I can't. I'm going to meet Olivia for a drink." I knew he wasn't telling the whole truth, but I was sure I'd find out soon enough. If they truly were in a good spot, then Shannon's attitude toward me would improve, or so I hoped.

"That's good. Maybe Dean and I should join you two."

"Girls only." I smiled.

He kissed me on the forehead again. "Then I won't intrude." Bryce took a step back and walked to the bathroom.

Before closing the door, he turned around and said, "I love you, Crystal."

"I love you plus one."

His smile widened, revealing his perfect white teeth and charming dimples. Then he disappeared into the bathroom. Something didn't feel right. Like my momma used to say, *Always trust your gut*, and for some reason, ever since I met Bryce, I hadn't been doing that.

24
KAREN

"Good night, my sweet boy," I said flicking off the lights in Riley's dinosaur-themed bedroom. He was all tuckered out after a night of just the two of us playing in the backyard, eating pizza, and watching his favorite movie, *Harry and the Hendersons*. It was a favorite of mine as a child too. Mark was still in Miami and wouldn't be back this week. He said he had a plastic surgery conference to attend. I wasn't sure if he actually did or he just didn't want to be around me. We hadn't been getting along so well after I urged him to take a vacation and questioned him about his kinship with Olivia. He had said he was too busy for a vacation and that he was just being nice to her, as she's my friend and his client.

I closed Riley's bedroom door and made my way to the kitchen, pouring myself a glass of red wine. The doorbell rang. I quickly set down my drink and ran to the front door before whoever was on the other side could ring it again.

I opened the door and there stood Shannon. Her eye

makeup was halfway down her face. Her hair was disheveled. Her eyes were bloodshot and wet with tears.

"I had nowhere else to go." She sniffled.

I didn't even hesitate before inviting her in, guiding her into my house. Sure, we had been fighting, but fights were almost always temporary. She flicked off her shoes and collapsed into the couch.

"Let me get you some water."

"I went to have dinner with Bryce tonight," she said and then broke into a sob.

I filled two glasses with ice water in the kitchen and hurried back to Shannon before she fell completely apart on my couch. She quickly took a gulp, while I took a seat beside her on the couch.

"What happened?" I asked.

"I proposed to him," she cried.

"You what?" I whipped my head toward her. *Save the judgment*, I reminded myself.

"I know. I'm a fucking idiot." Shannon took another big gulp of water.

"No, you're not. You're just a woman with a broken heart." I placed my hand on her knee.

"He said no, by the way." She looked at me with a crumpled face.

"I figured that much." I gave her my most sympathetic look.

"And he threatened me." Shannon's face turned from sadness to anger.

"He what?"

"Well, I think he threatened me. Told me to stay away from him and Crystal, and something about becoming a widower." She set her glass down, folded her arms across her chest, and leaned back into the couch.

"Bryce is an asshole. Always has been," I said, setting my glass down and matching her posture.

She turned her head toward me and let on a small smile. "You're right, aren't you?"

"Yes. He's kind of slimy too."

"He *is* slimy, isn't he."

I nodded and put my hand on hers. "You're going to be just fine. Trust me. The men in our lives don't define us. We define ourselves," I said to her, but in a way, I was saying it to myself.

"But I lost my chairwoman position because I'm divorced," she cried.

"You didn't lose it because you were divorced. It was because you missed two meetings. I'm sorry I didn't tell you right away. I wanted you to be happy and focus on the gala. I didn't want it to interfere with your big night," I said.

"Olivia said it was because my divorce got in the way, and that it was unanimous." Shannon bit at her lower lip.

I let out a groan. "Don't listen to Olivia. I voted against it, but it was in the bylaws. That's how Olivia got the motion through."

"Karen, I'm really sorry for the way I acted today. I'm so embarrassed by tonight, today, last night." She lowered her head and shook it.

"It's fine. Really it is. I understand. Life is hard and living in Buckhead is even harder. I'm here for you no matter how bitchy you get," I said with a laugh.

She laughed too and immediately wrapped me in her arms for a tight hug. She was going to be okay.

My phone buzzed, and I picked it up from the coffee table. It was a text from Keisha.

Have you seen this?

"Oh, my fucking God," I said out loud as my mouth dropped open.

Shannon looked at me with worried eyes. "What is it?"

I shook my head. "You don't want to know."

25
JENNY

Detective Sanford pulls his phone from his pocket and places it on the table. He clicks around and pulls up a saved video.

"One of my officers came across this." He faces the screen toward me. "Can you tell me about it?"

I close my eyes, take a deep breath, and then reopen them. On the screen is a still image of Shannon. The video is titled *Woman Commits Suicide**.

"Yes." I nod.

26
OLIVIA

I took a seat at a table in a small cocktail bar on Peach Street and ordered two vodka martinis. Crystal had phoned earlier, asking me to meet, and I was more than happy to do so. I knew I had done well at the salon earlier, saying all the right things. These women would come around now and realize I wasn't so bad after all. They should know that it's just easier to have me on their side, and Crystal needed someone to take her under their wing. I was that person. Sure, my wing wasn't big, white, and feathery like an angel's. It was more like a bat's—quick and dark with claws hiding beneath.

"Hey, how are you?" Crystal said, taking a seat and placing her purse on the back of her chair. She was underdressed again. I was wearing a little red cocktail dress, and she was wearing a jean jacket. Now that we were allies, it was something I could help her with. I refrained from looking her up and down and instead smiled.

"I'm good. I'm glad we could get together. I ordered you a vodka martini."

"Oh, thank you. I've never had one. I'm more of a beer type of girl."

I held the smile on my face. It was nearly impossible to not snarl. A 'beer type of girl'? Something else I could teach her. The server set a vodka martini in front of both of us. I quickly took a sip.

"You're going to love it."

Crystal picked up her glass and held it to her lips. She was apprehensive, but she tipped the martini back anyway. Her face crumpled up as soon as it hit her tongue. She set the drink down, coughed, and tried to compose herself. "That'll take some getting used to."

"It's rather sophisticated, so I guess it's not for everyone. Do you want to order a beer instead?"

"Oh, no. This is fine. I've got to start fitting in somehow." She laughed.

"No need to worry about that, Crystal. With me by your side, you'll fit in just fine," I said.

She took another sip but this time kept her composure. Maybe she was teachable, like a charity project of mine. Or a small pet.

"So, I asked you here tonight because I just wanted to make sure you were okay." She dropped her chin in a sympathetic way.

"Oh, you mean because of Shannon's behavior? She doesn't faze me anymore. Shannon is a total mess, and she's so obsessed with Bryce. It's sad. *I* should be the one worried about *you*. How did her dinner go with him? Are you and Bryce okay? She didn't do anything, did she?"

"No . . ." Crystal said awkwardly. "Not that. Bryce and I are fine. It seems their conversation was productive. I was talking about what happened between you and Dean at the gala." She took another sip of her martini.

I waved my hand at her, dismissing her comment. "What, that? That was nothing. Dean had had a little too much to drink, and he was just upset about all the drama. He hates drama," I explained.

Crystal crinkled up her face as if she were trying to understand what I was saying or make sense of it. She wasn't the brightest crayon in the box, that was for sure. I took another sip of my martini and signaled the waiter for two more. I was going to need it to get through this conversation.

"You're sure?" she asked.

"Sure of what?"

"He grabbed your arm really hard. Has he done that to you before?" She stared right into my eyes.

I didn't know what her angle was, but I didn't like it. Why was she sitting here asking me these questions? My relationship was none of her business. The server set down two more martinis just as I finished my first.

"Yeah, I'm sure," I said, rolling my eyes at her.

"You can talk to me, Olivia. I was in an abusive relationship. I understand what it's like." She placed her hand on mine.

"Who? Bryce? Is that why Shannon is so hung up on him? Stockholm syndrome?"

She pulled her hand away and finished her first martini. "No, Bryce has never been physical with me. I was referring to a past relationship. I just wanted to talk to you to make sure you were okay." Her face softened and she smiled at me.

I gave her a small smile, weighing out my options. The best way to get someone to like you was to make them feel sorry for you. Perhaps the right play just landed in my lap. If it wasn't for Dean pushing me to make nice with her, I would have told

her to fuck off right then and there. But power required looking ahead rather than living in the moment, so I had to play
the game, and I was more than willing. Social climbing wasn't
a sprint, it was a marathon.

"Thank you for being here for me. Your companionship is so
interesting. I'll be honest with you. Dean has never been physical
before, but he did scare me last night. He's been growing more
and more angry and short with me recently, and I'm not sure
why. Maybe it's me," I said, hanging my head in fake shame.

"No, don't say that. You are not responsible for the way
other people act, including the ones you love." Crystal reached
across the table and squeezed my hand.

"I just love him so much," I said, getting my voice to crack
at the end perfectly.

"I'm sure he loves you too. And listen, I don't know what
your relationship is like with Dean, but I am here for you if you
need to talk or need help. Anything."

I took a sip of my martini and nodded. My relationship
with Dean was fine, and it wasn't any of her business. But if she
wanted to be the useless rock in my life, I'd allow it.

"Thank you. I appreciate that. I'd really love for us to be
close. I know what it's like to be the new person in town." I
squeezed a single tear out.

"Oh," she said, handing me a napkin.

I dabbed the tear away. It was like a bullet in the chamber
of a gun, always loaded and ready to spill out if needed.

"I'm sorry. It's just you being new here brings up really bad
memories for me." I took a sip of my martini.

"Do you want to talk about it?" she asked.

"I shouldn't, but yes. When I moved here, Shannon was
absolutely awful to me. She pretended like I didn't exist for so
long, and then when she did start paying attention to me, she

bullied me, calling me the most awful names and making me the butt of every joke. It wasn't until I discovered Glow that she started treating me better. But it was two years of torment." I shook my head.

Crystal reached across the table and put her hand on mine. "I'm so sorry, Olivia. I had no idea you went through that."

I wanted to flick her hand away, but I let it rest on mine. "Thank you. I know you're not as sophisticated or glamorous as I was when I arrived, but I promise to never treat you like that. You and I have to stick together," I said, holding a martini glass up.

She clinked hers against mine, gave a small smile back, and took a sip.

"You should come to Glow the day after tomorrow. Jenny told me they're doing manis and mimosas. Sounds like a fun time. There's always an event at the salon," she said with a laugh.

How dare she invite me to the very event I created! Who did she think she was? Was she trying to be the new me? Trying to take my reign? Silly girl.

"I would love that," I said with a big fat fucking smile. My lip nearly split.

27
SHANNON

Karen had begged me not to watch it again, but I couldn't help myself. Each time I viewed it, I died a little more inside. How could I have become this person? You never get to see the way people see you, but I did. The video played again. First, it was me onstage at the gala, drunk and sloppy; then, it was me in the restaurant proposing to Bryce, drunk, delusional, and sloppy. The whole thing was edited so some parts would play over and over again, like a track on an album. Someone had anonymously uploaded it to YouTube under the title "Woman Commits Suicide*" with * *Social Suicide* in the description. How clever. I rolled my eyes. I pressed stop on the video and sunk deeper into my couch. It was already up to over ten thousand views. Karen had said she reported it and would work on getting it taken down, but the views just kept going up, and it was being posted on other sites and apps. I scrolled down, venturing toward the comments section. I knew it wasn't a good idea to read them, but I couldn't help myself.

What a stupid bitch.

Too bad she didn't actually kill herself.

OMG! I would die.

This is cringe gold.

Clickbait at its finest.

Lol. This is fake right. It has to be. No one is that pathetic.

Nice tits.

Money can't buy class. That's for sure.

Anyone know her name?

I squeezed my eyes tightly together, pushing tears out of the corners, and took a deep breath. Bryce had to have done this. He was at the gala and the restaurant, and he threatened me. I hated him, but right now, I hated me more.

My phone buzzed. A text from Karen was on the screen.

> Checking to make sure you're all right. They should be taking it down.

Did the video really matter? So many people saw me like that in person. I just hadn't seen myself, and I was truly embarrassed for who and what I had become.

My phone buzzed. It was a text from Jenny.

> Thinking about you. Hope
> you're okay.

I hadn't been okay for a while. I just didn't know it. But I couldn't deny what was right in front of me anymore. That video was proof, and I was a tiny bit grateful for it. I needed to change. I needed to be better. I couldn't go on living if I didn't.

28
KAREN

I was running about fifteen minutes late to my spray tan appointment with Jenny, thanks to dealing with YouTube all night. The video had finally been taken down after accumulating over one hundred thousand views. Poor Shannon. I had read the comments, and I knew she did too. Each one was viler than the last. I had decided to get a pedicure after the spray tan, just so I could be there when Shannon arrived. She hadn't spoken to me since she left last night, but she had said she'd be in today to be there for Jenny and to apologize to her and Keisha for the way she had acted at the book club.

I threw open the recently repaired salon door and walked right past the black curtains because the front area was empty. Keisha was sitting in a pedicure chair with her feet massaging in water, drinking a glass of lemonade, and looking completely lost in thought.

"Hey, sorry I'm late for my appointment with Jenny," I said, looking around the salon. Jenny was nowhere in sight.

"Actually, Jenny went to the doctor for a follow-up. Are you good with me doing it?" Keisha said, taking her feet out of the water.

"Yeah. How is Jenny?" I tilted my head.

"She's a bit jumpy and shaken up still, which I'd expect." Keisha pulled in her lips. "I'm trying to do everything around here to help out as much as possible, but she's not really accepting much help." She stood up and dried off with a towel before slipping on a pair of sandals.

"Jenny's a tough woman. I can't even imagine what she's going through. That must have been terrifying." I fidgeted with my fingernails.

"She's a little too tough if ya ask me." Keisha raised an eyebrow. "She's shut the whole thing out and refuses to talk about it." Keisha rubbed her forehead. I could tell she was worried sick about Jenny. We all were.

"Well, people respond to things differently. I'm sure she'll be all right," I said with a nod.

"I hope so. Speaking of how people respond to things. How's Shannon after the . . . video?" Keisha's eyes went a little wide. She wiped down the pedicure chair.

"She's upset. She was with me when you sent it. She had come over to apologize."

"That was painful to watch." Keisha cringed.

I nodded. "It was. It's taken down now."

"Who do you think uploaded it?"

"Shannon is convinced it was Bryce. He was at both events, and he threatened her at dinner," I explained.

"These people, I swear." Keisha shook her head in disgust, then glanced at me. "No offense. You're nothing like the others here—and I mean that as a compliment."

"Thank you." I smiled. "But Shannon will be in later this

afternoon. She wants to apologize to you and Jenny for what happened at the book club."

Keisha beckoned me with her hand, and we walked to the spray tan room in back.

"That's nice of her. Not necessary, but nice."

"Despite how horrible that video was, it seems to have pulled her back to reality. I think she's finally seeing things clearly now and realizing her marriage is truly over."

Keisha nodded and then closed the door behind her and began to ready the spray tanning machine.

While she prepared, I found myself watching her, captivated by her beautiful profile, wishing that she might look back at me once more. Then Keisha said something entirely unexpected. "Why do you spend so much time with these women, Karen? Don't be fooled, I see what goes on around here and I can tell that you're different from the others. You see past all their bullshit and pointless rivalries." She almost spat the words, such was her vehemence.

Initially stunned, it took me a moment to gather my thoughts enough to respond. "The truth is, I've begun to question my place in the world more and more these days. It's not just Buckhead, or my friendships. It goes deeper than that. I find myself questioning everything, even my marriage . . . I just wish I didn't feel quite such a stranger to myself."

Keisha glanced at the ground, hesitant to say more, before returning my gaze.

"I know what it's like to question your identity, Karen. I know what it's like to not feel seen for who you really are. But I want you to know that in my eyes, you're amazing." And then she smiled this warm, open smile that made me realize that Keisha meant every word.

After an awkward pause, I began to remove my

clothing for the spray tan. Keisha turned toward me, and rather than start, she hesitated, holding the nozzle by her side, her eyes scanning me from head to toe. I should have felt uncomfortable, but I wasn't. I knew that Keisha wasn't judging me; her eyes were filled with a frank curiosity . . . and something else. Could it be longing? I felt my heart rate rise.

My eyes met Keisha's. Her full lips fell slightly apart, moisture forming between them. And I could say the same for mine. I hadn't had that feeling in a very long time—if ever. Just then, I realized what was wrong with my marriage. It wasn't my hormones. It wasn't the stress of raising a child. It wasn't my husband. There wasn't anything actually *wrong* with me.

Keisha started to compose herself, tightening her lips and avoiding eye contact. But I knew it was now or never.

I closed the distance between us, standing just inches from her. There was a moment of stillness, of reckoning between us, before Keisha took one small step forward. Tentatively, our lips met as her right hand caressed the side of my face. I found myself instantly responding. I kissed her so hard and with such passion that all the sexual frustration melted out of my body like an ice cream cone on a hot summer day. She dropped the spray tan unit, and it clunked when it hit the ground. Tanning liquid spilled onto the floor, and we stood in a puddle of it. She wrapped her arms around me, pressing her lips firmly against mine. Our tongues tingled. Our lips moistened. She grabbed my breasts for a moment, then slid her hands down my stomach. I took off her shirt and bra, revealing perky B-cup breasts. I immediately dove onto them, but she brought my face up to kiss her again and again. I had never been with a woman before, minus some experimentation in college. Perhaps it wasn't just experimentation though, because I seemed to know exactly what to do, as though I should have been doing this all along. Her hand slithered across my belly, then down to my pelvis. Just as she was about to venture farther, the front door chimed.

29
SHANNON

I marched right into the salon. No one was at the front desk, so I called out and saw myself to the back, pushing the black curtains to the side. I had no time to waste. I was a woman on a mission. I had apologies to make and a life to turn around. It was dead quiet when I entered the back area. Then I heard giggles from the tanning room. Keisha came out first, her feet a strange brown-and-orange color and a wide smile plastered on her face.

"Did you miss the target?" I pointed at her feet. She looked down.

"The machine malfunctioned and spilled," she said with a laugh. "Did you have an appointment?"

"Nope. I need nothing done—just a lemonade, and I owe you an apology." I took a seat in one of the pedicure chairs. "Keisha, I'm sorry. I should have never acted the way I did yesterday."

"You are forgiven. And lemonade, you got it," she said, pointing at me.

She poured me a glass and handed it over. "I'll turn on the bubbles," Keisha added.

I slid my feet into the warm water. That was easier than I thought it'd be, but then again, Keisha was never one to hold grudges. She was carefree and a breath of fresh air in this town. I knew she had seen the video, but she pretended she hadn't. Keisha was good like that. She could forgive and forget.

Karen emerged from the spray tan room. Her skin flushed. Her lips were plump. And her eyes lit up. She smiled as she walked in a white tank and blue jean shorts, and I noticed her feet were orange and blotchy too.

"Spray tan machine got you too, I see," I said, staring at her feet.

She looked down and blushed. "Yeah, it malfunctioned in the middle of my session."

"That's what Keisha was saying," I confirmed. "You're staying, right?"

"Yeah, I was going to get a pedicure." She glanced at Keisha with a half smile.

"Great, have a seat next to me. We have loads to talk about." I patted the chair beside me.

Karen climbed into it. Keisha brought her a glass of lemonade and filled her foot tub. I turned on the massager on my chair, and Karen did the same.

"Are you doing okay? You seem to be in a much better mood today," Karen commented. Her eyes bounced over to me.

Keisha picked up Karen's foot and massaged it ever so tenderly, paying special attention to each of her toes.

"I think I am." I nodded.

"The video was taken down."

"I know. Thank you," I said with a small smile.

"How are you feeling about everything that happened?" Keisha asked.

"Good," I said. They both smiled at me. "And not good." They both frowned.

"Why the former?" Karen asked.

"And why the latter?" Keisha asked.

They gave each other a look of understanding and me a look of compassion. Why were they finishing each other's sentences? I wanted to assure them that I was fine—that I was better than fine, that I was so grateful for being able to see myself the way others had seen me. It was a wake-up call and a tough pill to swallow, but I knew that despite how I was feeling right now—embarrassed and pathetic—it would make me a stronger person. It made me realize that I didn't need Bryce. That I could be confident and powerful all on my own, just as soon as I got my shit together. I needed a makeover, not for looks, but for life.

"*Good* because I realized I don't need a man to be me. *Not good* because it took two completely humiliating incidents and a semiviral video to learn that." I gripped my glass a little tighter, then took a deep breath, and let the tension flow out of me.

They exchanged concerned glances.

"I think it's great that you know you don't need a man to be you and to be happy," Keisha encouraged while massaging the top of Karen's foot. Her toes curled in ecstasy.

"I never said I was happy." I took a large drink, swallowing so quickly that the gulp hurt the back of my throat. Everything was so hard to swallow these days.

"Okay then, you don't need a man . . . to be you," Keisha corrected. I caught Karen wink at her. I wasn't sure why she did, but I thought it was cute. I had been a fan of women supporting other women (before Crystal came along), so to see this sweet exchange brought me a little joy. I wanted more of that in my life, and I hated that I had started to become a person who despised other women. I didn't want to be that, but sometimes you become the person you hate the most.

"And who cares about all those people?" Karen piped in.

"I do," I said.

"Yes . . . yes, but you can prove them all wrong. Prove that what they thought about you and what they thought about Bryce was wrong," she added.

"You're right, I guess. But how? They all think I'm a joke now—a has-been, a washed-up divorcée and ex-chairwoman."

Karen and Keisha gave me sympathetic looks.

"Being yourself is the strongest, most powerful thing you can do. It's like signing your autograph on something you created. You're saying, 'This is me, and I'm so fucking proud of it. I'm proud of me,'" Karen exclaimed with so much conviction in her voice she could have led a riot. Where did this come from? She was always outspoken, but not with this much confidence. Whoever this new Karen was, I liked her. I reached over and grabbed her hand and squeezed it, exchanging a pleased look with her.

Last night, everything felt like it was going to hell. But today, things felt a little better, like everything was going to be okay. Life was funny that way. Living in Buckhead was like a roller-coaster ride. You'd wait in line for a very long time, and then finally, you were in. You were on the ride of a lifetime. But this ride wasn't consistent. It was ever-changing. Sometimes you'd scream. Sometimes you'd be sick to your stomach. Sometimes you'd beg the operator to stop the ride, so you could get off. Sometimes you'd smile and laugh out of pure enjoyment. Sometimes you'd have to hold on tighter than usual for fear of falling off. And sometimes you'd just let go, waving your arms and hands freely, without a care in the world. I was letting go, or at the very least, I was starting to.

30
CRYSTAL

I headed straight to the salon after taking care of some errands and things around the house. I needed to talk with all of them. I needed to tell them what was happening with Olivia. She wasn't safe in that relationship. I could feel it. I wanted to help her, and I wanted to get the girls to rally with me. I had been in a bad relationship before, an awful one. It nearly destroyed me. From that relationship, I learned that monsters don't change. They can hide who they are, they can morph into something else, but their ugliness never goes away. They're predators to the core.

I flung open the door of the salon and wandered through the curtains, finding Karen and Shannon sitting in pedicure chairs sipping lemonade, while Keisha massaged Karen's feet. They all looked over at me as my heels clacked along the hardwood floor. It would appear Shannon had made peace with them. Perhaps Bryce was telling the truth. Maybe they did agree to move past the gala night and learn to get along. I hoped it was true.

"I'm so glad you're all here," I exclaimed. Karen and Shannon held up their glasses. I walked over to the pitcher of fresh lemonade and poured myself a glass.

"So, you saw the video?" Shannon tapered her eyes.

"What video?" I asked. "No, I wanted to talk to you all about Olivia."

Shannon's eyes stayed tight for a moment as she looked me over carefully, then she relaxed them and took a sip of her drink. I didn't have a clue what she was talking about, but before I could ask, Karen spoke up.

"What's going on?"

The back door swung open, and in walked Jenny dressed in white tennis shoes, tan shorts, and a striped sleeveless top with a turtleneck. She pulled off her sunglasses, revealing a fading black eye. It was almost completely covered with makeup, but I could still see it.

"Hey, Jenny. How are you feeling today?" I asked.

I poured her a glass of lemonade and handed it to her.

"Thanks, and I'm fine. Even the doctor says so." She nodded and brought the glass to her lips, taking a long drink.

"No need to be tough, Jenny. We're all here for you. Whatever you need," Shannon said.

"Seriously, please don't worry about me." Jenny took her cross-body bag off and placed it on the back of her salon chair. Then she began tidying up. She was always cleaning, even though the salon was spotless.

"Crystal was just about to tell us all something about Olivia," Keisha said, changing the subject.

"Can we go one day without hearing about or from Olivia?" Shannon asked.

"Be nice." Karen patted Shannon's hand.

"No, she has it in for me." Shannon shook her head.

"You were saying, Crystal," Karen added.

Jenny stopped cleaning to give me her full attention, and Keisha stood up from massaging Karen's feet and wiped up some of the water that had spilled on the floor.

"Wait, hold on." Shannon put her hand up. "Jenny, I want to apologize for my behavior yesterday. I'm sorry."

"It's fine, Shannon." Jenny nodded.

"Aren't you going to apologize to Crystal?" Karen whispered, although it was loud enough for everyone to hear.

Shannon shook her head again. "Anyway, you were saying, Crystal . . ."

The talk Bryce and she had didn't go well enough for her to apologize to me, but I'd take what I could get with Shannon. At least she was acknowledging me.

"I had drinks with Olivia last night, and she said something about Dean . . . and I'm just worried about her." I fiddled with my glass and took a small sip, then clutched it tightly.

Shannon adjusted her feet. "Well, what did she say exactly?"

"She said she was scared. That Dean had never been physical with her before the night of the gala, but he had been verbally abusive, and she was afraid of him one day taking it too far."

"This might be out of line, but it's more likely that Olivia would be handing out the beatings, not Dean," Shannon said with a laugh.

I let out a huff of annoyance and tapped my foot on the floor repeatedly. I drank my whole glass of lemonade and then poured myself another.

"Now, now, ladies. Olivia's our friend. If she's in trouble, we should be there for her," Jenny said.

"Like she was there for me when my husband left me for her?" Shannon pointed at me. I took another large gulp of lemonade.

"Let's not get hung up on the past," Karen said.

"The past? What do you mean, the past? The fucking past is standing right there," Shannon pointed at me again.

There was no way I was going to get through to them. Shannon was clearly mad about something. Karen was a bit more understanding.

"You know what? If you ask me, Olivia could use a good beating." Shannon cackled. Jenny, Keisha, Karen, and I held our breath at her comment and just stared.

"Anyway, I really think we should try to be supportive and encouraging of Olivia." I took a seat in a salon chair, crossing one leg over another. They all looked at each other, waiting for someone to speak up. I bounced my foot up and down, hoping they would get on board. I knew Olivia was no ray of sunshine, but women needed to stick together. Perhaps Olivia's behavior was a result of her toxic relationship with Dean. I didn't know her well enough to know otherwise, but I tried to see the good in people. There had to be good in Olivia.

"I don't think Olivia needs any encouraging." Shannon raised an eyebrow.

Jenny waved a hand at Shannon, dismissing her comment. "I'll give Olivia a call today and make sure she comes to Manis and Mimosas tomorrow morning."

"That's great, Jenny." I smiled.

"I'll try to be nice," Shannon added, but it was unconvincing. I nodded at her.

"I'll make sure she feels welcome," Karen said.

"And I'll make sure you're all tipsy enough to tolerate her tomorrow," Keisha said with a laugh.

31
JENNY

Splashing some water on my face, I glance at myself in the mirror of a sterile bathroom. Although I'm looking at my reflection, all I can see is through it. I quickly apply some lip balm to my dry lips and pull my hair from its ponytail, running my hands through it to give it some life. I don't know how I got dragged into all of this. I should have kept my distance from these women. I should have stuck to my role as the help, rather than becoming a confidant or a friend. What was I thinking?

Inside the interrogation room, I take a seat again. It's mere seconds later that Detective Sanford enters the room. He shuts the door behind him and sits across from me.

He drops his notepad on the table and scans over his notes. "Now where were we?" Sanford taps his pen on the paper, "Oh, yes. That's right. Olivia and Dean. Tell me more about that." He looks at me, the corners of his eyes slightly wrinkling.

"There were definitely marital problems between them," I say.

"Did Olivia tell you that?"

"She told all of us that."

He scribbles down some more notes. "The day Crystal came into the salon and explained what Olivia told her about Dean. It seemed like all the women were getting along again, or at least were planning to."

"That's right." I nod. My lips form a straight line.

"Then what happened?" He taps his pen on the table.

"The husbands happened."

32
JENNY

Keisha and I were prepping for our monthly Manis and Mimosas event, setting out fresh fruit and baked goods and putting champagne and orange juice on ice. I had resorted to biting my nails early that morning and fidgeting with everything in sight—including adjusting and straightening up my station at least seven times. After the break-in, I felt uneasy. The salon didn't feel like it was mine anymore. I felt violated. Sure, the building was still standing and Glow was back to its pristine condition, but it just felt like everything had been taken from me. Keisha rubbed my shoulder as she passed by, her way of ensuring I was okay. I knew she worried about me because I wouldn't talk to her about what happened. I wanted to forget it. Although I pretended like it wasn't on my mind, it was. Sometimes, I'd flash right back to that moment when I was gasping for my last breath. My life felt like a nightmare, only I was awake for it.

"How do you think it'll go today?" Keisha asked.

I pulled my fingers from my mouth. "I think it'll go well, or at least I hope it does."

Mary, the salon assistant, popped in with a fresh carafe of coffee from a local café and set it on the table. I'm not sure why we even provided it. No one ever drank the coffee anyway. It was all about the mimosas. We kept a few contract manicurists on for events like this. Mary escorted them in, and they began to set up their stations. They mostly kept to themselves, but they did great work. Several bottles of nail polish slid from one of the manicurist's kits onto the floor with a crash. My body jumped and my shoulders tightened. I felt like I was always on edge now. The manicurist apologized and cleaned them up.

"You ready for this?" Keisha asked, looking me in the eye.

"Ready as I'll ever be." I gave an unconvincing smile.

"Should we have hired security?" Keisha laughed.

"That wouldn't have been a bad idea."

The front bell jingled.

In walked Shannon, wearing a Chanel tank top and Givenchy black linen pants. She pulled off her oversized Prada sunglasses in a dramatic fashion.

"Hello, ladies! I'm ready for Manis and Mugshots." She laughed. "I'm kidding. I'm sure we'll all be on our best behavior."

Shannon greeted us and immediately walked to the snack table, grabbing a croissant and pouring herself a cup of coffee, which surprised me. Like I said, no one ever drank the coffee. She was changing—or at least trying to—and she was already doing so much better now that she was focused on herself instead of Bryce. One of our manicurists began working on Shannon's left hand.

"When's the guest of honor arriving?" Shannon raised an eyebrow.

"Be nice," I said as I straightened up the food and beverage table.

"I'm always nice . . . except when I'm not," she snickered. "You doing okay, Jenny?"

I let out a quiet huff. I was tired of people asking if I was okay. I always said I was, even though I knew I wasn't. I didn't like all the attention on me, which is why I wore a turtleneck again today and used our thickest concealer to cover my eye. My lip had healed nicely, just a little swollen, so it looked as though I had recent lip injections.

"Yes, I'm fine," I finally said.

The front door chimed, and moments later in walked Karen wearing yoga pants, sandals, and a tank top. Her hair was tied back in a low ponytail, and although she was in workout clothes, she had clearly put in an effort as her face was in full makeup—natural-looking, but still full.

Karen walked over to Shannon, giving her a partial hug, and then did the same to me. Her hug was a little longer than usual. That's what I got now, long hugs and are-you-okay's. She nodded at Keisha and gave her a coy smile. They must have bonded at the gala. Plus, yesterday was the first time Karen had her spray tan done by anyone other than me. Although, she didn't look any more tanned. Keisha poured Karen a mimosa. They were becoming friends. Good. At least some people were getting along.

"You're dressed for the gym, Karen. Did you intend on breaking a sweat at this soiree?" Shannon chuckled.

"No, there won't be any fighting today. We're all grown women. We're classy, and we can be civil," Karen assured.

"Classy?" Keisha laughed.

"Ish." Karen shrugged as she took a seat. Keisha grabbed her hands and began massaging lotion into them.

The front door chimed, and I heard one set of heels and one set of sandals make their way quickly from the front area to just before the curtains. There were faint whispers, and then, all at once, the black curtains burst open, flooding the room with natural light. I let out the breath I didn't even realize I was holding. I pulled my shoulders back and smiled. This was my salon, and it was all I had left in the world. In walked Olivia, wearing a red skirt and a white long-sleeved top, followed by Crystal.

Olivia gave a big toothy grin. "I'm so glad we could all get together," she declared.

"You're looking so much better, Jenny. You were unsightly before," Olivia said with air kisses on each side of my cheek.

I could always count on Olivia for her brutal honesty. "Thanks," I said. "I'm feeling much better too," I lied.

"Shannon, I hope you're not still upset with me." Olivia brought her hand to her chest. "It devastated me how the gala ended. Unfortunately, I don't think people will ever forget that." She shook her head.

"I'm perfectly fine, Olivia." Shannon rolled her eyes.

"You're so strong. After that, I could never show my face again," she said with a laugh.

Shannon leaned forward in her seat like she was about to fight, but I gave her a stern look and she readjusted herself in her chair. She pulled her lips back into a smile, almost like a ventriloquist's puppet would. Crystal gave everyone a hug, except Shannon. She had started to lean in, but Shannon gave her the look a mother gives to a child when it's about to do something wrong—a don't-you-fucking-dare look. Crystal recoiled and nodded instead. Shannon nodded back and took a sip of her coffee. So they were still on tenterhooks with one another. That was to be expected, as getting along with your ex-husband's new wife took time—lots of time.

Crystal sat down at a nail station across from Karen. Olivia planted herself in front of Shannon. I should have had the contract manicurists make a straight line of these stations today rather than having two lines across from each other. With this group setup, some cattiness was inevitable, especially with the alcohol. I should have made it a dry event too—Manis and Milk, or Manis and Melons. What was I thinking? It was too late for should-haves and would-haves. I was going to get through this, and I was going to ensure these women got through it too.

I grabbed the pitcher of mimosas and made my way around the room, topping off glasses.

"Is anyone else coming?" Shannon asked, glancing at the clock. It was 9:15 a.m. Manis and Mimosas had started fifteen minutes prior, and it was odd that none of my other clients had arrived.

"I'm sure they are," I said, placing the empty pitcher down.

"They're not," Olivia piped in as one of the manicurists filed down her talons.

"What do you mean, they're not coming?" Shannon's brow furrowed and her lips pursed together.

"I told all of your other clients that this was a closed event. I figured we needed time for just us today." Olivia smiled.

"What do you think gives you the right to do that?" Keisha's words cut through the acetate-scented air.

"I'm a top client here and an angel investor." Olivia jutted her chin up.

Keisha stood beside Karen. Shit. I thought I only had to worry about Olivia and Shannon. I completely forgot about how overprotective Keisha was being with me since the break-in. She treated me like I could fall apart at any moment because she knew me best.

Just as Keisha took a step toward where Olivia was seated, Karen grabbed her by the hand and said, "I need a wax."

Keisha stopped dead in her tracks. She looked back at her

hand, the same one that Karen was holding. She glanced up at Karen and took a deep breath. Karen nodded and gave an encouraging smile.

"Right this way," Keisha said, leading her down the hallway to the waxing room. Thank God for Karen. I'm not sure if I would have been able to diffuse that. I knew Keisha had had enough of Olivia and was tired of her trying to walk all over everyone. Olivia's eyes lit up with a job-well-done attitude. I had had enough of her too, but she was right, she was a top client and an investor. I wouldn't say *angel*, more demonic. So I did what I always did—I put on a smile and took care of her.

33
KAREN

I followed Keisha into the waxing room. It was small and brightly lit with a massage table in the center of it. A few cabinets lined the walls. As Keisha closed the door behind us, she let out a deep breath. I held mine for a moment, just long enough to have a few doubts slither across my mind. Was I doing the right thing? Did right and wrong even matter? Was I ready to throw away the life I had? Was there a life to even throw away? I hadn't been happy in so long, I forgot what happy was . . . until Keisha. The thoughts disappeared faster than they surfaced, and I exhaled the doubts.

"I saved you," I said, pulling my hair free from its ponytail and twirling a piece of it around my finger.

"The only person you're saving is Olivia, from me kicking her bony ass," Keisha said matter-of-factly before cracking a smile.

"I know she gets to you. She gets to all of us." I propped up Keisha's chin with the ends of my fingertips, ensuring her icy-blue eyes met mine.

"Jenny can't handle her bullshit right now. I know she says she's fine, but she's not," Keisha confessed.

"Of course, she's not. It's only been a few days," I rationalized.

Keisha nodded, dropping eye contact for a moment before her eyes returned to me.

Typically, I had a hard time looking someone in the eye and holding a gaze. Eye contact, such a standard way of communicating but so difficult to master. I'd always be the first to look away, to pretend something caught my eye . . . but not this time. With Keisha, I couldn't look away. Her eyes held everything—my courage, my trust, my fear, my curiosity, my desire. I had thought about little else since our last meeting. It wasn't simply the kiss, incredible though it was, but something more than that. We go through life searching for a sense of belonging, of connection, and so often we are disappointed. How can anyone even begin to define what draws two people together like magnets? I spent my teenage years reading romance novels, believing in a fairy-tale version of love that never quite came to pass for me. So, just like that passage in Corinthians, I committed to putting away childish things and settled instead for being a good partner, wife, and mother. I buried that secret place inside of me that longed for real connection, real intimacy. Now, in Keisha's presence, I had begun to question my choices. Perhaps all the love stories of my teenage years weren't so foolish after all? It's like when you take that leap into a body of unfamiliar water. You have no idea what you're getting into, and that's how it was with Keisha. Would I drown or somehow learn to swim in this new sea? Or would I be thankful after I got out that my feet were planted back on solid ground again? It didn't matter though. None of it mattered. I was going to jump.

I could feel my cheeks redden and my heartbeat quicken.

"And Olivia doesn't get to me," Keisha said.

"She doesn't?" I raised an eyebrow.

"You do."

Before the words finished echoing throughout the small room, her lips were on mine. They were soft and warm, just like I remembered. Her hands slid the straps of my tank top down my shoulders, revealing my small breasts. Someone could have walked in at any moment. But I was so lost in the moment that I didn't care. She pushed my red locks back, and her plump lips followed the trace of her fingertips, leaving light cherry-red lipstick marks on my neck, shoulders, collarbone, and breasts. My breath became ragged and quick. My head spun. My body tensed up. She pushed me back onto the massage table. I fell hard, nearly rolling off. We giggled and then quieted ourselves. She finished removing my tank top, softly rubbing and kissing each of my breasts. I straightened out on the table as if I were adjusting myself for a bikini wax . . . Keisha pressed my legs apart. A sinful smile spread across my face as our eyes met. Wrapping and tucking her fingers beneath the waistband of my yoga pants, she pulled them toward her, curling them down my hips.

I took a deep breath. We were doing this.

34
CRYSTAL

I held the glass ever so gently, careful not to mess up my freshly done manicure. I went for a soft pink color—no acrylics, no fancy designs or bold colors. Just something simple and practical. I raised the mimosa to my lips and took a long drink, while one of the manicurists worked on my other hand.

So far, so good. We made it past the first potential blowup. I thought for sure Keisha was going to throw Olivia out, but thank Jesus for Karen stepping in. Keisha and Olivia both have strong personalities—who knows what would have happened? I had no idea Olivia manipulated this event. It was completely out of line, as Glow is Jenny's salon, and she should have asked Jenny first. However, in a way, I could see where Olivia was coming from. Maybe she genuinely wanted it to just be us girls. Maybe she wanted to open up about what was all going on with her and Dean. It wasn't the best way to do it, but I think her intentions were good . . . at least I hoped so.

The conversation had never really picked up. Remarks

were made here and there, but overall, the only noise was from the manicure tools buzzing and the quiet chatter between the contract workers. The tension was so thick that even the hired help felt uncomfortable. Their eyes bounced around the room and then back at the hands they were working on.

Jenny continued to tend to the refreshment table and make small talk when she could. Shannon was sipping at coffee, and Olivia was deep in thought, perhaps figuring out what to say next.

"I caught your big-screen debut," Olivia finally said.

Shannon's lips pressed firmly together. "It's been taken down."

I still didn't know what they were talking about. "What video?" I asked.

"Don't act like you don't know." Shannon tilted her head.

I looked at Jenny, then Olivia, and then back at Shannon. My eyes were wide and bewildered.

"Anyway . . . you having any luck on the dating scene, Shannon?" Olivia smirked.

I took a deep breath.

"I'm not looking to date right now. I'm focusing on myself." Shannon raised her chin.

Good for her. I gave her a slight nod and a smile without realizing it. I hadn't meant for it to be rude. I was proud of her strength, but Shannon glared at me and returned to her coffee. Something was up. I dropped my head and quickly looked away.

"Well, if you need any help." Olivia pointed at me. "Crystal over here is really good at picking men." She threw her head back in laughter. "I'm only kidding."

Shannon turned red . . . not from embarrassment, but from anger. I turned red . . . not from anger, but from embarrassment. A vein emerged in the center of Shannon's forehead, and her mouth began to open. Jenny instinctively stepped toward

Shannon. My body tensed up. Oh God . . . this was it. Shannon was going to lose it. What the hell was Olivia doing?

The front door chimed, interrupting the impending outburst. The door closed with a bang that sucked all the air out of the room. All that lingered was tension.

"Hello," a man's voice called out. We all exchanged glances. Olivia's face went white.

"One sec," Jenny said as she made her way to the front. Before she could get there, the curtains burst open and in walked Dean Petrov. He was dressed in a white bedazzled T-shirt and a pair of Philipp Plein jeans. He looked like a real douche.

"Hey, Jenny. I heard about what happened. You doing all right?" he asked.

Jenny nodded as Dean waltzed past her.

"Hey, baby," Dean said to Olivia. She gave a coy smile as he leaned down to kiss her on the cheek.

"What are you doing here?" Olivia asked.

"Thought I'd get myself a manicure too." He winked.

"This is a women-only event," I said, surprising myself.

Dean crinkled his face at me. "Well, I pay the exorbitant fees for this place. Jenny, are you fine with me staying?"

Before Jenny could get a word in edgewise, Olivia spoke up. "Of course, you can stay, baby. Right, Jenny?"

Jenny and Shannon exchanged glances. Shannon shrugged her shoulders in an I-don't-care-what-you-do kind of way.

"Yes, that's fine. We have plenty of room, since Olivia decided to make this a private event," Jenny said with a bit of tautness in her voice. "Take a seat." She motioned to the chair beside Olivia. Dean sat down with a big grin on his face.

I wasn't sure why he was here. Was he keeping an eye on Olivia? Trying to ensure she wouldn't tell us anything he didn't want us to know? I tried to relax my face. I was scowling at him and didn't even realize. A manicurist began filing his nails, and Jenny brought him an IPA. He thanked her and took a big swig, making a refreshed *ahhh* sound afterward.

"What were you ladies talking about before I crashed the party?" Dean asked. He looked at each of us.

"Well, your wife was telling me I should get dating advice from Crystal, since she's so good at picking men . . ." Shannon spat out the words.

I knew she wouldn't let go of that dig so easily. It was a low blow and completely uncalled for. Shannon was being as pleasant as she could be—which for a normal person would be a bit cold, but for Shannon, it was rather nice. Sure, she hadn't been particularly warm or welcoming to me, but I wouldn't expect that from her considering our history. I could tell she was at least trying. She didn't hug me or talk to me, but she did nod. A nod was a start.

Dean tightened his eyes. "Is that true?"

"Oh, babe, I was just messing around. But seriously, I wouldn't want to see Shannon lonely," Olivia said with unconvincing sincerity. She grazed her long nails down Dean's bicep, stroking his arm gently.

"Aaah . . . I'm sure you're real concerned about my well-being, Olivia," Shannon said sarcastically.

"I am, Shannon. You're my friend." She smiled a devious smile.

"We have very different definitions of *friend* then," Shannon fired back.

"You would know," Olivia quipped.

"Who wants more mimosas?" Jenny interjected.

Dean whispered something into Olivia's ear. I couldn't hear what he said, but she immediately stiffened up and dropped her hand from his bicep. She tapped her nails on her glass. Jenny refilled our drinks and took a seat in a pedicure chair across from Shannon. She turned on the bubbles and dipped her feet in the tub. I could see this whole situation was taking a toll on her. She should have taken a week off of work after the robbery. I had no idea how she was handling all of this.

My nails had been dry for a while. I was just sitting there monitoring the tension between Shannon and Olivia while also keeping an eye on Dean. I should have just left, but I felt somewhat responsible for what was occurring. My being with Bryce is what had caused the rift between Shannon and Olivia. I didn't understand why, but it would seem I didn't really understand anything about these women—or Buckhead.

"Do you need anything, Jenny?" I asked, cutting through the silence.

"I'm okay," she said.

"Let me get you a mimosa," I offered. I got up from my chair and poured her a drink.

"That's not necessary," Jenny said. I handed it to her. "Oh. Thank you, Crystal." She accepted the drink with apprehension and took a gulp of it.

"Are you sure you're okay?" I whispered.

Her eyes bounced around. She couldn't downplay what happened. I was there. I saw it. It was horrifying.

"I'm fine, really," she said, taking a sip of her mimosa.

I knew she was lying, but I didn't press any further. We all healed differently.

These women needed to learn to get along for Jenny's sake, so I vowed to be the bigger person by leading by example. I was going to bring these full-grown women back to the basics— elementary school manners.

"Can I get you anything while I'm up, Shannon?" I asked with a smile.

"Yeah, you can get me my house back. Keep the husband. He's useless anyway." Shannon waved her hand at me in a dismissive way. I swallowed hard and walked back to my seat.

Olivia's mouth fell open and she was about to speak, but Dean gave her a nasty look and she instead filled the open space of her mouth with the lip of her glass, chugging the rest of her drink.

35
OLIVIA

I couldn't believe the nerve of Shannon. Where did she get off? She was nothing without Bryce, and she was just sitting there, defiant. If Dean weren't here, I'd put her back in her shitty place. I knew exactly why Dean came. For starters, I invited him. His attendance made it look like he controlled me, and it gained sympathy points from Crystal. Second, I knew how Dean was. I counted on Dean to be Dean. And when he did, people might not see me as the evil one after all. He was tired of me causing trouble. He wanted me to act like a lady—quiet, calm, and collected. He wanted me to fit in with the other women. He wanted me to not bring any extra attention to us. He had always been secretive, but lately, his secrets were like a shadow over our relationship. I felt in the dark, and I was tired of feeling that way. Dean knew who I was when he married me: fiery, fearless, and a woman who will do whatever it takes to get what she wants. That's why he fell in love with me in the first place.

I felt Dean's eyes on me. I looked over and gave him a

crooked smile. He smiled back and nodded as if he were pleased with me—like I was some animal or small child that was obeying his silent commands. That's the thing with looks though: they're quite deceiving.

I felt Crystal's eyes on me. I glanced over at her. She was watching my and Dean's moves intently. It was her pinched forehead, tightly pressed lips, and slightly narrowed eyes that indicated to me she was concerned. Clearly, our chat the other day had had an impact on her. Good.

Then, I looked over at Shannon, and I nearly laughed out loud. It was obvious she thought Bryce was responsible for that video, what with the way she was being so accusatory toward Crystal. But no . . . it was me. I'd take that little secret to the grave. A friend of mine who was at the restaurant caught the whole thing on video and sent it to me. I just couldn't help myself. After all, Shannon had done something similar to me years ago, and I never forgot, nor will I ever. I can tell that video really got to her too. She's different today—weaker, I think.

The front door chimed again, and before Jenny could get out of her chair to go and greet the guest, the curtains were already thrown open. In walked Mark. This should be interesting. Mark was clearly in love with me, and why wouldn't he be?

"Hey . . ." Mark said, scanning the room. His eyes stopped on Dean and me. "What are you doing here?"

"Just enjoying a manicure and a drink with my wife," Dean said, nonchalantly.

"What brings you here, Mark?" My voice was light and full of seduction. If Dean wanted to play games, I could play games too.

"Well, Karen and I have hardly seen each other, so I figured I'd join her for a manicure." *Lie.* Mark glanced around. "Where is she?"

He clearly wanted to see me. I hadn't been in contact with

Mark since our last encounter, even though he had texted me many, many times. That was also a ploy of mine—make him wait and he'll never tire of you.

"She's in the back getting a wax," Shannon piped up.

"Well, all right. I'll just wait right here, if that's all right with you, Jenny?" Mark took a seat directly across from me. Dean and Mark exchanged prideful looks. Mark's face softened when his eyes met mine.

"The more the merrier, I suppose." Jenny's voice trailed off as she pulled her feet out of the tub of water. She dried them off quickly, grabbed two beers, and brought them to Dean and Mark.

"I don't think you'll need any reconstructive surgery," Mark said, staring at Jenny's face.

She furrowed her brow. "What are you talking about?"

He swallowed hard. "Olivia mentioned you might be in need of it . . . ya know, after the incident."

Jenny narrowed her eyes at me. "She's mistaken."

"Oh, honey. I mentioned it to Mark out of concern. That's all," I said with a smile.

Jenny forced a small smile and took a seat. *She'd never challenge me again.* She was too weak for that now.

"Karen's getting a wax . . . you two must have a hot date tonight." I toyed with Mark.

He let out a laugh, then coughed, and straightened himself in his seat. "Actually, no we don't. Haven't had one of those in a while."

"Sounds like you're not tending to your wife's needs?" Dean snarked.

"You'd know better than anyone," Mark retorted.

"What's that supposed to mean?" Dean raised his voice. He frightened the manicurist so much that she jumped back and let out a gasp.

"He's just messing with you." I placed my hand on Dean's forearm to try to calm him down. Mark was walking too close to that line. I took a mental note to punish him later for it. I knew he'd enjoy it—additional flogs for being a naughty boy—and I'd be sure to charge him extra next time. The money was for the pleasure and to keep my mouth shut. He didn't love Karen, but he wasn't ready to leave her. She was too vanilla for him. I didn't want to be with Mark. I just liked to play. I enjoyed having secrets of my own.

Dean shook my hand off his arm.

"Calm down, Dean," I pouted.

"Yeah, take it easy, man. I was just messing with you," Mark said.

Dean waved his hand, dismissing him, and took a swig of his beer. "So, how's business been?" Dean directed his question to Mark.

"Busy. Been traveling back and forth to Miami. The office there is sure taking off. Might have to relocate if it keeps going this way." He took a swig of his beer.

"You and Karen are moving?" Shannon jumped in. Her face immediately wrinkled up in worry. Of course she'd be sad about that. Karen was basically her only ally and her only lifeline to any sort of social status in this town. As much as I would hate to lose the extra income, I think Mark and Karen moving would be a blessing for me.

"We haven't discussed it yet," Mark said matter-of-factly.

"I think that's exciting. Miami would be a good fit for you two," I said.

Mark gave me a somber look. "You want me . . . I mean *us* . . . to move?"

"What do you care what my old lady wants?" Dean raised an eyebrow.

"Obviously, because I'm one of his patients," I quickly answered. "And please never call me 'old lady' again."

"It's a term of endearment, babe." Dean bumped his shoulder against mine playfully.

"I don't like it."

"It suits you." Shannon smiled.

I let that one go because Dean was sitting right beside me and I knew he wouldn't appreciate the cattiness, so instead, I smiled back. "Well, if you two move, I'll just have to travel to Miami for my treatments."

"It's always a pleasure," Mark said.

"Karen would never leave her successful business behind," Shannon said.

Everyone ignored her—as they should.

Crystal was still watching Dean and me intently. Shannon snacked on her second croissant, and Jenny was straightening up around the salon while keeping a close eye on all of us. Where the hell were Karen and Keisha? Waxes don't take this long. Ha! Unless Karen has a field down there. She's always been a bit unkempt.

"I think you could find a qualified plastic surgeon around here." Dean took another swig of his drink.

"And I think it's her body, so it's her decision," Mark challenged.

"He's right." I smiled.

"I think since I'm the one paying for it and she's my wife, I have more of a say than she does, Mark." Dean gritted his teeth. "Besides, it's none of your business."

Shannon sighed. "No one cares which plastic surgeon makes Olivia look like more of a blow-up doll. Can we talk about something else?" She rolled her eyes.

Dean, Mark, and I ignored Shannon again, while Jenny

engaged her in a side conversation. Crystal was still acting like a fly on the wall, quiet and observing.

"We can discuss this at another time, Olivia," Mark said with a small smile.

I nodded.

Dean looked at Mark and then at me and then at Mark and then back at me. The vein in his forehead throbbed. His face reddened. "Why don't you both fuck off."

"Already did," Mark said under his breath. I just barely heard it, but no one else did. Mark was getting ballsy. He was never like this. What had gotten into him?

"What did you just say?" Dean spat as he stood from his chair. "Say what you said to my face." He closed the distance between himself and Mark. Dean was always such a hothead, like an alarm on a fancy car, prone to going off with even the slightest of unwanted attention.

Crystal's eyes widened as she scrambled in her seat, grabbing her phone from her purse. It was the first time she had moved since Dean had arrived. She typed vigorously into it, and I thought for sure she was dialing the police, but her fingers tapped repeatedly. She must be texting, using her phone as an escape from the physical world, or she was trying to get the hell out of here.

"That's enough!" Shannon shrieked. She jumped from her chair and threw her hands on her hips. "You are not doing this in here!"

Jenny joined her by her side. "If you two are going to fight, you can leave." Her voice was shaky.

Mark threw his hands up in an I-give-up kind of way. Dean seethed and stood there for a moment. It seemed like he was deciding whether he wanted to stay or he wanted to use Mark as a punching bag for all his frustration. He returned to his chair, slammed his beer, and took a deep breath.

"Good. Glad that's settled," Shannon said. "Would you mind giving me a trim, Jenny?"

Jenny nodded. Shannon took a seat at a hair station, and they began quietly talking again, while Jenny pulled out a pair of scissors and a comb.

I returned my attention to Dean. Something was eating at him. I wasn't sure what, but he was off. His issue was bigger than Mark's small quips or the drama surrounding me and the girls, and I was determined to find out what that was.

36
SHANNON

Jenny took a pair of scissors to my hair and neatly began dry cutting the ends. She combed out small sections, sliding them through her fingers, and slowly cut, careful to only trim off a half an inch. She was so meticulous about everything she did. I noticed she was concentrating extra hard, like her mind wasn't really here.

"This event is a disaster," Jenny quietly confided in me. I looked in the mirror at Olivia, Dean, Crystal, and Mark. They couldn't seem to hear us over the chatter from the manicurists, most of whom were packing up. Two of them were finishing up with Dean and Mark's manicures. Crystal's head was buried in her phone. Dean, Mark, and Olivia were embroiled in a heated exchange of indignant looks.

"I'm not going to sugarcoat it. It is, but it's not your fault." I gave Jenny a look of understanding in the mirror.

"I don't seem to have control of this place anymore," she said, glancing over to make sure no one could hear her. Her forehead was wrinkled, eyebrows pinched together, shoulders tight, and lips pursed. "I feel like I lost it during the break-in."

"You do have control, Jenny, and you didn't lose anything. Your salon is still here, and so are we." I smiled. "If you ever need anything, and I mean anything, just let me know." She looked at me in the mirror and gave the smallest smile back. She was still tense and overly focused, so I know my words didn't get through to her. It was obvious Jenny was still hurting, but I didn't press it.

"Thank you," she said.

"Anytime."

The front door chimed again.

"Shit." Crystal got up from her chair. "Thanks, Jenny. I'll call to make an appointment tomorrow." She walked quickly toward the curtains, but it was too late. Bryce walked in wearing a navy-blue suit and a jack-off smile.

"Great," I said, sarcastically. Jenny squeezed my shoulder in a comforting way. She pulled the cape from me, signaling the haircut was finished.

"Let's go, Bryce. I told you to text me when you were here." Crystal grabbed his hand and tried to pull him out of the salon.

"Hold on a sec, babe. Since when do the men crash the women's manicure party?" Bryce chuckled. He took a couple steps into the salon, stopping right in front of Olivia, Dean, and Mark. Crystal let out a huff of annoyance.

"Nothing wrong with taking care of your hands and nails. These bad boys need to be well taken care of. They're like God's hands, sculpting the human body to perfection." Mark held them out and admired his hands in the most arrogant way.

"You're comparing your botched tit jobs to God's work now?" Dean belly laughed, clearly pleased with his comment.

"Your wife sure likes hers," Mark quipped.

The vein in Dean's forehead made an appearance again and his face reddened. These men were buffoons. How could I have ever been so hung up on someone like them?

"Now, now guys. It seems you two have been hanging with the ladies a little too long," Bryce said, gesturing toward Olivia, Jenny, and me. "We're men, not a bunch of females with too much time on our hands." He laughed heartily.

And the biggest buffoon of them all, Bryce. What did I ever see in him?

Dean relaxed and nodded.

"Does your mouth taste funny, Bryce?" I stood up from the salon chair and faced him. It was like I put on a pair of glasses and could finally see him for what he truly was—an asshole. I was no longer blinded by his charm, good looks, or his gaslighting. Bryce redirected his attention and took a couple of steps toward me. Crystal rubbed her head as if she were warding off an impending headache.

"No, why?" Bryce's face was smug.

"Huh . . . just figured it would with all the bullshit you've been spewing." I placed my hands on my hips and stood up tall.

"You should be pretty familiar with the taste. You ate it up for years," Bryce said with his crooked politician smile.

"Bryce, stop," Crystal begged.

He waved his hand at her. "Shannon's a big girl. If she can dish it, she can take it. Isn't that right? You can handle yourself?"

"You know I can." I raised my chin.

"That's not what you said the other night when you proposed marriage to me." Bryce looked around the room with a sly smile.

Olivia started laughing, and Crystal's mouth fell open.

"You proposed to Bryce?" Crystal asked.

I knew then that she hadn't seen the video and that this was news to her. I felt like an absolute idiot.

"I wasn't serious," I said, but my face reddened, betraying my words.

"Right, sweetheart, right." Bryce straightened his tie.

"I thought you said you two worked everything out . . ." Crystal furrowed her brow.

"We did. Shannon just isn't over me," Bryce said.

"I am so over you, and one day Crystal will be too. Because you're a fucking asshole, Bryce!"

"Shannon, stop. Please don't talk about my husband like that," Crystal spoke up, surprised by the words that came out of her mouth.

"Don't be an idiot, Crystal. He did it to me. He'll do it to you too. The next woman always thinks they're the special one. Trust me. You're not, and you should know better than anyone."

Crystal gave me a peculiar look, as if she were trying to figure out if I knew. I narrowed my eyes at her, trying to convey that I in fact did. I had been keeping a secret of hers for a very long time, one she didn't even know I had.

"All right, that's enough!" Olivia stood from her chair and walked over to Crystal, putting her arm around her. "I'm not going to stand here and listen to you talk about her that way. Crystal is my BFF, and I won't stand for it."

Crystal furrowed her brow. It was obvious she was unaware of her supposed close relationship with Olivia.

"Get off your high horse, Olivia," I said.

Dean stood from his seat. He grabbed Olivia by the arm and gave it a pull. "Let's go. I told you to stay out of this."

"Get your hands off her." Mark jumped out of his seat.

"No, Olivia's right." Bryce pointed a finger at me. "You're not going to talk about my wife like that."

Mark grabbed Dean by the shoulder and spun him around. He pulled back his clenched fist and launched it right into

Dean's face, knocking him to the ground. Without missing a beat, Dean got up and tackled Mark, crashing into a pedicure station and spilling the tub of water onto the floor. Crystal yelped. Bryce took a few steps away from the commotion. Olivia screamed at Dean and tried pulling him off. As Dean cranked his arm back for a punch, he elbowed Olivia right in the eye, and she fell onto her back.

Karen and Keisha waltzed into the room with glowy skin and bright smiles. Their faces dimmed and their mouths dropped open when they saw Olivia on the ground, holding her face and crying. Dean, realizing what he just did, climbed off of a bloodied Mark to tend to his wife. Crystal scurried over to Olivia. Bryce was off to the side like a true politician—causes a commotion and then just watches the chaos unfold, keeping his hands clean while everyone else got dirty.

"That's enough. All of you!" Jenny grabbed the empty glass pitcher and slammed it against the ground. It shattered into a thousand shards. Everyone froze in place and looked at Jenny, eyes wide, mouths open. None of us had ever heard her raise her voice, let alone break something. Like Olivia's entire body, it was completely unnatural. However, I reveled in it. Women weren't meant to be quiet.

37
KAREN

My first instinct was to run to Mark, who was sitting on the floor holding his bloody nose. Regardless of what had just happened between Keisha and me, Mark was my husband. I grabbed a wad of napkins from the refreshment table and held them against his nose. Jenny was frozen in place, just staring off, while Keisha tried to talk her out of her trance.

"Oh God! Are you okay?" I asked, helping Mark tip his head back to stop the bleeding.

"Yeah, I'm fine," he huffed.

"What the hell happened?" I asked Mark.

"He started it." Mark pointed accusingly at Dean.

"Yeah, well, maybe next time you'll keep your mouth shut when it comes to my wife," Dean said in between planting small kisses on Olivia's face. He apologized profusely in quiet whispers, calling her his baby and telling her how much he loved her.

My lips pursed as I looked at Mark, his wispy brown hair, hurt ego, wandering eyes . . . Why was he so concerned with

Olivia? I couldn't blow up at him now because she was clearly hurt. Her eye was red and puffy and most certainly would bruise. Crystal brought a glass of ice and a napkin to her. Dean took the napkin and wrapped it around a handful of ice. He pressed it to her eye and told her to hold it there. She winced.

Jenny finally relaxed. Her muscles were so tight that when she loosened up, she almost fell to the ground. Keisha caught her.

"Are you okay?" Keisha asked.

"Yeah, I'm fine. I'm just not feeling well." Jenny's voice was quiet. Keisha poured a glass of orange juice and handed it to her. She chugged it and then filled it up with champagne, sipping at it before she downed the whole thing.

I felt terrible for Jenny. She wasn't like the rest of us. We were used to the drama, the dysfunction, the gossip, the deceit. She wasn't. She wasn't from here. Crystal wasn't either, but she had Bryce to help her navigate the complexities of Buckhead. Buckhead wasn't a place you lived. It was a place you survived.

I helped Mark to his feet. Before leaving, I gave Jenny a hug and told her how sorry I was. Her body was stiff. She wasn't herself. I gave Keisha a small hug too and whispered in her ear how much I enjoyed our time together.

"I'm sorry too," Crystal said. She gave Bryce an elbow to the ribs. He looked down at her and straightened up.

"I apologize, Jenny, for my part in all of this as well," Bryce said in his politician voice, which contained a smidgen of seriousness, a dollop of charm, and a dash of insincerity. "Guys, you got anything to say?" Bryce looked at Dean and Mark. They both apologized. Dean helped Olivia up from the floor and carefully checked her swollen eye. Jenny nodded, acknowledging their apologies, but it seemed she was just going through the motions.

"Why don't we just chalk this up to *boys will be boys?*" Bryce said with a laugh. "Come on. We're all neighbors. We work hard, and I'm sure we're just a little stressed out. That's all." He patted them on the back.

I rolled my eyes. *Boys will be boys.* How completely disgusting.

"You're right, Bryce. Sorry about that, Mark. I've just been under a lot of pressure at work," Dean admitted. He held out his hand. Mark eyed it with apprehension.

"It's my fault too. I shouldn't have egged you on. It's all this travel back and forth to Miami that's getting to me," Mark explained while reaching out to shake Dean's extended hand. They shook and brought it in for a half hug with a solid pat on the back.

"That's the spirit," Bryce said. "Why don't we go out for some beers?"

They nodded. "Are you okay with that?" Dean asked Olivia. He gave her another kiss on the side of her head.

"Yeah, I'll be fine," Olivia said dismissively.

"I can take you home," Crystal offered, and Olivia nodded.

"Perfect. It's all settled then," Bryce said with a well-done attitude. He clapped his hands together. "By the way, I wanted to extend an invite to all of you. Crystal and I are having a housewarming party in two weeks. We put on a new addition and completely renovated and redesigned the entire place. It was important to me to ensure Crystal feels my home is her home." Bryce smiled a crooked smile. He looked over at Shannon and raised his eyebrows in a challenging way.

Shannon folded her arms into her chest. Her eyes shot daggers at Bryce. She opened her mouth for a moment, the words she wanted to say lingering at the tip of her tongue. But she stopped. She closed her mouth tightly and said nothing . . . nothing at all. She didn't need to say the last word to have the last word.

38
JENNY

Detective Sanford drops his pencil and leans back in his chair, stretching out his arms as if he were giving the air an invisible hug. He lets out a deep breath, clearly exhausted from this case—most likely, just from hearing how much back-and-forth there was. How they were all on tenterhooks with one another. How it was inevitable that something was going to happen that would change our lives forever. He rubs his eyes and leans forward, resting his elbows on the table.

"You're telling me after all that—the fighting, both verbal and physical; the lies; the infidelity—the husbands went and grabbed beers, and the wives were just fine with everything that had happened?"

"In a way, yes, but things were never exactly 'fine.' It was like when you boil a pot of water—that slow simmer. You can see the bubbles starting to form at the bottom, but they're not quite there," I explain.

"Had it always been like a simmer?"

"No."

"What do you think caused this never-ending tension?" He furrows his brow.

"The new wife, Crystal."

"Why?" Sanford leans back in his chair again.

"It was the first time a wife had been replaced in this group of women, and I think it made the rest of them question their relationships, their purpose, and who they'd be if they weren't a wife. It brought fear into the group, and fear makes people crazy."

I look over at the clock. It's 2:00 p.m. I've been here for six hours, and we haven't even scratched the surface. When I volunteered to come and speak with the lead detective on the case, I didn't think it would take this long. As much as I want to help, I'm tired. I yawn so wide my eyes close and tears come out the corners. I rub at them to keep myself awake.

Detective Sanford looks over at the clock and returns his eyes to me. "Do you need a break?"

"Yes, and I'm famished."

"I can take care of that. Pizza or burgers?" he asks, raising an eyebrow.

"Pizza," I say with a small smile.

"I took you for a pizza girl." He smiles back. Detective Sanford gets up from his chair and starts walking toward the door. He stops and turns back toward me, hesitating for a moment.

I knew he really needed my help. Buckhead was complicated, intricate, like a spider's web—so beautiful to look at, but so easy to get entangled in. Only the spiders knew how to navigate the web without getting stuck. And I was a spider.

"What do you know about Crystal's life . . . before Buckhead?" he asks.

I try to recall the small tidbits I had learned here and there. She was a bartender in Texas. That was about all I had known about her. No one ever really asked about her past, unless it had to do with how her relationship started with Bryce.

"Actually, not a whole hell of a lot."

Detective Sanford purses his lips and nods. "I thought so. It seems she had a complicated history of her own." He opens the door and closes it behind him, letting his words hang in the air.

39
KAREN

I wrung the mop out into the sink of the back closet one final time and left it propped up. Closing the door behind me, I walked back into the salon area. Shannon tossed a bag of used napkins, crumbs, and empty champagne bottles into the trash can. Jenny vigorously wiped down the tables and stations with a damp rag. Even though they were clean, she just kept on scrubbing. Keisha collected dirty dishes and put them all into a bin.

"You guys really don't have to help," Jenny said, blowing small pieces of hair out of her face and wiping her glistening forehead with her arm.

"Nonsense." Shannon gathered the remainder of the trash.

"We're not leaving you to clean up our messes anymore. We're grown women," I confirmed.

"Yeah, and you pay me," Keisha added with a laugh.

"Okay. Okay." Out of breath, Jenny took a seat in her salon chair and let out a huff.

The rest of us followed suit, so we were all sitting in a circle.

We looked around the salon, which was pretty much spotless again. No evidence was left as to what had transpired an hour before. The blood from Mark was cleaned up, as well as everything that had been knocked over and left in disarray. The nail stations were all put away. The contract manicurists had packed up and left quickly.

"Are you going to the housewarming party, Shannon?" Keisha asked. Her question was sincere.

"No. You'd have to hold a gun to my head to get me to go to that." Shannon took a sip of water and turned her nose up at the thought of it.

"I don't blame you," Jenny said. "What Bryce did today was completely out of line."

"And let's not forget the gala and the video." Shannon crossed her arms in front of her chest.

I nodded. "It wasn't just Bryce today though. My husband's an idiot as well. I don't understand his need to protect Olivia and this little feud he has going with Dean." I folded my arms to my chest, matching Shannon's posture.

"She is his client, right?" Keisha asked.

"Well, yeah . . ."

"And you two are friends?" Keisha crossed one leg over the other, bouncing her foot.

"Barely." I rolled my eyes.

Before Shannon and Bryce split and Crystal entered the picture, Olivia, Shannon, and I were close. But our friendship had been fractured since it was made public that Shannon and Bryce were splitting, and we just drifted further and further apart. I still felt close to Shannon, even though at times she needed her space, but Olivia was driving a wedge between all of us.

"Maybe that's it. Maybe he feels like he needs to protect

her as a client and as your kind-of friend." Keisha tried to make sense of my dilemma.

"Or he's sleeping with her." Shannon blurted out.

My eyes widened, and my mouth dropped open. "Do you think he is?" I stood from my seat and began to pace. Sitting still was always difficult for me, hence my need to run. I tried to piece together the last few months since Mark had really started acting strange.

"Ummm. No, I mean, I don't know. I was just thinking out loud. You know me, Karen," Shannon said with an uncomfortable laugh.

"Yeah, let's not get ahead of ourselves," Jenny chimed in.

I paced harder, my shoes smacking across the floor. Was he cheating? With fucking Olivia? Would he do that to me? Would he do that to Riley? Oh, Riley. My heart stung for a moment, thinking of my little boy. Could I even be mad after what Keisha and I did earlier?

"I should find out. Shouldn't I? Like hire a private investigator or something?" I stopped and looked at each of them for confirmation.

Jenny nodded.

Shannon shrugged her shoulders.

Keisha pinched her forehead and looked at me with judgy eyes. She didn't need to say anything. I knew what she was thinking.

"It couldn't hurt," Shannon said. "You know . . . to be sure." She rummaged through her purse and pulled out a business card. "Here."

"What's this?" I took the card and held it up. It said, *William Bellinger, Private Investigator.*

"I used him a while back." Shannon pulled out a tube of red lipstick. She slowly pressed it against her lips, tracing them back and forth.

"Wait—on Bryce?" Jenny asked.

"Among other things," Shannon said with a flick of her wrist.

"Maybe I should hire a private investigator to figure out who broke into my salon. I think that's the worst part, the not knowing. The feeling like they could come back at any time," Jenny said, but I don't even think she realized she was saying it out loud, because she wasn't looking at any of us.

Keisha grabbed Jenny's hand, snapping her out of her daze. "If it'll make you feel better, you should."

She looked at Keisha. "Oh, yeah, maybe I will. But Karen you definitely should," Jenny said.

I nodded and slid the card into my pocket. I didn't know if I would use it, but it didn't hurt to have it. If Olivia was really sleeping with my husband, what else was she doing?

40
CRYSTAL

Olivia sat across from me in a throne-like purple chair in her large and lavish living room. *Opulent* wasn't a big enough word to describe her and Dean's home. Everything was trimmed in gold and mixed with onyx and white marble. I'm not quite sure who her interior designer was, but I'm sure she had the Trumps' number on speed dial. It was exactly how I pictured her decor taste would be. The house was a monstrosity of architectural design, big in every way imaginable—ten bedrooms, eight bathrooms, an outdoor pool, a walking garden, and tennis courts. Just like Olivia, it was over the top and in your face. I hadn't known her long, but I knew that much about her.

She was holding a nearly melted ice pack against her eye. We had been sitting here for thirty minutes, talking on and off, mostly about the greatness of the house she resided in. I wanted to leave, but I didn't want to abandon her like this. Olivia wasn't a very kind person, but she was still a person. I knew what Dean had done to Olivia was an accident. However, what he did to

Mark was deliberate, and I could see the rage boiling within him. I feared one day that anger would spill over onto Olivia, if it hadn't already.

"Are you sure you're okay?" I asked again for the hundredth time.

"Yes. It was an accident."

"This time it was, but what about the next time?" I shifted uncomfortably on the couch.

Olivia took a deep breath and removed the ice pack from her face. She set it on the coffee table in front of her, leaned back in her chair, and gently pressed her fingertips to her bruised eye. She winced but continued to press her fingers into her skin. It was clear it was painful, but she kept doing it, which was rather odd. She stopped and looked directly at me.

"There won't be a next time," Olivia said.

"And you're sure of that?"

"Yes, Crystal. I'm not some little girl who can't take care of herself."

"I'm not implying you are, and I thought the same thing . . ."

Olivia's face lit up, and she leaned forward in her chair. "Did something happen to you?"

I shifted again uncomfortably. "Umm. No . . . I was just trying to relate to what you're going through," I said unconvincingly. The corner of Olivia's lip perked up. She leaned back in her seat.

"I'm not going through anything," she said firmly. "So just drop it."

I looked around the room awkwardly. An older woman walked in and handed us both a glass of sweet iced tea. Olivia took her glass without acknowledging the woman. I thanked her.

"I'm sorry, Olivia. I just wanted to make sure you were okay. I don't mean to butt in." I took a sip of the iced tea.

Olivia nodded. "It's fine. I just don't feel comfortable speaking ill of my Dean. He's my husband. I'm sure you'd feel the same way about Bryce." She raised an eyebrow from behind the rim of her glass.

"Of course," I said, setting the drink down on a coaster.

"I'm happy we're friends," Olivia said, looking me up and down.

"Me too." I pulled in my lips and fidgeted with my fingernails, unsure of what else to say.

"I like to keep my inner circle small, so you're quite lucky to be a part of it." Olivia cocked her head to the side with a smirk.

"Yeah . . . Well, do you need anything else?" I stood from my seat and readied myself to make a quick exit.

"Have dinner with Dean and me tomorrow night. Bring Bryce. We'll do a double date."

I stammered, trying to come up with an excuse as to why it wouldn't work. I really needed a break from everyone, and I didn't care for Dean. Buckhead was driving me crazy, but after some hesitation, I reluctantly said yes.

"Great, how about seven?"

I nodded. She rose from her seat and closed the space between us in three steps. She wrapped her arms around me, then released me from her embrace. Before I could turn away to collect my purse, she grabbed my shoulders and looked me in the eyes.

"Perfect. We'll have our chef make osso buco. You probably don't know what that is, but trust me, you're going to die when you try it." Olivia's lips spread wide, revealing a large, toothy smile, like a primate does just before it attacks. I smiled back. From the couple of weeks I had known Olivia, I had noticed she had this way of being both cruel and kind at the same time, like a personality paradox. The way she acted wasn't natural . . . but it was intentional.

41
OLIVIA

I waltzed into the dining room wearing a tight-fitting red dress and a face of resolve. I was adorned in diamonds around my neck, wrists, and fingers. My hair was flawlessly blown out, and thanks to Jenny's skillful makeup application, there was no sign of yesterday's mishap on my face. I had to ensure everything was perfectly in place. The white silk tablecloth sat beneath the gold-trimmed chinaware. Several bottles of red wine were set out on the oversized mahogany table. Crystal and Bryce would be here any moment, and I was determined to have tonight go well. Crystal and I had gotten off to a rocky start, and I could tell she was apprehensive about me, always so shifty and uneasy. Tonight, I would fix that. Power couples had to stick together.

I really didn't need any more added drama. It causes wrinkles, and my Botox sessions were becoming more and more frequent. Crystal agitated me though. I wasn't sure why. A therapist would have to figure that one out. There was no reason for me to dislike her. With Shannon on her way out of our group, whether she liked it or not, Crystal would take her place. There was power in numbers, so I couldn't just kick people out without replacing them. Crystal was a replacement—for Bryce and for my circle of influence.

The doorbell rang. I was about to call for the help to answer the door but decided it would be more personable to answer myself. I took a deep breath and twisted the corners of my lips into a welcoming smile. It was forced, but it was inviting.

I threw open the large arched door, revealing Crystal and Bryce on the other side. A soft-pink dress enveloped Crystal, while Bryce wore his usual campaign suit: fitted navy with a red power tie. Bryce gleamed his trademark wide toothy grin. Crystal smiled awkwardly, her lips quivering in every direction, trying to find the right curve they should be in when greeting someone. She handed over a bottle of Veuve Clicquot. *Dom would have been a more suitable choice.*

"Thank you. Come in, come in." I threw my arms around each of them. "Dean, they're here," I called over my shoulder as they crossed the threshold.

"Thanks for having us," Crystal said.

"No, thank you for coming. We're so glad to finally have you both over for dinner."

"Glad you two could make it." Dean trotted down the spiral staircase. He was dressed in black slacks and a white button-down—not as formal as Bryce, but Dean was never all that formal. Dean gave Crystal a hug and shook Bryce's hand, and then guided them into the living room for drinks, pointing out the thirty-foot ceilings and superb architecture of the house along the way.

"Crystal and I are looking forward to our housewarming party. We're excited to show you all the addition we put on as well as Crystal's eye for design. Right, sweetheart?" Bryce wrapped his arm around her and pulled her into the crook of his shoulder.

"Right," she said.

I clasped my hands together as they each took a seat on an oversized couch. "An eye for design," I said, raising an eyebrow. "I didn't realize you were a designer, Crystal. Very surprising. I did all the interior design for this house. What do you think?"

She swallowed hard. Dean handed out crystal champagne glasses. Crystal took a drink from hers before answering. "I didn't study interior design or anything. Bryce is just really proud, and your place looks . . . expensive," she said, taking another drink.

"Thank you." I gave a delightful smile. "It was just what I was going for. I wanted guests to feel like it was a rare treat to be in our home."

"A toast," Dean proclaimed, holding his drink out. We all followed suit, raising our glasses. "To good friends, new beginnings, and long lives."

Our heads nodded and our glasses clinked, and we drank to that.

"Did we mention our housewarming party is a costume party?" Bryce took another sip of his champagne.

"No, and I already bought a dress, a very expensive dress," I said with a huff of annoyance.

"Save it for another occasion." Dean walked to me and wrapped his arm around my waist, pulling me in tightly, almost a little too tightly.

"I'm sure you could still wear the dress. Costumes are optional," Crystal spoke up.

"Nonsense. They're required. With it being the weekend after Halloween, we figured it'd be perfect," Bryce campaigned.

"Yeah, babe. It'll be fun. There's nothing better than pretending to be someone else," Dean said.

"Except when you're me. Then being anyone else is a down-grade." Bryce howled with laughter.

Dean laughed harder, and I let out a cackle. Crystal did one of those closed-mouth laughs—the one that's forced for politeness. She clearly didn't appreciate his sense of arrogant humor. I rather liked when people knew their place in society. Bryce was at the top and he knew it. Shannon, on the other hand, had no self-awareness. She was an ex-wife, a has-been, a "whatever happened to?" And she had wronged me. No one gets away with that.

I would never be like her and that is why she needed to be severed from this group—like a lizard caught by its tail. The only way the lizard survives is if it sheds the tail. Shannon was the tail, useless and unnecessary. And if she wouldn't sever it herself, I would, because I knew she would only bring the rest of us down. But enough about Shannon. This night wasn't about pushing Shannon farther away. It was about bringing Crystal closer.

"Are you ready for your party?" I asked with a gleaming smile.

The help refilled each of our glasses, while Dean and I took our seats in our throne-like purple chairs beside one another. He held my hand and we sat as one, a queen and her king. I smiled at him. He smiled back, pleased with me this evening. Dean was so dead set on maintaining our relationship with Bryce and whomever he happened to be married to. Crystal would be my new BFF, whether she liked it or not.

"Not quite. Still have some finishing touches, and we're having a company come in and decorate the whole place for Halloween this next week," she explained. "It's going to be rather on theme. Skeletons, spiderwebs, chandeliers, and everything red and black: curtains, carpet, roses. We're even having the pool dyed red for the night." Her face lit up as she spoke about it, like a child would in a toy store. Then again, Crystal was a child. I smiled and took another sip of my champagne.

"That sounds lavish. We can't wait to see it." I pursed my lips together.

Dean grazed his thumb over my hand affectionately.

"It was Crystal's vision," Bryce said proudly. He put his hand on her leg and patted it lovingly.

She beamed at him. "Couldn't have done it without you."

"Or his checkbook," I coughed.

Crystal's face scrunched up as she looked at me. She didn't hear what I said, but her brain was still trying to put it together. Dean grumbled under his breath.

"Excuse me . . . I swallowed wrong." I pretended to clear my throat. Sometimes, I just couldn't help myself.

"Let's not forget about the fireworks show," Bryce said.

"Save something for the party," Crystal teased.

"Wow. This is going to be the party of the year from the sound of it," Dean said, pumping Bryce up.

"Gala night usually is, but we all know how that went." Bryce gave a half smile.

Crystal shifted uncomfortably in her seat. The help once again refilled our glasses. I sat up taller.

"You don't have to remind me. Shannon made such a fool of herself that night. How could anyone forget? Plus, the video." I let out a laugh.

"What video?" Bryce asked.

Shit. Crystal gave me an odd look.

"And then she proposed to you," I quickly added, but I was sure it was too late. Damn it. Crystal's little brain was putting things together. She stared at me as she brought the champagne flute to her lips.

Bryce burst into laughter, and Dean did too.

"Can we change the subject?" Crystal huffed. It was less of a question and more of a demand. Bryce whispered something into her ear. I couldn't hear what he had said, but he did change the subject, so I can only assume it was an apology of some sort. Why was Crystal loyal to Shannon? Why did she care? Perhaps she just felt guilty. What Crystal did to Shannon was the worst thing you could do to an elite housewife. Actually, the worst thing she could have done to Shannon was kill her. Heck, maybe now that was the only way to make things right. It would be the humane thing to do, and it would be for the best for all of us. Put Shannon out of her misery, like an old mangy dog.

42

CRYSTAL

A woman wearing black pants, a black shirt, and an expressionless face set a plate of warm food in front of me. The steam rose, sending an intoxicating smell of meat, veggies, and white wine straight to my nose. I thanked her. She barely nodded and quickly disappeared. Olivia and Dean's help were like ghosts, or at least treated that way. They said nothing and just moved things where they were told to move them. It was clear that's how Olivia liked it. Bryce and I had a cleaning lady, a full-time chef, a gardener, and a pool boy, but I made sure I got to know all of them on a personal level. Only Olivia would enjoy treating the living like they were already dead.

"Everything looks so delicious." I unfolded my napkin and placed it on my lap. Olivia and Dean were seated across from Bryce and me at a decadent dining room table that could seat eighteen. I was surprised they hadn't sat at the far-reaching ends of it. However tacky, it would have been a true power move. I assumed that's where they sat when it was just the two of them, a mile apart from each other. I giggled to myself but quickly extinguished it by separating my lips with a glass of red wine. It went down smooth, unlike everything else this evening—the atmosphere, the opulence, the company. That damn video was mentioned again. I hadn't seen it and I didn't know what it was about, but now I knew Olivia had something to do with it. She always had something to do with everything, and I knew whatever it was, it was no good.

"Thank you," Olivia said, taking a bite of her food. "Eat up."

I nodded and picked up my knife and fork. The knife slid through the meat like butter. I could feel Olivia staring, and when I glanced up, her large eyes with rich chocolaty irises were laser-focused on me. She gave me a small smile; however, her overly injected lips made her smile look bigger than it actually was. I stabbed the fork into a piece of veal and brought it to my mouth, making eye contact with her. The meat slid off the fork with ease, and the flavors burst on my tongue, forcing me to let out a sound of delight.

"Yum, oh my God." I swallowed.

"I told you, Crystal. Can't you just die?" Olivia said, pleased with herself.

"You're right about that, Olivia. This is incredible. We have to have our chef get the recipe from your chef," Bryce said as he took several more bites.

"That'll cost ya." Olivia gave a playful wink. She took another sip of her wine and flicked her long, luscious hair over her shoulder.

Dean laughed. "Of course, we'll get you the recipe." He wiped his face with a napkin.

"Tell me. Are things okay at the salon after the mishap yesterday?" Bryce asked.

I let out a small awkward cough. I hadn't had a chance to

talk to any of the women aside from Olivia, and I really didn't want to discuss the salon.

"I went and saw Jenny today for a Brazilian blowout and makeup. It seems to me everything is just fine," Olivia said matter-of-factly, folding her hands in front of her.

Bryce nodded and continued eating. "That's good to hear. Do you feel the same way, Crystal?" He looked to me, waiting for my confirmation.

"I haven't had a chance to speak to any of the girls aside from Olivia, but if Olivia says it's fine, I'm sure it is." I took a large gulp from my wineglass.

"You should probably go in tomorrow. Get nice and pampered, and I'll throw in some extra money for Jenny for her trouble yesterday," Bryce said.

He was always all about his reputation, about smoothing things over, fixing things—and how did he fix things? By throwing money at them. It annoyed me, but now wasn't the time to call him out for it, so I just nodded and smiled instead. It was a nice gesture, even though it was for all the wrong reasons. I nearly rolled my eyes, but I caught Olivia looking at me again, so I forced them to stay in place.

"That is so sweet of you, Bryce." Olivia fluttered her eyelashes. "Maybe we should do the same, Dean?" She turned toward him.

Dean nodded and spoke with a mouth full of veal, "Of course."

I didn't believe Olivia and Dean intended on delivering that promise. It seemed like their offer was more for show than making things right. Then again, Bryce's gesture was for show too. Perhaps we're all more alike than I thought.

"Speaking of things we should do, I was talking to Bryce and Mark, and I think we should up our life insurance policies, Olivia," Dean said nonchalantly while chewing his food.

I shot a look of confusion at Bryce. "Why were you talking about that with Dean?"

Bryce grabbed the napkin from his lap and wiped his face. He was sure to chew his food thoroughly and swallow before speaking, the complete opposite of Dean. "Mark's cousin sells insurance and isn't doing so hot, so he mentioned it to us when we all had beers. They've got Riley, and we just redid the house. So, I think it's a good idea."

"Or maybe Mark's planning on killing Karen," Olivia said, tossing back her head in laughter.

Dean laughed along with her.

Bryce chuckled but shook his head and looked back at me. "We're all just getting older, and it never hurts to get covered. Plus, with what happened at the salon. We can never be too careful."

"Ain't that the truth," Olivia said with a nod. "Death don't knock first."

"If anything were to ever happen to me, I'd want to ensure you were taken care of," he said, reaching out and holding my hand.

"But you're changing the policy for both of us?" I questioned.

"Yes. Not to bring her up, but Shannon and I did the same thing. We both wanted to make sure the other was set if something were to happen. For Shannon and me, kids were never in the picture, but I think they are for us. I'm thinking long term, sweetheart." He planted a kiss on my cheek.

I glanced over at Olivia. She was leaning on her elbows, her chin propped up with her hand, hanging on Bryce's every word. So was Dean. I looked back at Bryce. His eyes were squinty, yet large, begging me to say yes and waiting for my approval.

None of this made any sense. We didn't have any kids right

now, and if I were to die, Bryce would be fine. He was the one with all the money. I wasn't about to hash this out in front of Olivia and Dean, so I nodded and told him I'd take a look at the policy.

"That's my girl." He pulled me in and kissed the side of my head.

"So, what about us?" Dean said to Olivia.

"What about us?" She returned to picking away at her food, barely eating any of it. My plate was nearly clean, but Olivia had only consumed a few bites.

"I think we should do the same. My job isn't always the safest, and I want you to be well taken care of if something were to happen to me . . . and vice versa." Dean planted a kiss on Olivia's cheek.

This whole conversation was odd and definitely not a topic for a dinner party. Who the hell talks about their life insurance policies with people they barely know?

"I think you and Bryce are right. What's wrong with betting on death?" Olivia laughed.

"Hear, hear." Dean raised his glass.

Olivia raised hers. Bryce raised his and then looked to me. I followed suit, begrudgingly.

"Cheers to death." Bryce chuckled. They all tipped back their glasses, extinguishing their laughter with red wine.

I cringed at the very idea of it—toasting to death. I perched the glass to my mouth, letting the red liquid pass my lips, slither across my tongue, and slide down my throat . . . What did I get myself into?

43

KAREN

I shut off the lights and closed the door to Riley's room, quietly whispering, "Good night, my sweet boy." I tied my hair back into a low ponytail as I made my way down the hallway into the kitchen. Grabbing a bottle of opened red wine, I poured two glasses. I drank one and refilled it again, letting out a sigh of relief. I had been waiting for that glass of wine all day, something to numb the worry, the anxiety, the confusion, the heartache— all of it.

The eight miles I ran earlier that morning did nothing but aggravate my knee. Playing in the park all afternoon with Riley only helped busy my mind for brief moments: when he would ask me to watch him jump off the swings, cross the monkey bars, or run as fast as he could to some inanimate object ahead of him. Doing an extravagant house showing this evening just made me feel emptier and more confused. They were brief reprieves from the worrying. I tried reading a book when I put Riley down for a nap, but no matter what I read, the words on the page kept rearranging themselves into questions: Is Mark cheating? Is he sleeping with Olivia? Would Olivia do that to me? Did I even love Mark anymore? Did I really care if my marriage was over? Was my marriage over? Who would I be without Mark? How would Riley react? Did Keisha and I have something real? If we did, could we make it work? How would people treat me as a gay woman? Would it affect my business?

I felt so alive when I was with Keisha, like I was truly living the life I was supposed to live, like I was me for once. So it had to be real, and if it were, could I be mad at Mark if he was cheating too? I took a deep breath, followed by a long sip of wine. I tossed the empty bottle in the trash, grabbed both wineglasses, and made my way to the living room. Mark was lying on the couch waiting to start an episode of *Dead to Me*.

"Hurry up, I'm going to press Play." He turned his head to look over at me.

I handed him his glass and took a seat at the end of the couch. He pulled in his feet to make room for me. His hair was a scruffy mess, and he was already dressed for bed in flannel pants and a white T-shirt. Despite the way I was feeling about Mark and Keisha, he was still handsome to me. He still had that boyish charm to him.

"Ready?"

I nodded, and he pressed Play.

The colors swirled on the television. Noise emanated. But nothing of substance registered with me. I was in a trance, my mind trapped within thoughts of what would be. I brought the glass to my lips and took another drink. It didn't go down smoothly. It got caught in the back of my throat as if I had forgotten how to swallow. I coughed violently, struggling to breathe, struggling to get it down or get it out—much like the lies I had been telling myself all these years and the truths

I hadn't been telling Mark these last few weeks. Mark paused the television and sat up. He grabbed the glass from me, set it down on the table, and patted my back as I tried to catch my breath and clear my throat. Swallow. Breathe. Cough. Mark disappeared and returned moments later with a glass of water. He propped it up to my lips and tipped it back. I gulped half of it down. He pulled the glass away and placed it on the table. I could breathe again. The liquid free from my throat. The lies still buried within me. Rubbing my back, he asked if I was okay.

"Yeah, I just swallowed wrong," I said breathlessly, not looking at him.

Was he, too, holding on to lies? We were husband and wife, vowed to love one another till death do us part, but we couldn't even be truthful—or perhaps it was just me. Had I not held up my end of the deal?

"Are you sure you're okay?" He pushed loose pieces of my hair from my face.

I looked over, surveying him, trying to find the deception. Was there any?

"Are we okay?" I asked.

Mark pulled his head back as if he were caught off guard by my question. Maybe I was wrong. Maybe I was the only one in the wrong.

"Yes . . . at least I think so. Why do you ask?" He returned his hands to his lap and leaned back a little, increasing the space between us.

"I don't know. You've just been distant, and we haven't been intimate in months," I confessed. I needed to put it all out on the table, or at least most of it. I needed to make sense of my feelings for Keisha and my lack of feelings for Mark.

"I know. I've been overworked, and I haven't been the best husband. I was planning to cut down my hours in the Miami office come the New Year, and I was going to surprise you for Christmas with a vacation for just the two of us." He let out a deep breath.

"Really?" I felt entirely guilty now. A little over a week ago, we got into a fight over the idea of him taking a vacation, and now he wanted to take one and cut his hours. Was he telling the truth? Had I blown things out of proportion? My eyes glistened from the condensation of my guilty conscience.

"Of course." He reached for my hands and held them, rubbing his thumb tenderly on me.

I wanted to tell him right then and there what I had done, what was going on between Keisha and me. I wanted to talk to him about how confused I was. He was my husband after all. He would understand.

He leaned in and gave me a soft kiss on my lips.

As we pulled away from each other, I looked him in the eyes, ready to tell him the truth. "Mark—"

"Actually, there was something I wanted to talk to you about," he interrupted.

"What is it?"

"Ya know my cousin, Sal?" he asked.

I nodded.

"Well, he sells life insurance and he's not doing too hot, so I'd like to switch and up ours, ya know, to help him out."

I furrowed my brow.

"Well, what do you think about increasing our life insurance payouts?"

"I don't really think about it." I pulled my hands away from his and grabbed my wineglass.

"I talked to the boys about it, and Dean is upping his and Olivia's life insurance policy. I think we should too." He leaned back and took a drink from his wine.

"Well, it makes sense for them. Dean has a shady job—whatever it is he does—and Olivia can't stop getting plastic surgery," I said with a small laugh, perching the glass back on my lips.

"But we have Riley. And what if something were to happen to one of us or, worse, both of us? I want to make sure he'd be well taken care of."

I glanced around the room, thinking it over. What he was saying did make sense. We had never really talked about life insurance policies before, but we were getting older, and we did have Riley. Maybe it wasn't such a bad idea after all.

"Okay." I nodded.

"Great. I'll get the paperwork drawn up for us." He kissed me on the cheek and reached for the remote. Before I could confess to him what I had intended, he pressed Play. It was probably for the best. Mark was a calm man, almost too calm. It was why he was the best plastic surgeon on the East Coast. Steady hands, still nerves. But I always sensed there was another side to him, a side even I wasn't privy to, a dark side.

44
SHANNON

Jenny combed a deep conditioning mask through my hair, carefully spreading it through my ends. Karen was seated beside me, while Keisha worked on trimming her hair and waxing her brow. I really didn't need anything done today, but I figured some pampering would do me some good. I spent the night thinking of ways I could take down Bryce, but when I awoke this morning, I figured I had better start spending my time on something more positive. A good night's rest and some Valium can do wonders for the mind. Rather than bringing Bryce down, I would try to refocus my energy on lifting myself up. *Try* was the key word. I'm sure if I saw Bryce's smug face again, I'd feel differently.

Karen screamed in pain as Keisha pulled a strip of wax from her brow. "Ouch, what the hell, Keisha?"

"Sorry, you need to relax. You're holding so much tension in your face." Keisha waved her hands, fanning air on her, while Karen pressed her hand against the splotchy red skin.

"Beauty is pain, Karen," I reminded her with a wink in the mirror.

"You would know, Shannon," she spat back at me.

"Ooooh, someone woke up on the wrong side of the doctor today," I teased. Karen took a deep breath. She closed her eyes and relaxed her face. It uncrumpled and became smooth again. Another deep breath in and out, then she reopened her eyes. Perhaps she had found out about Mark. It was clear he was cheating—at least to me it was. Bryce had cheated on me for months. I knew from the first time he was unfaithful. Intuition. I knew it. I didn't believe it. But I knew.

"What's going on, Karen?" I raised an eyebrow.

"Nothing."

"Lies. You're tense and snappy. Now spill. If you can't spill here, you can't spill anywhere," I said, setting my glass down.

"It's Mark."

"Ugh. It's men. It's always men." I rolled my eyes.

"He told me last night that he was cutting his hours in Miami in the New Year and that he was planning a surprise vacation for us," she confessed.

"Wow, Karen. A devoted husband *and* a surprise vacation. You sure have it tough." Keisha's tone was full of sarcasm.

"Oh, stop," Jenny said.

"I'm just kidding, obviously. Go on," Keisha said.

Keisha had a point. Why would Karen be upset over that? There was more to this story. There was always more to every story in Buckhead.

"No. Never mind." Karen shook her head.

"Don't be coy. Just tell us," I said.

Karen took a deep breath. "Well, he admitted to being a

bad husband because he's been so overworked, so he was going to start focusing on us. I think I jumped the gun on believing he had done anything wrong. It's me that's wrong."

Keisha gave Karen a confused look, which quickly turned to disapproval when her lips tightened and she cocked her head. She was hurt by Karen's words. I wasn't sure why, but she was.

"That's good news then," Jenny said. "What's the problem?"

"I'm not sure I believe him." Karen took another sip of her coconut water.

"Why?" Jenny asked.

"Because he's a man." I laughed.

Jenny patted my shoulder playfully. Karen ignored my comment. Keisha smiled.

"At least someone appreciates my humor," I added.

"You know I do," Keisha said.

"Not the time." Karen huffed.

"Man bashing. There's always time for that." I held my hand up for a high five. Keisha did not leave me hanging either. It went from a high five to a fist bump.

"Will you guys stop?" Karen let out another huff.

"Fine. Fine. Fine. When you're ready to join in on the fun, I'll be waiting." I gave her a coy smile.

"Me too," Keisha added with a wink.

Keisha clearly did not like Mark. Or maybe she knew something about Mark that the rest of us didn't. Maybe she was the one sleeping with him. Or perhaps she just really liked Karen and didn't want to see her get hurt. Regardless, something was off. I could feel it in my gut. It was that same feeling I had when Bryce was cheating on me, like there was a heavy rock inside my stomach weighing me down.

"Tell us why you're not sure if you believe him," Jenny said as she placed a cap over my head. She dragged the stand-up dryer over and set it up, turning it on a low setting.

"Well, last night he said . . ." Karen started. The front door chimed.

"Hello," Crystal called out.

Oh, great. I wasn't ready to deal with her today. Even if I didn't want Bryce anymore, I also didn't want him to be happy. He didn't deserve that, and it seemed as though she fulfilled him. If he knew what I knew about Crystal, I don't think he'd be so content. But I could be civil . . . for now.

Crystal slid through the black curtains dressed in ripped, fitted jeans; an off-the-shoulder top; and a pair of tennis shoes. Nothing on her was designer. Perhaps all wasn't well in paradise. Bryce always made sure I was dressed head to toe in high-end clothing. But it seemed like he was fine with Crystal looking like she came right from the farm.

"Hi, Bryce said he made an appointment for me today," Crystal said, unsure of herself and her place here.

"That's right." Jenny motioned with her hands. "Take a seat on the couch, and I'll get you started in a few minutes." Crystal sat on the plush white couch kitty-cornered to us and right in front of the bar. "Do you want anything to drink?"

"Just a sparkling water." She repositioned herself on the couch.

Jenny grabbed a San Pellegrino from the minifridge. She removed the cap and handed it to Crystal. Keisha plucked away at the hairs the wax didn't pick up on Karen's face.

"Now, what were you saying?" Keisha said to Karen.

"Well, last night Mark randomly brought up upping our life insurance policies after he said all that about cutting his hours and spending more time with me. Isn't that odd?" Karen winced while Keisha plucked.

I furrowed my brow. Crystal coughed on her sparkling water.

"Are you okay?" Jenny asked.

"Yeah. But that's odd, Karen. Last night Bryce and I had dinner with Olivia and Dean. They brought up the same thing to us, about wanting to up the life insurance policies."

Everyone turned to look at Crystal. I took a sip of my water and let out a laugh.

"What's so funny?" Karen asked.

"Your husbands want you all to up your life insurance policies. Sounds like someone's going to get offed." I cackled.

"That's not funny." Karen playfully slapped me on the knee.

"Bryce mentioned he did the same thing with you," Crystal said. I turned to look at her and found it was me she was referring to.

"No, he didn't."

Jenny took a step back.

"You sure about that?" Karen said with a laugh.

"Of course." I sat up taller and pulled back my shoulders.

"Ever sign something he put in front of you without reading it?" Keisha raised an eyebrow.

I thought back to our marriage. I liked signing my name, Mrs. Shannon Madison. I signed anything and everything I could. It made me feel powerful. I even had a gold-plated pen specifically for signing my name on packages, receipts at designer stores—and yeah, anything Bryce put in front of me.

"Fuck," I said.

Karen and Keisha laughed. Jenny patted my shoulder. Crystal averted her eyes from me and returned to taking small sips of her sparkling water.

"At least he didn't have you sign a postnup," Karen offered.

"What a slimy bastard." I shook my head.

If he really had me sign something like that without telling me, what else did I sign? He always thought he knew best. That arrogant prick. Where did he get off increasing my life insurance coverage? Was he hoping I'd die while he was off banging Little Miss Barnyard? At least I didn't have to worry about it now that we were divorced. No one would profit from my death.

45
JENNY

I toss the pizza crust into the box and take a swig of Coca-Cola to wash it down. Detective Sanford devours his piece of pizza, crust and all. He wipes his hands on his pants and picks up his pen again.

"So, the husbands convinced all the wives to increase their life insurance policies?" he asks.

"Yes." I nod my head and wipe my hands with a napkin.

He scribbles some more words down on his notebook, then drops his pen, and reaches for another piece of pizza. The cheese oozes off the end of it, but he's careful to grab it all and plop it back on his slice. He folds the pizza in half the long way and takes a large bite, smacking his lips together and chewing it vigorously. He eats pizza like he investigates a crime, thoroughly and with care not to leave anything behind.

In between bites he asks, "And you didn't find that odd?"

I lean forward in my chair, placing my elbows on the table. "I found everything about Buckhead odd."

Detective Sanford nods and continues to eat his pizza as he turns things over in his mind. Buckhead was like a Rubik's Cube—few figured it out, few understood it. I knew what I knew because I was a silent observer—through the text messages they sent, the phone calls they took, and the emails they drafted, I saw everything. All while they sat in my salon chair. Not only that, but the pauses between their words, looks exchanged with one another, and their body language told me everything else.

"Why did you come to Buckhead in the first place?" he asks. I'm not sure if he's just filling in the lulls in our conversation or he's generally curious; or perhaps he thinks I had something to do with all of this.

"Just needed a change in scenery," I say. "I always liked the South. I was born in the Midwest. Couldn't stand the cold weather any longer. When I decided I was going to open up my own salon, I knew it'd be somewhere south."

"Where in the Midwest?"

"Wisconsin."

"Brrrrr. I feel cold just hearing the word *Wisconsin*." He laughs.

I gave a small smile.

"And what do you do when you're not working?" Detective Sanford finishes up his slice of pizza.

"Not much. I'm typically always working."

"Glow is your whole life?" He leans back in his chair, and his eyes bounce all over me as if he's trying to figure me out. Trying to put me together like a puzzle.

"It's a big part of it." I lean back in my chair, matching his demeanor.

"It must have been rather aggravating to have these women stirring up drama and bickering over everything. Then to have their husbands physically fighting in your salon, the place you worked so hard to make successful." He raises an eyebrow.

"I knew it came with the territory, so it didn't bother me. I found it more annoying than anything that these grown men and women couldn't act like adults." The corners of my lips perk up.

"Right . . ." he says.

"These women paid well. They tipped well. They made me very comfortable, financially. So, as long as they weren't killing each other in my salon, I didn't care what they did." I grab another slice of pizza and plop it on my paper plate.

"Well, lucky for you the murder didn't happen at Glow then." Detective Sanford raises his brows.

"You know what I mean." I fold my arms in front of my chest.

He lets on a smirk.

"We've determined the murder weapon was a Glock 19. Do you know anyone that would have access to that?" he asks.

"Any one of them could have had access. Guns are easy to come by in this country, especially in Georgia," I say, twisting up my lips.

Detective Sanford nods and grabs another slice of pizza.

46
JENNY

I refilled the spray tan machine and set out a pile of folded, freshly cleaned towels. Exiting the room, I returned to the main salon area. Shannon had left a few minutes before, and Crystal was gathering her things, while Karen and Keisha sat on the couches socializing.

"Spray tan room is all set to go. It shouldn't malfunction again," I said to Keisha. She nodded and thanked me.

"Thanks so much for fitting me in today," Crystal said as she admired her fresh hairstyle in the mirror. Like Shannon, she had also come in for a deep conditioning treatment.

"Not a problem."

She gave me a hug and said goodbye to Keisha and Karen, disappearing behind the black curtains. Keisha and Karen stood from their seats.

"I'm going to catch up on some cleaning and take a nap. Are you okay to cover the salon for a couple hours?" I asked Keisha.

She waved her hand at me. "Take all the time you need. You look exhausted."

"Are you sure?" I cocked my head at her.

"I'm positive. Besides, if I need you, I'll just bang on the ceiling with a broom." Keisha laughed.

I smiled and said goodbye to both of them and walked through to the back of the salon. I had had four additional locks installed on the back door—a chain lock and three dead bolts. I slid the chain over, and after three clicks from the bolts, the door was open. I could never be too safe now. Out in the alley, I climbed a flight of stairs and unlocked the door to my apartment. There were three dead bolts there too. No one had ever seen my apartment, except Keisha. I was rarely up here myself— just to sleep, basically. My whole life was the salon.

The sound of the door closing echoed throughout my apartment, thanks to it being barely furnished. There was a small table with two chairs in the kitchen. The living room had only the essentials: a couch, a coffee table, an area rug, a couple of pillows, one throw blanket, a laptop, and a stack of books and magazines. I didn't even have a television.

I had one framed photo on the wall. I walked to it, admiring the smiling faces in the picture and the gold frame that outlined it. It was a photo of my sister, her husband, and their two young kids. She looked like a younger version of me by a couple of years. Her children were blond with big blue eyes and even bigger smiles. Her husband towered over her petite size with light-brown hair and green eyes. I had never met the children, my niece and nephew. It was difficult for me to take time off from the salon. She hadn't been down to visit me since before she started her family. It was challenging for her to travel with young kids. We were sisters, connected by DNA and a shared upbringing, but other than that, we were strangers. I guess that's what happens when a person makes work their whole life. I pressed my fingertips to the glass, touching it for a moment. Letting out a deep breath, I allowed my hand to fall back to my side and made my way to the kitchen. I poured myself a glass of red wine from an already opened bottle. Prior to the break-in, I wasn't a big drinker. Well actually, prior to the break-in, I wasn't a lot of things. I wasn't scared, jumpy, or anxious. I didn't wake up drenched in sweat in the middle of the night. I didn't double- and triple-check that doors were locked. I didn't tense up every time the bell chimed at the salon. That night had taken a piece of me, and I wasn't sure I was ever going to get it back.

With wine in hand, I walked back into the living room and took a seat on the couch. Firing up my laptop, I opened a browser and typed *eHarmony* into the search bar. It autofilled before I could finish typing it, as I had visited the site nearly two years ago.

It was on one of the many nights Keisha and I had had drinks after a long day of work. She kept pushing me, telling me I needed to start dating, that I wasn't getting any younger. Not much had changed. After my third drink, I agreed to let her help me set up a dating profile. We spent hours on it and somehow actually made me sound interesting. We messaged one eligible bachelor that we both agreed could potentially be a good match for me. Keisha wanted to message a dozen. She believed the more hooks we put out, the more we'd catch. I wasn't look- ing for quantity. I was looking for quality. If I'm being honest, I wasn't sure I was really looking at all, but I was trying to be open to it. That was the first and last time I had looked at the site. I had never revisited it, never followed up to see if he had messaged me back. I wasn't ready, or maybe I feared the rejection. Maybe what terrified me more was the opposite of rejection. What if he had wanted to get to know me? To date me? To love me?

Logging into my account, I typed in my password and username. It took me a few moments to figure out how to navigate the site. I found the little envelope with the number one over it. I had a message. It was eighteen months old, and it was from a man named Henry. I remembered him. He was our front-runner that evening and the only man we messaged. He worked in finance. Never married. No kids. Dog lover. Tall. Athletic. Ready to settle down and focus on the things that mattered in life, like love, laughter, and family. He had worked hard, solely focused on his career for many, many years. He was perfect.

I slowly read the message.

Hello, Jenny. I was so pleased to receive your message. It sounds like we have more in common than we care to admit. Overworked, me too. Ready to live, me too. The belief that cats are for people that never had the love of a dog, me too. I'd love to take you out to dinner sometime, so we can discuss anything but work and talk about how great dogs are 😊. Look forward to hearing from you.
—Henry

My lips spread into a massive smile, one I couldn't contain. It was the first time since the attack that I felt anything other than anxiety. I reached for my wine and took a drink of the liquid courage. Setting the glass back down, I cracked my fingers and took a deep breath. This was it. I was finally going to put myself out there. Keisha was right. I needed more than Glow.

Moving the cursor over to his name, I clicked on it. The screen loaded and it said, *Profile No Longer Exists*. I refreshed and clicked it again, receiving the same error code over and over. I took another drink of wine, then opened a new tab. I brought up Facebook and typed his first and last name into the search bar. His profile was the first one.

Just as I was about to click *Add Friend*, I stopped. His last post on his wall caught my eye.

So happy to announce that Ashley and I are engaged.
She's everything I have ever wanted in a partner.
Here's to a lifetime of love, laughter, and all the dogs.

Below the photo was a picture of him in a suit and his smiling bride-to-be. She was blond and petite . . . like me.

I closed the laptop and tossed it on the coffee table with a thud, knocking over the wine and spilling it onto the area rug. I didn't flinch. I didn't attempt to immediately clean it up. Instead, I wrapped a blanket around myself and laid down on the couch. Squeezing my eyelids closed so that they held back my tears, I sank deeper and deeper into myself, finding what it was that I truly had at my core: nothing, just a deep emptiness. I knew I couldn't go on living like this.

47
KAREN

Keisha pulled out her phone and put on a Spotify playlist of early 2000s R&B songs, while I leaned against the table in the waxing room. Placing her phone on the counter, she turned to me.

"What's the music for? Trying to get me in the mood?"

"I don't need to try, honey." She winked. "The music is to cover the screams of pleasure I'm about to bring out of you."

I raised an eyebrow. "Is that so?"

She walked to me and put her lips on my neck, licking and kissing all the way up to my hairline. "I'd say so," she whispered hot breath into my ear. The hair on the back of my neck stood. My heart raced. I tingled all over.

"How much time do we have?" I asked, my breath already ragged.

Keisha glanced over at the clock on the wall. "Thirty minutes. Jenny said she needed a couple hours, but she's never away from this salon for more than thirty minutes during working hours."

"How's she holding up?" I asked, while Keisha slid her top

off, revealing a black lacy bra. She pulled mine off too, revealing a red lacy bra. We had clearly known we were going to see each other today or at least hoped we would, hence the lace rather than the usual cotton bras I wore.

"She's not herself. Hasn't been since the attack. And she's overworked and stressed with all the drama in the salon lately."

I felt a pang of guilt.

Keisha unzipped her pants and slid them down her toned thighs. I followed suit, revealing my creamy-white runner's legs. I really needed to actually get a spray tan one of these times. The girls were going to get suspicious if I kept going in for "spray tans" and coming out my usual pale self.

"I'm going to try to help put an end to the drama. I'll see if I can get everyone to get along and be cordial with one another in the salon . . . for Jenny's sake."

"Good luck." Keisha laughed.

"What's that supposed to mean?" I took a step back, looking at her, trying to focus on her icy-blue eyes, but her full lips that begged to be kissed always grabbed my attention.

"I'm just saying it's not going to be easy. Every one of you has been off since Bryce traded Shannon in for Crystal." Keisha bit her lip and put her hands on her hips.

"Even me?" I stammered.

"Yes, even you." Keisha shifted her hips. I leaned back on the table.

"How so?" I raised my eyebrows.

"Well, you're sleeping with me."

"You think me sleeping with you is just me 'being off'?" I made air quotes with my fingers and then returned my hands to my hips.

Keisha let out a huff. "No . . . I don't know. You think your husband is cheating on you and you're pissed about it, despite the fact you're sleeping with me. What do you expect me to think?"

I rubbed my forehead with my fingers. She was right. I didn't know what to say or what to think or even what I wanted *her* to think. "It's just really complicated," I finally said.

"What's complicated? You either want to be with me or you don't. You either want to be with your husband or you don't. What is it you want?"

I looked around the room and then back at her, my gaze drawn to her full lips again. Her eyes begged for an answer. I thought about my life with Mark. The passion had disappeared long ago. Then there was Keisha. When I was with her, I didn't question myself. I didn't think there was anything wrong with me. I just thought about the moment. About us. About how I felt. About how natural it was. Not forced. Just the way it should be. Effortless. But I had to think about my business, my son, and my life as a whole. But that could wait for now.

"I want you. I only want you," I said as I closed the gap between us, kissing her so hard she'd forget why we were fighting in the first place. It worked. She kissed me back. Her hands all over my body, unclasping my bra, on my breasts, beneath my panties. My hands following suit on her body. Lips on lips. Tongue on skin. Our breathing heightened, while "If I Ain't Got You" by Alicia Keys played softly on Keisha's phone. She pushed me onto the table, and our hands ventured south while she kissed my lips, sucking on my bottom one. I closed my eyes, trying to concentrate on my breathing. Trying to wait for her, so we could finish together. We were in this together.

The door slamming against the wall stopped us dead in our tracks. I sprang away from Keisha and quickly covered myself with my hands. Keisha startled, swiftly doing the same.

"What in the fuck is going on here?" Olivia's eyes and mouth were wide open. She stood there taking it all in—Keisha and me, half-naked, struggling to catch our breath. She looked at each of us, raising an eyebrow, her mouth transforming from a perfect circle to a devilish half smile.

"I didn't realize finger-banging was a service offered here," she said with a laugh, then she turned on her heel and walked out of the room. I glanced at Keisha, exchanging a look of horror, and I quickly threw on my clothes.

"Olivia, wait!" I ran out of the room, chasing after her.

48
OLIVIA

Sitting in Jenny's salon chair, I waited impatiently for her to arrive. We had an appointment. I was late. She was *later*, and Jenny was never tardy. Her time wasn't important like mine. I sent a few text messages, then admired myself in the mirror. My hair, although long and luscious, needed a little volume. My latest Botox injections had started to wear off, allowing me to express my emotions more visually—like the shock I felt thirty minutes ago when I walked in on Keisha and Karen. Who would have thought? Mommy Dearest and Little Miss Perfect Realtor diving all the way to the bottom of Lake Muff. Karen begged me to keep it to myself, and I obliged after some groveling on her part. As long as I held other people's secrets, I had power. I wasn't sure yet what I would do with this new power, but for now, I'd hold on to it. What would Mark think of all this? I mean, he had his own little dark sexual fantasies. Such a submissive man. I'm actually not surprised he turned Karen gay.

"Hi, so sorry I'm late." Jenny emerged from the back. Her

hair was tied up in a haphazard ponytail. Her clothes were rumpled. Her eyes were bloodshot. Her face was blotchy. It looked like she had been crying. She immediately wrapped a cape around me, pulling my hair out of it and fluffing it.

"What will it be today?"

I examined her reflection in the mirror while she waited for me to answer. There was clearly something wrong. Did I care? Probably not. Did I want to know what was bothering her? Knowledge was power.

"Are you okay?" I asked. My face turned sympathetic. It was something I had practiced through watching reruns of *Grey's Anatomy*, when the doctor had to tell some poor patient's family their loved one didn't make it. The look on the doctor's face was always one of sympathy. It required a slightly pinched brow, fused lips, a small rise of the forehead, and eyes that were engaged with the one you intended to be sympathetic for. I had mastered it.

"Yeah, I'm just feeling a little overwhelmed, and I've just been off since the break-in," she confessed while combing through my hair.

Oh yes, the break-in. I nearly forgot about that because it didn't affect me in the slightest. I was beyond tired of hearing about it. It wasn't that big a deal. Like, she was fine. Sure, a little beaten up. But the skin heals perfectly, and I should know. Mine's been cut into a dozen times and look at me, I'm stunning.

"That must have been horrible." I feigned interest.

She slightly nodded. "Yeah, I'm still working through it."

Ugh! When I made this appointment, I didn't realize I'd accepted an invitation to Jenny's pity party. For Christ's sake! I suppose I brought this on myself. They were just supposed to break some things and leave. That's it! Just enough to rattle her. It was punishment for her kicking me out of the salon. She wasn't supposed to be at Glow when it happened, and those buffoons I hired messed the whole thing up. When I saw Jenny after the attack, I felt the tiniest pang of guilt. Like when I cheat on my diet—that type of guilt, small and fleeting.

"What's there to work through?" I pried, holding eye contact with her. She glanced around, then at my hair, and then back at me.

She hesitated, and I thought for sure she was going to close up and change the subject, but I have a way with people.

"Umm . . . going through that made me feel violated. I'm not sure if that's even the right word." Jenny brought out a container of large hair rollers and sectioned off the hair on the top of my head.

"Understandable." I raised an eyebrow but quickly lowered it to its sympathetic position. "I'm sure you're feeling alone as well."

Jenny's eyes widened slightly as she rolled one of the curlers and pinned it.

"Yeah, even more so now. It made me realize that I needed more outside of these four walls," she said, looking around.

"So, it was a good thing it happened?" I perked a lip up.

"I wouldn't say that at all." She shook her head.

"My mistake."

She continued to roll curlers into my hair quietly. Every curler had the same amount of hair in it. Jenny was so meticulous and fervent about her work. If only she could apply that same type of passion to her personal life, then maybe she wouldn't be feeling sorry for herself.

"I think you just need a night out."

She shrugged her shoulders. "I don't know. Maybe."

"Perfect. It's settled then. You'll come out with us girls. Me, Karen, and Crystal, and you can bring your little Keisha friend." I grabbed my phone and started typing up a group text message.

"Oh . . . no . . . no . . . no," she said, shaking her head.

"I won't take no for an answer." I raised an eyebrow and hit Send on my phone. Jenny's phone buzzed. She picked it up, and I could see her cringe as she read my message.

> Hey ladies. Jenny NEEDS us!
> She's in dire need of a night out,
> Buckhead style. Meeting
> at Death & Company tonight at
> 9 p.m. See y'all there.

She forced a smile as she set her phone down and went back to working on my hair.

"You're going to have a killer time," I said with a wink.

I knew she had no interest in spending any time with me outside of Glow, but I didn't care. This would be fun and would surely make up for the little strangulation incident I caused. Jenny and I had been butting heads for a while, so it was time to get her to fall back in line—behind me.

49
CRYSTAL

I tied my black robe tightly around my body and leaned over the island counter to look at the sprawled-out documents. I was careful to reposition my head of towel-wrapped hair so it wouldn't spill out. The documents on top were the ones Bryce had just laid out, detailing our new life insurance policy. The papers below were everything concerning our housewarming Halloween party: caterers, menus, guest lists, vendors, invoices, etc.

"How does it look?" Bryce asked as he pulled his tie loose from his neck and unbuttoned the top three buttons of his white-collared shirt.

I scanned the papers quickly. Increase of life insurance coverage to ten million dollars on me and ten million dollars on Bryce. Lots of terms. I wasn't sure what I was looking for, but I continued to bounce my eyes around the text. It felt like the terms and conditions on an iPhone update: too long and too complicated. Yada yada, I accept. There were tiny Post-it Notes stuck to the spots where I was meant to sign.

"It looks official," I finally said as I looked up at Bryce. My eyes refocused from the strain of reading the tiny black text.

"It is. Need anything explained?"

I shook my head. I signed the papers, gathered them up, and handed them back to him.

He leaned over, giving me a kiss on the cheek. "Perfect. I'll get these filed in the morning."

I unwrapped the towel from my head, tossed it over my shoulder, and began finger-combing through my damp hair. My phone buzzed a third time.

"Who's that?" Bryce asked.

I shrugged. Bryce took it upon himself to grab my phone. He keyed in my four-digit password and read the message. I didn't mind that he went through my phone. I had nothing to hide. But on some level, it did bother me. He was throwing insurance papers in front of me and now he was reading my messages—messages I had been trying to avoid.

"It's Olivia. She wants you to join the girls for a night out with Jenny."

Letting out a groan, I started separating invoices into paid piles and unpaid piles. I still had a party to plan, and after yesterday's dinner with Dean and Olivia, she was the last person I wanted to see. I was exhausted just thinking about how draining she could be.

"You should go. It'll be fun." Bryce poured himself a glass of scotch.

"I think we have different definitions of *fun*." I rolled my eyes.

He walked over to me and set his drink on the island. He put his hands around my waist and nuzzled my neck. I giggled as his five o'clock shadow brushed against my skin.

"Come on. That's nice of Olivia to plan a night out with Jenny. She needs it."

"I don't know about that."

He spun me around to face him. "What do you mean?" Bryce kissed my forehead.

"From what I've learned about Olivia, she doesn't do anything to be nice," I said, raising an eyebrow.

He lifted my chin with his hand and kissed my cheek and the tip of my nose. "Oh, stop. This isn't a Disney movie, sweetheart. Someone doesn't always have to be the villain." He gave a coy smile.

"I wouldn't be so sure of that."

Bryce frowned at me—not a real frown, but a frown he made when he wanted to get his way. I rolled my eyes again and turned back toward the counter, sorting through all the papers and making a checklist of things that still needed to be done.

"Please," he whispered in my ear as he gently kissed my neck. I tried to resist but that was the thing about Bryce, he was hard to say no to.

"Please," he said again.

He slipped his hand in between the opening flaps of my robe. His fingertips grazed my bare thighs, making their way to the center of me. He swirled his fingers on my sensitive skin.

"It'll feel good to say yes. I promise," he whispered.

His fingers ventured farther. I let out a gasp.

"Is that a yes?" he asked while he kissed my neck.

I shook my head. My breath quickened. He kissed my neck harder, sucking and biting.

"Is that a yes?"

I gasped louder and louder. My back arched. My pelvis rocked. My gasps turned to screams. My body tensed all the way up like a marionette with its strings pulled taut. Then all at once, I erupted, and my body relaxed.

"Yes?" he questioned.

I nodded.

"That's my girl." He pulled his hand from my robe, kissed my cheek, grabbed his glass of scotch, and left the kitchen. Like I said, Bryce was a hard man to say no to. He was going to be the death of me.

50
SHANNON

After spritzing a few sprays of Tom Ford's Fucking Fabulous on my neck, wrist, and cleavage, I waved my hands to dry the perfume and rubbed my wrists together. I sprayed a little extra between my legs . . . just in case. I took a second look at myself in the mirror. This was me now, a fortysomething divorcée. Keisha had made a house call earlier to do my hair and makeup for the evening. She did a classy updo, wrapped up so well I couldn't tell where it ended or started. She was careful to amplify my best features, and by that I mean the features Dr. Richardson had done his fair share of work on. A light smoky eye, red lips, peach blush, and highlights on my cheeks, tip of my nose, and brow bone. I was dressed in a brand-new little black Givenchy dress, accessorized with a Tiffany & Co. pearl necklace and a Saint Laurent clutch. I was going on my first date since Bryce made the worst decision of his life—leaving me.

"His loss," I said out loud as I turned from side to side, admiring the curves of my body.

I wasn't sure if I was seriously looking for a partner, but I decided it wouldn't hurt to see what was out there. Plus, what a crime it would be to deprive the world of me! I had already wasted far too much time lying around my apartment feeling sorry for myself. It was time I put myself out there. Just because I was divorced didn't mean I was about to roll over and die. It was time to build myself back up. Then everything else would fall into place. I pulled out my phone and double-checked the last email I had received from Jonathan. We had met online a few weeks ago, chatting on and off. He was quite the charmer, saying all the things a woman wants to hear. Earlier this week, I finally accepted his invitation to meet in person.

I grabbed my bag and slung it over my shoulder, checking the time on my phone once more. The driver would be here any minute. I hadn't been on a first date in over fifteen years. Had anything changed? Did the men still pay? Or had the progressive females of the world ruined that for the rest of us? Women had to deal with periods, childbirth, and menopause. The least we could get is the occasional free meal. I had been all for being an independent woman. I even attended the Women's March, but personally, I rather enjoyed being wined and dined.

My phone buzzed. It was a text from the driver announcing his arrival. I took a deep breath and smoothed out my dress. This was it.

"Time to meet my future ex-husband," I said with a laugh.

51
JENNY

I walked in through the back of the salon, dressed in a pale-pink midi dress and nude heels. My hair had soft waves throughout, and I had lightly accessorized with a thin silver necklace and stud earrings. At my station, I finished off my look by applying mascara, blush, eyeliner, and light-pink lip gloss. The bruises around my neck had faded enough that a heavy foundation completely covered them. The same went for my eye. It was almost like it never happened . . . almost. Even though I didn't want to go out, I figured I'd at least look the part. I poured myself a vodka soda, and before I finished capping the bottle, the front door chimed.

"You better have one of those for me too, bitch," Keisha's voice called from over my shoulder. I turned around to find her dressed in a black miniskirt, a lace tank top, and black heels. Her hair was bigger than it usually was. Her makeup was heavier too. She put her hands on her hips and made her lips extra pouty.

"I know. I know. This wasn't my idea. Olivia cornered me," I said, putting my hands up, signaling my surrender.

She looked me up and down, shifting her stance. Her pout turned into a large grin.

"Oh, I can't be mad at you." Keisha ran to me and gave me a hug.

After our embrace, I poured her a drink too. We brought the glasses to our lips and gulped down half of them.

"How are we going to make it through tonight?" I asked, wiping away the liquid that had accumulated above my lip.

"I think the question is, *are* we going to make it through tonight?" Keisha raised an eyebrow.

We each took a seat at the bar and turned ourselves on the swivel chairs to face the front of the salon. The limo Olivia arranged for would be here in ten minutes. She insisted that we arrive in style. She also demanded that everyone dress up for our night out, and by dress up, using the term "Clexy," her made-up word for classy meets sexy.

"Why the hell did Olivia plan this again?" Keisha took a sip of her drink.

"I don't know. She said I needed a night out after what happened with the break-in," I confessed, taking another drink.

Keisha nodded. "It hurts me to agree with Olivia, but you do. I think a distraction would be good for you."

"Yeah, maybe. It's better than being inside my own head," I said.

"I wish you'd open up and tell me." She placed her hand on mine. I looked to her and then lowered my head.

"I . . . I . . . know." I hesitated. "I'm just feeling overwhelmed and alone. Like it's made me question what I've done in my life." I took a deep breath. "I love this salon. But this salon doesn't love me. I can't love something that can't love me back. This can't be all I have." I let out a sigh.

Keisha put her arm around me and pulled me in. "You have me."

I leaned into her. "I know. Honestly, most days I don't even feel like I have this salon. Olivia's always bulldozing over me, and lately, it feels like Glow's just a wrestling ring for my clients and their husbands." I shook my head and took a sip of my drink.

"This salon is yours, and don't you forget that," Keisha said.

I nodded.

"And like I said, you have me. Men are a dime a dozen. You can get one of those tonight. You found your BFF already. Finding a man—now, that's the easy part." She laughed. "Why do you think I switched to women? I wanted a challenge," she said with a laugh.

I laughed too.

"That's the spirit." Keisha squeezed my shoulder. "Now, let's add some more spirits to the spirit." She poured vodka into both our glasses and held hers up for a toast. I straightened myself and held my glass up too.

"So, you think I still have time?" I asked. "Like it's not too late for me? I haven't missed out on my chance for more in life?"

"It's not over till you're dead." She clinked her glass against mine, and we tossed back our drinks.

52
KAREN

"Limo's here," Mark called from the living room as I spritzed a floral-scented perfume on my neck and wrists. Giving myself a once-over in the oversized floor mirror, I ensured the emerald lace dress and gold sparkly heels I was wearing was the look I was going for—just a night out with some girls, not me trying to seduce Keisha. I quickly applied a bright-red lipstick and took a deep breath. I was nervous—nervous to be around Olivia. She had promised she'd keep Keisha and me a secret, but Olivia's word was about as strong as a toothpick. I was also anxious to see Keisha. I wasn't sure how we were, after how we had left things. I had taken off after Olivia to make sure she kept her mouth shut, and by the time I was done talking to her, Keisha had left through the back for a house call with Shannon. So I never got a chance to speak with her, and I wasn't sure we'd get that chance tonight.

I walked out into the living room. "Better hurry. They've honked twice." Mark raised an eyebrow. He was lying on the couch reading *Gravity's Rainbow* for the second time.

"I know. I know." I transferred a wallet and some other essentials from my oversized day bag to a small evening purse.

"What's the occasion?" Mark lowered his reading glasses, examining me from head to toe.

"I told you. Olivia planned some girls' night out for Jenny." I zipped up my purse and flung it over my shoulder.

"That's sweet of her." Mark pushed his glasses back up the bridge of his nose and refocused on his book.

I rolled my eyes and opened the front door. "Don't wait up," I called over my shoulder as I closed it behind me. The limo was parked in the driveway with "Dangerous Woman" playing loudly. Olivia popped her body out of the sunroof.

"'And you make me feel like a dangerous woman,'" she belted out as if she were Ariana Grande herself, minus the voice. Olivia was tone-deaf and not just when it came to singing, obviously.

"Get in, loser. We're going drinking," she said, giving her best Regina George impression. However, it wasn't much of an impression, considering being mean and female were her two greatest strengths. I gave a partial smile and walked to the limo. Olivia disappeared inside, slinking back into her seat. Just as I arrived at the door, the driver was there to open it. I shuffled in and was greeted with a drink.

Crystal, Olivia, Keisha, and Jenny were all seated in the limo, holding glasses of champagne and wearing Buckhead smiles.

The driver closed the door behind me. "Let the party begin," Olivia declared. She downed her glass. We followed suit with far less enthusiasm.

I scanned the limo to gauge everyone's face. I tried making minimal eye contact with Keisha. As I finished my sweep, I landed back on Olivia and was met with a grin fit for only the devil herself.

"How's it going, Karen? Anything new with you?" The end of her question was laced with the implication that she already had her own answer to this inquiry.

"Just was finishing up some paperwork and spending time with Riley before our bacchanal this evening."

"How sweet of you. Mother of the year if I ever saw one." She smiled back at me, closing our interaction.

"Did you invite Shannon?" Jenny asked from the other end of the limo.

"Of course, darling. This is your night after all. However, she had a prior engagement, if you will, that may or may not involve a gentleman caller." Olivia winked.

Olivia's knowledge of Shannon brought out gasps and whispers from each of us.

"She's going out on a date?" Keisha asked.

"Good for her," Jenny encouraged.

"Yeah, I'm happy for her," Crystal said.

"I can't believe she didn't tell us." I crumpled up my face. "She told you?"

"She did. But Shannon was very sorry to miss your night out, Jenny." Olivia refilled her glass. "Who wants more champagne?"

We each held out our glasses to Olivia, waiting for her to pour ours. Instead, she handed the bottle off to Keisha, tasking her to replenish the drinks. I shook my head. For a moment there, Olivia almost had me fooled.

53

CRYSTAL

We finally pulled up to Death & Company. The limo ride had only been twenty minutes, but with Olivia, everything seemed so much longer. The conversation on the way was filled with awkwardness between Keisha and Karen, snappy and double-edged remarks from Olivia, and peacekeeping comments from Jenny. I stayed quiet for the most part, only answering questions that were directed toward me—like when Olivia asked about how Bryce felt that Shannon was dating again. Bryce didn't know Shannon was dating again, and frankly, I thought he would be relieved to learn that. Perhaps it would ease the tension between me and Shannon. And maybe someday we could have a relationship or at least be in the same room without her jumping down my throat.

"Let's go, bitches," Olivia said as she exited the limo. I caught Keisha shaking her head as she followed her out. Olivia handed the driver a one-hundred-dollar bill. We all resituated our dresses, ensuring everything was in place, and followed

Olivia to the door. The bouncer didn't even stop to ask her name. She handed him a one-hundred-dollar bill, and we instantly crossed beyond the red velvet rope.

The swanky cocktail bar was bustling. There were two bartenders with perfectly sculpted beards and a couple dozen patrons standing around. The place was ritzy and chic, like a 1920s throwback speakeasy, replete with red accent walls, rich wood, and dim lighting.

A woman dressed in all black, carrying a clipboard, greeted Olivia. "Right this way, Mrs. Petrov," she said as she led us to a large VIP table off in the corner with a reserved sign. There were already glasses and ice buckets full of bottles of vodka, champagne, and white wine set out. We took our seats as the woman in black poured each of us a glass of champagne. "Do you need anything else right away?"

We all shook our heads, except Olivia. "Yes, we'll have five shots of tequila with the wheels."

I cringed. I had no intention of getting drunk tonight. I just wanted to have a drink or two and leave. But I already knew that was going to be tough to pull off with Olivia here calling the shots . . . literally.

"Count me out," Jenny said.

"Absolutely not. This is your party, and it's my treat. I insist. Come on, Jenny. Loosen up. No man wants to date a woman that's stiff as a board." Olivia's voice had an air of lightness, but it was laced with annoyance.

Jenny dropped her shoulders and put her hands up. "Fine. One shot."

Olivia clapped her hands with a job-well-done attitude.

"I'm trying to keep it low-key tonight too," I said to Jenny, letting her know that she wasn't alone. She gave me a small smile.

"No one is keeping it low-key tonight. I didn't spring for

a limo and VIP treatment at the most exclusive cocktail bar in town for a low-key night," Olivia interrupted.

The shots arrived just as she finished lecturing. She raised hers and narrowed her eyes at each of us, her way of telling us to follow along. We raised our glasses slowly.

"To an extravagant night, courtesy of me," Olivia toasted. Of course her toast would be to herself. We repeated her words anyway and tipped back the shot, forgetting about the lime and salt.

After my face regained its composure, I looked to Olivia. "Thanks for planning this, and I didn't mean anything by the 'low-key night' comment. It's going to be a great evening."

"I know it will, Crystal." She raised her chin slightly. "I'm sure where you come from, you're used to beers and dive bars. This is surely a special treat for you." Olivia attached a smile to her condescending comment. I brought the glass of champagne to my lips and glanced around the bar.

Over Karen's shoulder, I spotted Shannon sitting at a table alone, sipping at a vodka soda. I quickly looked back at Olivia as not to bring any attention to Shannon. She must be meeting her date here. I stole another glance at Shannon. She checked her phone several times and blew out her cheeks. What were the odds we'd all end up at the same bar? Did Olivia know Shannon was having her date here? Did she plan it or was it all pure coincidence? From what I had known about Buckhead thus far, there were no coincidences.

54
SHANNON

I was now working on my second vodka soda, casually glancing around the bar and back at my phone. I told myself I would switch to water after this drink. I noticed a rather handsome-looking man sitting at the bar alone. He also appeared to be checking the time. I gave him a second look to ensure he wasn't my date. He wasn't. My date was ten minutes late. I let out a huff but pulled it back in, deciding if his excuse was valid, I'd give him a chance. I was still nervous and anxious about joining the dating scene again after such a long hiatus, but the vodka was helping.

A cackle of a laugh caused my body to immediately tense up. I'd recognize that nails-on-a-chalkboard laugh anywhere. It was Olivia. I looked over my shoulder and spotted her sitting at a booth with Crystal, Karen, Keisha, and Jenny. They were chatting; however, the conversation looked stilted and one-sided. Karen and Keisha were exchanging glances. Jenny was fiddling with her jewelry. Crystal was refilling her drink, and Olivia was laughing—alone I may add. What were they doing here? And why were they all together? As far as I knew, Olivia wasn't getting along with anyone.

I noticed Crystal's eyes peering in my direction, and I quickly turned away, hoping she hadn't seen me. I glanced back again. Crystal looked away. Jenny and Keisha were chatting. Olivia was on her phone. Karen was refilling her drink. Good. She hadn't noticed me, or at least if she did, she didn't tell the others. She and I had something in common. We both were able to keep secrets. I took another drink and looked at the time on my phone. He was now fifteen minutes late. I brought up my email, and just as I was about to write him to ask where he was and/or to cancel the date altogether, a message popped up.

> Hey so sorry, I'm running late. Got held up at the office. I'll be there in fifteen minutes. Promise I'll make it up to you. —Jonathan

> You better be worth the wait.

Before I hit Send, I decided to add a wink face emoji at the end. I had to learn how to flirt again, and from what I'd read online, emojis could be very flirty, if not downright provocative. A plain old eggplant was code for penis. I considered adding that too but stopped myself. I hit Send and smiled as I set my phone down. An email alert chime went off. I picked it up and read his message.

> Don't worry. I am 😉

My smile grew wider. He added the emoji too. He must have been reading the same 'how to flirt online' articles I was. I was excited to meet this man. I ordered a third drink from the server but switched to Chardonnay, which was essentially grape water in my book.

55
OLIVIA

I put my phone down and refilled my drink, making sure to top off each glass with more vodka. Some tried to protest, but I was calling the shots tonight, and if I had to serve them myself to get them drunk, I was willing to stoop that low. Everything was going exactly as I had planned it. The women were just starting to loosen up. Well, kind of. Karen and Keisha were still exchanging looks as if they were trying to read each other's lesbian minds. What was Karen thinking? How could she do that to Mark? He was a decent lover. I'd know better than anyone— and she's a mom. She can't be off discovering her sexuality when she's got a kid at home and a plastic surgeon for a husband. I didn't like the way Karen and Keisha were acting on my night, so I decided it was time for a little fun.

"Karen, your spray tan looks phenomenal. Keisha did such a great job on it," I said with a smile, looking at her pasty white skin. Karen shifted uncomfortably in her chair, rubbing her hands over her bare arms as if she could cover them up. Crystal glanced at Karen's skin and her brow crinkled in confusion.

"Was the spray tan machine acting up again?" Jenny asked. I wasn't sure if she was covering for them or she, too, was confused.

"No, I had to cancel last minute for a showing," Karen lied. She shot me a dirty look. I smirked back, taking another drink of my vodka soda.

"I don't really think you need a tan. You have beautiful skin," Keisha said.

I rolled my eyes. Karen thanked her.

Moving on.

"Jenny, any guys out here catching your eye?" I motioned to the room of people.

She looked around the bar. "Not really."

"Oh, come on! What about that guy?" I pointed at a man standing by the bar. He was poorly dressed for a place like this—ill-fitting suit—and stood alone, awkwardly out of place. He was tall and looked thin, thanks to his clothing that was one size too big for him. Everything about him was average, just like Jenny. "He's perfect for you."

Jenny looked at him and then back at me. "You're right, I'll go talk to him." She raised her chin. She knew I was picking on her, but she was defiant. Grabbing her drink, Jenny got up from her seat and made her way over to him. I let out a huff. Little Miss Goody Two-Shoes.

"Get him, girl," Keisha hollered. Jenny turned back for a moment, delivering a small flirty smile. She took a seat at the bar next to him and immediately made conversation.

"Good for her," Karen said.

"He could use a little styling but aside from that, he's not bad." Keisha looked him up and down.

"They have a lot in common already," I said with a laugh.

"We should dance," I added, half standing up, moving my upper body, and feeling the music.

"Uh . . . let me finish my drink first," Crystal said awkwardly. She didn't look like the type of woman that could move her hips. She must be a total bore in bed. Poor Bryce.

"Yeah, me too," Keisha and Karen said at the same time. I grabbed Crystal's drink and slammed it. I grabbed Keisha's drink and slammed it. I grabbed Karen's drink and slammed it. They each gave me a disapproving look.

"There. You're finished. Let's go!" I got up from my seat and grabbed Crystal and Karen's hands. Karen pulled Keisha along too. I started dancing, shimmying my chest and swaying my hips with the girls begrudgingly in tow. Before I made it to the center of the dance floor, I spotted Shannon sitting at a table alone and it stopped me dead in my tracks. My lips instantly curved into a toothy grin as I walked over to her.

"Hey, Shannon. What brings you here?" I leaned over her like a dark shadow. Karen and Keisha greeted Shannon with hugs. Crystal awkwardly waved at her but kept a step away from the table.

"I'm actually meeting someone," Shannon said.

"We know." Karen smiled. "A hot date!"

Before Shannon could respond, I jumped in. "Where is he?" I raised an eyebrow.

She looked around uncomfortably. "He's running late."

"That's a bummer," Keisha said.

"Do you want to join us while you wait?" Karen put a hand on her shoulder.

"No, that's fine. He should be here any minute," Shannon said, looking down at her phone.

"Oh, come on. I insist." I smiled.

"Yeah, come sit with us." Karen playfully pulled on Shannon's arm.

"All right, just until he gets here."

We walked back to the booth and took our seats. Jenny was still chatting with that poorly dressed man. She's lucky I came into her life because she clearly has bad taste. What would Glow be without me? It'd probably be out of business, and Jenny would be some hairstylist in a Walmart salon. These women just didn't value me. I was sure I'd be like Van Gogh or Amy Winehouse, appreciated and recognized for my greatness after my death.

"Jenny," I yelled across the bar. She turned back and put her finger up as if to tell me to wait. Who did she think she was? I waited for no one.

"Jenny," I called even louder this time. Crystal covered her little country ears, acting as if I was speaking too boisterously for a bar atmosphere.

She turned around again and mouthed, "What?"

"Come here. Shannon's here." I pointed at Shannon. Keisha and Karen gave me *WTF* looks. Shannon waved. Jenny pulled out her phone. It appeared she and the man were exchanging numbers. They smiled at each other. She grabbed her drink and returned to our table, giving Shannon a hug and taking a seat.

"Shannon's just waiting for her date," I said.

"He's a bit late," Shannon confirmed.

"That's okay. I'm sure he's just caught up." Jenny patted the top of her hand.

She nodded but continued to scan the bar for her mystery man.

I let out a small laugh. "Are you ready for your party, Crystal?"

She nodded and took a drink. "I just have a few more things to plan, but it looks like everything is in order."

"I'm definitely excited for it. It's going to be the party of the year, since the gala was a bust. What's everyone going to dress up as?" I glanced around.

Shannon rolled her eyes but pretended not to be a part of the conversation as she checked her phone.

"Haven't decided on anything yet," Karen said.

Keisha and Jenny nodded.

"What about you, Shannon?" I asked, full well knowing she had no intention of going. I found the whole thing hilarious—being invited to a housewarming party at your former house by your ex-husband and his new wife.

"I'm not sure I'm going to be able to make it," Shannon said.

"Why not?" I brought my drink to my lips.

Shannon swirled her Chardonnay and took a small sip.

"That's completely fine. I understand," Crystal butted in.

Shannon nodded at her, checked her phone again, and glanced around.

"Wow, your date sure is late, isn't he?" I pretended to look around the bar.

"Yeah, he is," she said with disdain in her voice.

"I'm sure he'll be here." Karen offered more encouragement and false hope.

"Maybe he came in and saw you and left." I laughed. The girls shot daggers at me. "I'm kidding. Lighten up. Jeez." I stood from my seat. "I'm going to the bathroom. Watch my stuff."

As I walked away, I glanced back at the table, my eyes lingering on Shannon, my mouth curving into a malicious grin. I loved seeing her like this, pathetic and desperate. It's what she deserved.

56
SHANNON

My foot tapped the floor rapidly while I checked my phone and scanned the room. Where was he? He was now forty-five minutes late. I would have just left if the girls hadn't been here, but now I felt like I had to stay to save face. I hoped he would show because if not, this was rather embarrassing. I hated that Olivia and Crystal were here to witness this. Bryce would surely find out that the first date I went on didn't even show up for it. And Olivia just seemed to relish it when any woman around her failed, especially me. Like it somehow elevated her.

Karen, Keisha, and Jenny were being supportive of me in every way they could be. They tried to take my mind off the waiting by making small talk. Even Crystal got Olivia off my back about the housewarming party. I appreciated that from her, but we still weren't on good terms.

I checked my phone again and this time, I decided I would send him another message.

> Are you okay? Are we
> still on for tonight?

Seconds later Olivia's phone, which she left on the table, lit up. On the screen it said, *Email from Shannon.*

For a moment I was confused. I double-checked my email, paying close attention to my sent messages. I hadn't sent an email to Olivia in weeks. Maybe another Shannon emailed her. Pure coincidence. Who was I kidding? In Buckhead, there were no coincidences.

I typed up a second email.

> Forgot to mention. Just in case you
> show, I'm sitting at a table with some
> friends. You'll recognize the brunette
> as she sticks out like a sore thumb
> thanks to her overinjected face and
> bloated tits.

I hit Send.

Olivia's phone lit up. *Email from Shannon* popped up on the screen. My heart rate quickened, and I could feel my face flush. I looked around the bar and watched Olivia walk back from the bathroom. She looked like the Cheshire cat with her wide toothy grin. I nearly exploded, but instead, I took a deep breath and a large gulp of my drink.

"Who wants to dance?" Olivia asked as she swayed her hips to the music.

I took a moment to decide what I was going to do. That fucking bitch catfished me. I took a couple of small deep breaths while I decided whether or not I'd leap across the table and bash Olivia's plastic face in. My body was tense. I could fucking kill her right now. I took another deep breath, trying to center myself. I knew what Olivia had done, but Olivia didn't know that I knew. I had the upper hand here. I could fly off the handle, scream at her, make a scene, and leave the club, refusing to ever speak to her again. I considered that option.

But then I watched her. I watched her sway her hips, sing along to the music, and try to get everyone to dance. I watched her put her arms up and slither them around like fucking snakes as she tried her best to move with the beat. I watched her smile and laugh and soak in all the attention she was getting from random men at the bar. I decided at that moment I wasn't going to scream at her. I wasn't going to make a scene. I wasn't going to cuss her out. I was just going to pretend like everything was fucking peachy. I regained my composure. I forced my lips to curve into a smile. Standing from my seat, I joined her, swaying my hips. The girls followed us to the dance floor. Olivia raised an eyebrow at me and smiled back. She didn't know it yet, but her days were numbered.

57
OLIVIA

After a few songs, we returned to our seats. I was surprised Shannon joined in on the dancing. Then again, rejection and desperation will make you do things completely and totally out of character. She hadn't checked her phone in a while. Shannon had clearly given up on her date showing at all. Little did she know; her date had shown. I let out a giggle and took another drink. Shannon needed to be reminded of her place in Buckhead, and what better way to remind her than to diminish her self-confidence. She did the same to me once upon a time.

Four years ago, at Buckhead's gala of the year, Shannon got drunk (nothing has changed) and told everyone about my past, something I had confided to her. She told them how my father was arrested, how my family was slimy, and how he lost all of our money. She belittled me and ridiculed me the whole night, dragging me through the mud, reveling in it like it was a game. From that point on, people looked at Dean and me a little differently. We weren't the classy Petrovs, we were the smarmy Petrovs, and we ultimately fell into those roles. Because it's easy to become who people say you are. On top of that, for years the women in Buckhead called me *Nemo*—"new money," a constant reminder that I wasn't like them. I could have spoken to her about it, explained how she hurt me, but where was the fun in that? Forgiveness is boring, but revenge . . . now, that's a real thrill! Betray me once, and I will bury you, one shovel of dirt at a time.

I had heard Shannon a while back talking about online dating. From then on, I made it a point to routinely look her up on popular dating sites to see if she had created a profile. A few weeks ago, I struck gold when I discovered her. She never even questioned it. Desperate women don't ask questions. I wondered how long I could keep it going. Could I lure her somewhere? Or humiliate her to the point where she'd never be able to show her face again? Could I make her feel the way she made me feel? Forced into a role that I created for her? Or maybe I could finally unload that last spade of soil, the one that will keep her where she belongs—six feet below the rest of us.

"This was fun. Thanks for including me, Olivia," Shannon said with a smile. She wouldn't be thanking me if she knew the truth. Fun indeed.

"Anytime." I smiled back. "So sorry your date didn't show."

"Yeah, that sucks. His loss," Keisha piped in.

"Men are dicks," Karen said.

"It wasn't a total loss. Jenny met a guy." I laughed.

"Actually, he was really nice. We exchanged numbers." Jenny took a drink.

I gave her a puzzled look. Nice means zilch when it comes to dating. Has she learned nothing from being around us all these years? We don't date nice. We date rich. But then again, Jenny wasn't one of us.

"Good for you, girl." Keisha high-fived Jenny.

"If you say so." I rolled my eyes. "I'm going to go settle the bill. Anyone want anything else?" They all shook their heads and thanked me—as they should.

I walked over to the waitress who was chatting with her coworker instead of serving us. I had already decided I was going to dock her tip. I shouldn't have had to come find her to settle my bill. I was the customer—the very wealthy customer—and therefore, I deserved impeccable service. I tossed my Black AmEx card on the counter. "Ring it up."

"Do you want to know the total?" she asked meekly while her little coworker skedaddled off.

"Look at me. Do I look like someone that asks how much? No. Just run the card," I demanded, putting my hands on my hips and tapping my foot.

She swiped the card. Then she swiped it again and again.

"It says it's declined." She tilted her head.

"Bullshit. Run it again!"

She swiped the card again and again.

"Do you have another card?" she asked, handing the Black AmEx over.

I stamped my foot and took the card, shoving it back into my wallet. I handed her another one. She swiped and swiped.

"It's also declined."

"What the fuck?! That's impossible! Run it again, you idiot!"

She swiped it once more, slowly, as if she were mocking me.

"Declined. How do you want to pay for this?" Her meek voice had become more assertive.

I grabbed the card from her and bolted for the door, not looking back as the waitress squawked, "Hey, you have to pay!"

The limo was parked outside waiting for us. I jumped in

and before the driver could turn around and ask any questions, I told him to fucking drive. Without hesitation, he stepped on it.

Ten minutes later the driver pulled up in front of my house. I threw a twenty-dollar bill at him and ran inside. It didn't have the same effect as my hundred-dollar bill. I groaned.

"Dean, where the fuck are you?" My voice echoed throughout the house. I ran frantically from the foyer to the living room to the kitchen, until I finally found him drinking scotch in his study without a care in the world. He sat up straight in his chair, startled to see me. "You're home early, babe. Did you miss me?" He winked.

"Don't get cute with me, Dean. Where the fuck is the money?" I threw my purse on the ground. A few single-dollar bills fell out of it.

"What are you talking about?" He set down his glass of scotch and furrowed his brow.

"Both my credit cards were declined tonight. Why?" I threw my hands on my hips. "You tell me right goddamn now."

"Don't worry about it, Olivia. I'll take care of it." Dean stood up and walked over to me. He put his hands around my waist and tried to pull me in for a hug, but I wasn't having any of it. I pushed him back with all my might. He stumbled backward a few steps, bumping into the coffee table. I grabbed a glass mug from his desk and threw it at him as if I were pitching in the World Series. He narrowly ducked and it smashed into the bookshelf, shattering into pieces. His eyes widened as he looked at the damage and back at me.

"Are you fucking crazy?"

I flicked off my heels and grabbed one from the floor, throwing it at him in one clean swoop. He stepped aside, and it hit the bookshelf.

"Tell me what the hell is going on!" I picked up a pen cup from his desk and cocked it back, ready to heave it.

"Just hold on. Put that down and I'll tell you." He flinched as I simulated throwing it at him, but instead, I dropped it back on the desk, pens scattering everywhere.

"Money's a little tight. We had a screwup with our last shipment. A rather big screwup, so I'm having to foot those losses until we can make it up," he explained. He took a seat on the couch and patted the cushion next to him, motioning for me to come sit. I hesitated but then walked to him. I took a deep breath as I sat down and turned to Dean, looking into his eyes.

"Listen, I've never cared what you did because the money was coming in. But now it's not, so I want to know what it is you do, because you're clearly not doing it well," I said as calmly as I possibly could. It still came out with a tinge of frustration.

"It's better that you don't know, babe. You have no idea what you are talking about." He put a hand on my shoulder and rubbed it.

"Oh, fuck off." I pushed his hand away. "If you don't tell me what you do, I'm leaving you, Dean."

"Yeah right . . . and go do what? You aren't worth anything and don't know how to do anything. You may as well be a child who still needs—"

With zero hesitation, I slapped him across his face as hard as I could. His face turned as red as fresh blood, and it looked like he might hit me back. But then Dean hung his head and sighed. I pursed my lips together.

"Fine." He looked at me and threw up his hands. "Let's just say I move goods in and out of Atlanta that law enforcement would frown upon."

"What? Like drugs?" I furrowed my brow.

"Among other things."

"Okay. So, what? Are people not using drugs anymore? Is demand down? Is that why we don't have any fucking money?"

"No. Like I said, I ran into some issues with my last shipment. So, the people I work for are having me pay for it." He dropped his head into his hands.

I tried to make sense of everything he was telling me. We were broke. Forever? Or was this temporary? What would people say when they found out? Who was I without money . . . again? I'd be Nomo, not Nemo. No money, not new money. Shannon would revel in it. How the fuck did this happen? I told myself this would never ever happen to me again, and at that moment, I felt like the teenage girl who had had everything ripped away from her because of a fucking dumbass man.

"Wait. What about our savings?" I said, my face lighting up. We had to have savings, investments, all that stuff.

"What savings?" Dean laughed. "Look at the way you live. The Olivia specialty is throwing one-hundred-dollar bills around."

"Don't you dare put this on me! You oversaw the money, and besides, I thought you were your own boss. Who the hell are you working for? Who's 'making' you pay for this?" I wanted to know who this asshole was that was messing with our money, our livelihoods. I'd kill him.

"It doesn't matter. Everything is going to be fine. Just trust me. I'll take care of it." Dean put his hand on my thigh and rubbed it affectionately. I picked a spot on the wall farthest from us and focused on it. He wouldn't take care of it. I would take care of it. I couldn't trust a man to do a woman's job.

58
JENNY

The bar was less crowded as people were filtering out. There were only two girls on the dance floor. "Where did Olivia go?" I asked, realizing she had been gone for at least ten minutes. I glanced around, but she was nowhere in sight.

"Maybe she's out in the limo, waiting for us," Crystal said.

"Or maybe she's in the bathroom?" Karen offered.

"Yeah, maybe. I've got to go to the bathroom, so I'll check. You guys can go out to the limo, and I'll meet you there."

They nodded, finished up their drinks, and began gathering their belongings. I made my way to the bathroom and found myself alone in there. I walked to the sink and checked myself out in the mirror, ensuring my hair and makeup were still in place.

I pulled my phone out of my purse and texted the number from Shaun, the man I had met earlier.

> It was nice meeting you
> tonight :)

I sent the message, put the phone back in my purse, and smiled, knowing that I was finally ready to become more than Glow. Perhaps this night did me some good, and Olivia's idea wasn't so bad after all. I was still unsure of her intentions. Olivia just didn't do things out of the kindness of her heart.

I walked out of the bathroom and bumped into our server. Before I could ask if she had seen Olivia, she pushed a bill into my chest with attitude.

"You need to pay for this. You're the last one here, and your friend ran out on the check."

I took the bill from her and glanced at the total: $1,989. My eyes widened and my mouth dropped open. Are you kidding me? Olivia ran out on the bill. Did she do this to us on purpose? Was this her plan all along? I knew she was up to no good.

I pulled out a credit card and handed it to the woman. "Here."

"It had better go through this time," she huffed.

When she was done running the card and handing over the receipt for me to sign, I was out $2,500 as I still made sure to tip well. Her demeanor changed after seeing her gratuity. She smiled and told me to have a good night.

"One more thing. Be sure to tell Olivia that she's not welcome back here," the server said as I walked away. I nodded.

Outside, the girls were waiting on the sidewalk. "Where's the limo?"

"It's not here yet," Shannon said.

"I think it was already here." I looked up and down the street.

Their heads snapped in my direction.

"What do you mean?" Karen asked.

"Well, I'm pretty sure Olivia took it home. The server said she ran out on the bill."

"Are you shitting me? I've had about enough of her." Shannon pulled out her phone and started tapping buttons vigorously. "I'm calling us an Uber."

Karen was shivering and tiptoeing around, trying to warm herself up. Keisha put her arm around her and pulled her in. I raised an eyebrow but didn't say a word.

"Wait, did you pay for the whole bill?" Crystal crumpled up her face.

I nodded.

"Oh, for Christ's sake! How much was it?" Karen asked.

"Twenty-five hundred, including tip."

"Don't worry. I'll reimburse you for it." Shannon fiddled with her phone.

"Me too." Karen and Crystal nodded.

"Yeah, I don't have a rich husband, ex or otherwise, so . . ." Keisha said with a laugh.

"What a shit night!" Shannon stamped her foot.

"You can say that again," Crystal laughed. Shannon and Crystal exchanged tight smiles.

"Let's remedy it. How about we go have a drink at the salon?" I offered.

They all looked at each other and then back at me and nodded.

59
JENNY

Detective Sanford picks up the empty pizza box and tosses it on top of a small trash can beside the door. He wipes his hands off on a napkin and pitches it in the garbage can too. Retaking his seat, he flips through his notes. He glances at me. "Did you know Olivia and Dean were having financial problems?"

"I had a feeling they were."

"Why?"

"Because on the evening we were all going out, I ran the membership fees at the end of the workday, and Olivia's card on file was declined. I had meant to talk to her about it the next time I saw her. When she ran out on the bill, I put two and two together."

"Did you tell the other women about Olivia's financial problems?"

I shake my head. "No, it wasn't anyone's business."

Detective Sanford nods and jots down a few notes.

"Were you aware Olivia had created a fake profile impersonating a man on a dating site?"

I furrow my brow and shake my head.

"So, you probably weren't aware she was using that profile to talk to Shannon—or better yet, 'catfish' Shannon, as the kids say?"

My mouth fell open. "Are you serious? That's awful."

He nods. "We believe Shannon knew about it too."

I cock my head. I don't know where he's going with this or why he's telling me about it.

"Did you know about Karen's relationship with Keisha?"

I nod.

"Did you know Shannon had Crystal privately investigated?"

I shake my head.

"Did you know Olivia was sleeping with Mark?"

I nod. His questions are like rapid fire.

"Did you know Olivia knew about Karen and Keisha's relationship?

I nod. Without thinking, I stand from my seat with force and my chair falls backward, banging on the floor. I slam the palms of my hands on the table.

"What do you want from me?" I yell.

"I want you to help me understand these women. I want you to help me understand Buckhead. Because right now, I've got a dead body, a fuck ton of questions, and not enough answers. What happened in the days leading up to the party?"

I take a deep breath, pick my chair back up, and sit down.

"Start with the night you guys went back to the salon for a drink. What happened?"

60
JENNY

Keisha helped gather up the dirty glasses. Karen, Crystal, and Shannon had just left after coming to the salon for a few drinks. It was nice to unwind with them and vent about what had all happened that evening. Shannon had urged me to cancel Olivia's membership, and she made a good case for it, but I told her I'd sleep on it and wait until I spoke with Olivia in order to give her the opportunity to explain herself. I was livid with Olivia. I wasn't sure if she had done it on purpose, but all signs pointed to yes. She had been trying to cause problems all evening, she left without telling any of us, she skipped out on the bill, and she took the limo.

Keisha sat down, letting out a deep breath. "We survived an evening with Olivia."

"Barely." I laughed, pouring two glasses of water. I handed one to Keisha and took a seat next to her. We were silent while we slowly sipped our water.

"I have to tell you something." Keisha spun her chair toward me.

"What is it?"

She looked at me, then at her glass of water, took a sip, and returned her gaze.

"It's about Karen."

I took another drink. "What about Karen?"

"Something happened between her and me."

"What do you mean by *something*?" I raised an eyebrow. I had a feeling something was going on with Keisha these past couple of weeks. There was a glow to her, and she was practically giddy, which was not the norm for Keisha.

She blushed. "Remember when I told you the spray tan machine malfunctioned . . . ?"

I nodded.

"It didn't. I dropped it during my make-out sesh with Karen," she confessed.

I took another sip of my water and swallowed hard.

"And every tanning or waxing appointment Karen's had in the past two weeks . . . well, no waxing or tanning were done."

"I figured that much." I laughed.

"How?"

"First, Karen is like paper pale . . . for starters. Second, I've noticed how you two have been interacting. I didn't know Karen was gay."

"I didn't either, and apparently, neither did she. But I do have a way with women," Keisha said with a smirk.

"What's going on with you two then? She's married, and she has a kid," I said in an attempt to bring Keisha back to reality. I didn't want her to get hurt, but I knew there was a good chance she would. Women in Buckhead didn't leave their husbands.

"I know. She says she wants to be with me, but I'm a realist. I know making that decision won't be easy, and I want to be with her too. It's different with her," Keisha explained. She didn't smile. She was serious, and she was serious about her feelings for Karen.

"How is it different with Karen?" I crossed one leg over the other.

"With Karen, it feels like I'm falling, but not off a cliff or something like that. It feels like that sensation right before you fall asleep . . . you feel warm and safe and sure that when you close your eyes, everything is going to be okay, that dreams will be dreamt and morning will come."

I leaned over and patted her on the knee. "Damn, Keisha. You really are in love. I've never heard you talk like that."

"I know. I know. I'm a big sap." She laughed.

"You're not a sap. It's great. You're so lucky to have that . . . to experience that."

I smiled, but deep down there was a tinge of jealousy and a dash of frustration. Keisha was jeopardizing my business by fooling around with a client. Did she think about that at all? Did she think about how it would affect Glow if things went sour? Would I have to ensure Karen's appointments were only with me? Would Karen demand that Keisha be let go? Would other clients complain? These are things business owners think about. They treat their business like their child, putting it before anything and everything else. I know I wanted more than Glow, but this salon was my baby—and although I was happy for Keisha and Karen, I was irritated that they hadn't considered the consequences of their actions. Love and entrepreneurship didn't go hand in hand, because they both required sacrifice. And we only have so much we can sacrifice before we have nothing left to give.

I cleared my mind and took another drink of water. Keisha was my friend, and her happiness mattered more than Glow, I reminded myself. I took a deep breath, exhaling all the thoughts racing through my mind.

"Actually, I'm not that lucky. See, the other day, when Karen and I were"—Keisha coughed—"having a tanning session, Olivia walked in on us."

My mouth dropped open. "She knows about you two!?"

"She told Karen she wouldn't say anything to anyone. She said she'd take it to her grave . . . But she was toying with us throughout the entire evening."

"She was messing with everyone." I rolled my eyes. *Goddamn Olivia.*

"I'm not exactly sure where things are with Karen and me because Olivia interrupted us, and I feel like Karen is being apprehensive now. Like she doesn't know what she wants."

"If Olivia gave Karen her word, I'm sure she'll keep it, because she'd love holding something over her head."

"I'm actually a little worried about what she'll want in return for keeping our little secret." Keisha let out a huff.

I shrugged. "What would she even get out of telling anyone?"

"Drama." Her eyes widened. "It's like crack to Olivia," she said with a laugh.

I laughed too, for a moment, but then stopped, placing my hand on Keisha's.

"Regardless of Olivia, you need to talk to Karen and figure out where you both want things to go."

Keisha nodded and squeezed my hand, exchanging a small smile with me. "I know."

"But also keep a close eye on Olivia," I said with a laugh, but I was entirely serious.

61
KAREN

The sun was too bright. The birds were too loud. My own heartbeat was deafening. I could feel it in my neck, in my wrist, in the temples of my head. I glanced over at the clock on my nightstand—it was noon. Shit. I jumped up, noticing Mark's side of the bed was already made. He was that anal of a person that he'd literally make the bed while I was still in it. I covered my white nightgown with a robe and raced down the hall to Riley's room. His bed was made. His room was clean, and his backpack and coat were missing. I padded down the hallway to the kitchen and found a note on the countertop.

Didn't want to wake you. Took Riley to school.
There's coffee in the pot. —Mark

Next to the note was a glass of water and four Tylenol. I tossed them in my mouth and washed them down. I walked to the sink, refilled the glass, and drank the entire thing again, nearly drowning my insides. Just as I was pouring a cup of coffee, the doorbell rang. I set the pot down and walked through the living room. The doorbell rang several more times.

"Hold on. I'm coming!"

On the other side of the door stood Olivia. She was dressed in all black, wearing oversized red-rimmed sunglasses, a scarlet Chanel bag, and a smug look. She looked like the Grim Reaper herself.

"We need to talk," she said, pushing her way past me. Her heels clicked along my hardwood floor as she made her way into the living room and took a seat, crossing her legs at the knee.

"Come right in, Olivia," I said sarcastically closing the door behind her.

"Did you just wake up? You look haggard." She looked me up and down. Her forehead attempted to wrinkle, but the Botox hindered her ability to show her disappointment in my disheveled appearance.

"What happened to you last night? You left us with the bill and stranded." I threw my hands on my hips, ignoring her comment. I could look however I wanted to look in *my* own house.

"Yeah, sorry about that. There was an emergency with Dean." She waved her hand dismissively.

I took a seat in the wingback chair across from her.

"Is he okay?" I asked. I was trying to be empathetic, but I didn't even believe Olivia had feelings. However, it must have been quite an emergency for her to just take off like that, and I tried to give her the benefit of the doubt. Maybe something *had* happened to Dean. Maybe she had a perfectly good reason for her behavior.

She looked around the room for a moment, fiddled with her fingernails, and then refocused her attention on me. "Yes," she hesitated. "He got into some trouble with his work, but I don't want to go into details. It's all still pretty raw."

Her face showed no emotion, but that's how Olivia always looked. She could be taking her last breath, slowly succumbing to death, and she'd still look like that . . . plump pursed lips, cutting cheekbones, fixated eyes, and not a smile or laugh line to be found.

"I hope everything is okay. Do you want something to drink? Coffee? Water?" I was trying to be kind and accommodating.

"No, no." She waved her hand again. "I came here to talk to you about something."

"What is it?" I leaned in a little closer to her.

"I can no longer keep your dirty secret. It's weighing so heavy on my heart." She placed her hand over her chest.

I leaned away from her. Of fucking course she'd be here for that. What is it she wants? Because I know for a fact nothing weighs heavy on Olivia's heart. She doesn't have a goddamn heart.

"It hasn't even been twenty-four hours since you found out about Keisha and me," I said through gritted teeth.

"I know. I know. It's killing me though. How can you do this to Mark?" She tried to make her face look sad, but instead, her lips twisted and her eyes squinted.

"You have to give me time to figure this out."

Olivia looked at her watch and then back at me. She was always one with a flair for the dramatic.

"I just don't think I can. It's immoral. Even though we're really close, it's wrong. Trust me, I'm team Keisha and Karen. I would be the first to walk you lesbians down the aisle, but it's really eating me up inside."

Since when the hell did Olivia have morals? She wanted something from me. That much was obvious. This had nothing to do with right and wrong; this had to do with Olivia getting her way. I wasn't sure what she was after, but I was going to find out. I let out a deep breath.

"Just tell me what you want to keep your mouth shut." I shook my head.

Without missing a beat, Olivia responded, "Fifty thousand dollars."

"What? Are you fucking crazy?" I nearly jumped out of my chair. Where did she get off? Coming into my house . . . and demanding fifty thousand dollars. I could kill her.

"I'm not crazy, Karen." She jutted up her chin. "I have something you want, and you have something I want. It's business."

"How do you expect me to come up with that type of money?" I asked, trying to make her realize how literally insane this demand was. There was no way she was serious.

"Close a deal or ask your husband—or better yet, I will." She sneered.

"Why do you need the money? You have money!"

"Why do you need a girlfriend? You have a husband." She cocked her head. "We always want more. Don't we, Karen?" Olivia stood from her seat and walked toward the front door. "I expect full payment by Saturday night. If not, I guess I won't be taking your secret to my grave." She laughed and left the house, letting the wind slam the door closed behind her.

I brought a throw pillow to my face. "Fuuuuck!" I screamed.

62
CRYSTAL

"Go ahead and set the coffins up out back," I said to a man dressed in blue jeans and a flannel shirt. It was the day before our Halloween-themed housewarming party, and our home was filled with workers and decorations. It was an absolute madhouse. Bryce was at the office, leaving me to get everything prepared. The decor had to be finished today as the caterers, DJ, performers, pyrotechnicians, servers, and bartenders would be setting up tomorrow. Red curtains were being hung up on every wall on the first floor. There were spiderwebs, skeletons, crystal chandeliers, smoke machines, and a light-up dance floor, along with a DJ booth outside by the pool area. They were dying the pool red and covering the backyard with red carpet. There were black thrones and chaise longues for seating. This party was going to be elegant yet frightening, just like Buckhead. I had always wanted to get into event planning, and this party was proof that I could do it and do it well. I wanted it to be memorable.

"Is anything going upstairs?" a man carrying a skeleton asked.

"No, keep everything down here aside from the crime scene tape blocking off both sets of stairs. But you can leave the tape on the counter. I'll put that up tomorrow, right before the party."

"You got it." He nodded and proceeded to carry the skeletons to the dining room.

"Thank you."

I made my way up the spiral staircase. It was the only area of the house that wasn't filled with people and party decor. I walked down the hallway toward our master bedroom and noticed Bryce's office door was ajar. He never left it unlocked, let alone open. Had one of the workers gone in there? I pushed open the door gently, peeking my head in. It was silent and dark. The blinds were drawn. His desk was tidy, but there was a glow coming from the computer monitor. I had never been in his home office before. Bryce was adamant about his privacy and had said there was too much confidential stuff inside to leave it unlocked. He wouldn't even let the maid clean it. He had rushed out in a hurry earlier, so he must have forgotten to lock it.

I ambled to the desk and placed my hand on the mouse. I was just going to put the monitor to sleep, but instead, I hovered the cursor over a folder titled *Insurance Policy*. It caught my eye. I knew I shouldn't click it, but curiosity got the best of me. I double-clicked and it opened a window filled with documents, videos, photos, and Excel spreadsheets. I started clicking through the spreadsheets. They didn't make much sense to me, as none of them had anything to do with our life insurance policy. They just looked like expense reports. I began opening the documents. There were letters and memos to police departments and sheriff's departments. Some sentences stuck out more than others.

Suspend patrol of Highway 14.

Be on the lookout for a blue Chevy Cruze.
Person of interest.

Suspend patrol of Highway 12.

I moved on to the photos and began opening them. There were photos of trucks. Pallets of unknown items. Dean was in a photo. Then, my heart dropped. I couldn't believe what I was seeing. I blinked several times. There was a photo of the inside of a semitrailer filled with a dozen young girls. They were lying on the floor of it, dressed in raggedy clothes, with their feet and hands bound. My eyes widened. I sat up straight in the chair and clicked a video. There were trucks and shipping containers in the background. Dean came on the screen. He was carrying a woman. Her body was limp. Her skin was pale. Her eyes were open but inert.

"Shit. We've lost another one," he said to someone not in the frame.

He carried her off-screen.

"How many didn't make it?" a familiar voice asked. There was a loud thud.

"Six," Dean said as he walked back into the frame empty-handed.

"Fuck, Dean. All these girls are prepurchased. You're paying for this mess one way or another." The voice off-screen said again.

Dean hung his head.

"Do you understand me?" The voice questioned.

Dean looked up, staring just to the right of where the video recorder was set. "Yes."

"Good. I wouldn't want Olivia to end up in that pile too," he said with a laugh.

It was Bryce's laugh—I'd know it anywhere.

My stomach jumped into my throat. I bent down to the garbage can beside the desk just in time. I spilled my guts into the wastebasket. Tears streamed down my face as I retched harder and harder. When there was nothing left inside of me, I tried to regain control of my body. My breaths were quick and deep. My skin was damp from sweat and tears. My throat burned from the remnants of bile. I wiped the tears from my face, patted away the sweat, and swallowed hard. What did I marry? A monster. A total monster.

I quickly grabbed the video and sent it to my personal email. I closed everything out, put the monitor to sleep, grabbed the puke-filled bag inside the trash can, and slipped out of the office, locking the door behind me. I had to warn Olivia.

63
OLIVIA

I walked into the house through the garage, carrying a half dozen shopping bags from Chanel, Gucci, and Barney's. We didn't have the money for this little shopping trip, but I needed it, and I was sure we would have the money soon. I was taking care of things the only way I knew how: by any means necessary. Tossing the bags on the island counter, I walked to the oversized fridge, grabbing a bottle of opened pinot grigio. I poured myself a glass and took an indulgent drink. Tapping my scarlet nails against the glass, I pondered how I was going to pull everything together. Karen would deliver on the money. I was sure of that. She had her business to consider and that son of hers, and the last thing she would want to do is to ruin her perfect image. I thought the fifty thousand might have been too much, but then I remembered how much her husband was paying me on a biweekly basis and knew they could afford it.

Taking another slow drink, I let out a laugh. I was bleeding her family dry through their own indiscretions. I just needed to figure out who Dean was working for, who was ruining us. Whoever it was, I would make it my life's mission to ruin them. No one messes with my money and gets away with it.

Jenny had called me twice today. I avoided her phone calls, but I'm sure it was to tell me my card was declined for this month's membership fee. I would call her later and explain it away with an expired card or something, and then I would pay her in cash at the party. Thank God, I had been stashing the money Mark had been paying me. It would keep my lifestyle afloat until Saturday.

The doorbell rang.

A few moments later, I found Crystal standing on the other side of it. She looked like she had been crying, thanks to a blotchy face and red-rimmed eyes. Her skin needed a serious facial. A large tote bag hung on her arm, and she was dressed in yoga pants and a crewneck sweater. How could she let herself leave the house like that? How could Bryce let her leave the house like that? She did not deserve him.

"Can I come in?" She cautiously looked over both of her shoulders.

"Come in." I opened the door wider and motioned her in. Crystal scurried in like a little stray cat.

She followed me into the living room and took a seat on the couch across from me. Her eyes bounced all around like she was looking for something or someone.

"Do you want something to drink?" I asked, taking a sip of wine.

She shook her head. "Is Dean here?"

I raised an eyebrow and crossed one leg over the other. She had piqued my interest. "No."

"Okay." She glanced around the room again and hesitated for a moment.

"Listen. I don't have a lot of time. What's this about?" My patience had worn thin.

Crystal pulled out a MacBook from her tote bag and placed it on her lap. She held the sides of it tightly, glancing at it and then looking back at me.

"Did you know?" She squinted her eyes as if she were trying to read text that was too small—but really, she was trying to read me.

"Know what?" I uncrossed my legs, leaned in, and repositioned myself as if on the edge of my seat.

She opened the laptop, clicked around with the trackpad, and then set it on the coffee table, turning it toward me.

"I'm sorry. This is going to be really hard for you, but you need to know." Crystal clicked Play and a video began.

"Shit. We've lost another one," Dean said as he walked on-screen carrying a dead woman.

When the video stopped, Crystal closed the laptop and put it back in her bag. My eyes were wide. My mouth was open.

"Was that Bryce's voice?" I asked. I knew it was but wanted to confirm.

She nodded and hung her head in shame.

I looked surprised, and I was . . . but only by the fact that it was Bryce that Dean was working for. I had always known that Dean's money wasn't clean, though I've been careful over the years not to ask too many questions. As long as the money kept coming in, it made sense to look the other way.

"Where did you get that video?"

"Off of Bryce's computer. I found it today." Her lip quivered. Her eyes moistened.

I leaned back in my seat, crossed one leg over the other, and took a sip of wine. That slimy bastard. I should have known. Of course it was Bryce. It was why Dean had pushed me to get along with the wives, to make nice with Crystal, to keep things peaceful. Bryce and Dean needed us to keep up appearances, to look like upstanding citizens of the Buckhead community. They needed us to look the part, while they were off trafficking drugs, guns, and girls.

"What are you going to do with it?" I asked.

She glanced around the room helplessly, like a small child that just found out Santa wasn't real. "I don't know. Go to the police?" Crystal looked to me for approval, for solidarity, for help.

"You're going to turn your husband in?" I raised an eyebrow.

"I have to. The man on that video is not the man I married. How could he do that . . . to those poor girls? He's a monster." Her voice cracked at the end as she fought back tears.

I swiveled my wineglass, allowing the liquid to coat the sides of it, and took another sip.

"Have you talked to him? Given him a chance to explain?" I bounced my foot.

"He can't explain that away. Did you not watch the video?" She pointed at the laptop that was now stowed in her bag. Her eyes were wild.

"We should really think about this."

"He threatened your life, Olivia. I came here to warn you."

"I'm a big girl, Crystal. I can take care of myself."

Her mouth fell open. Was it really so shocking that I would choose to stand by my husband? He brought home the money. His work provided for us, and that's what mattered. I had even told him I wanted to be an active part of it. Honestly, I felt I could do it better than him. Trafficking needed a woman's touch.

"We need to go to the police," she urged.

I looked around the room, contemplating, and then back at her. "You should send me the video," I said.

"Okay." She pulled out her laptop and typed away at it. "There. Sent. So, you're going to go to the police then?" Crystal stowed the computer back in her bag.

I finished my wine and set the empty glass on the table. Standing from my seat, I crossed my arms over my chest and raised my chin.

"I think you need to leave. I don't appreciate you speaking ill of my husband."

"Olivia, how can you be okay with this? This is wrong! So wrong!" She stood from the couch. Her voice came out all whiny.

"It's business. And I wouldn't be so quick to turn your back on your husband. You saw what he did with those women. You wouldn't want to end up in that pile too," I taunted.

"How can you do this?" Crystal asked as she quickly gathered her bag.

"We're living the American dream."

"Breaking the law isn't living the American dream, Olivia," she hissed.

"America was built on the backs of others. We're just carrying on the tradition." I chuckled as I walked her to the front door.

Crystal turned toward me as she exited my home. "Olivia, please."

"I can't help you," I said, closing the door in her face.

I pulled my phone from my pocket and dialed. A woman answered.

"Hi, is Bryce in?" I asked.

"Yes, may I ask who's calling?"

"Olivia Petrov. Tell Bryce I'll be stopping in." I ended the call and smiled a big toothy grin.

64
CRYSTAL

After the door slammed in my face, I stood there for a moment, deciding what to do. I couldn't believe it. I couldn't believe Olivia would stand by her husband after what he'd done. There was something truly wrong with her. I wiped away my tears and took a step back. A voice from behind startled me.

"She refusing to pay you too?" a voice called out.

I turned around to find a man with a goatee and several neck tattoos. He was dressed in a white T-shirt and long shorts. He gave a crooked smile, followed by a *ha ha*.

"Afternoon," I said meekly, stepping around him.

He gave a nod. There was something familiar about him. I kept my head down, and before I turned in front of the garage, I looked back at him. He pounded on the door. My eyes traveled from the top of his head down, until I saw it. A blotchy, inky tattoo on the back of his calf. I stopped myself from gasping.

Olivia swung open the door just as I stepped out of sight.

Her voice was just above a whisper, so I could barely hear what she was saying.

"We agreed to five, but that was before the other half-wit you hired went Mike Tyson on the salon owner. Now, I've got heat on me." His voice was laced with anger.

My hand went to my mouth. How could she have done this to Jenny?

"Shut up and come inside," Olivia squawked.

The front door closed with a bang, and I scurried to my car. I had to tell someone. If she was capable of this, what else was she capable of? Olivia needed to be stopped.

65

SHANNON

The magazine was full of glossy photos of celebrities. I turned the page again and again, then tossed the magazine onto the coffee table. This week had gotten the best of me—between Olivia and her catfish bullshit and Bryce and Crystal's impending house-warming party that I was sure I'd never hear the end of. It was all too much. I decided I wouldn't be attending. I wouldn't be caught dead in Bryce's home ever again. I needed a vacation. I needed to get away from Buckhead. This place was killing me.

My doorbell rang. Good. My Chinese food was finally here, and I was starving. I got up from the couch, slid my feet into a pair of Gucci slippers, and cinched my robe tighter. I had stayed in my pajamas all day, having only the energy to put a robe on. Occasionally, I needed a day like that—a day of noth-ingness, where I eat bad food and consume copious amounts of terrible entertainment, from smutty gossip magazines to awful reality shows.

I got to the door and pulled it open, immediately

disappointed upon seeing who was on the other side of it. Great. Perfect. Just what I needed. Crystal stood there, holding a large tote bag. A little country bumpkin. The last person I ever wanted to see. I had been civil, but civility ended at my front door. I began pushing the door closed, right in her face, but I noticed the tears pooling in her eyes, the quiver of her lip, and the lack of color in her skin. So I stopped.

"Can I come in?" A tear escaped and ran down her cheek. I didn't hesitate for a moment. I wrapped my arms around her and pulled in for a hug. She fell apart, and I held her tighter, ushering her into my apartment and closing the door behind us.

The video stopped playing. She looked over at me as we sat on the couch, the laptop open in front of us on the coffee table. The Chinese food was sitting beside the computer, unopened, and it would remain so. I wouldn't be able to eat now. I swallowed hard.

"Did you know?" she asked.

I shook my head, unable to speak, still processing what I had just seen. We sat in silence, each of us unsure what to say.

"How could I have not known? I was married to him. I should have known." My voice trembled.

"I didn't know either, and I married him too." She grabbed my hand and squeezed it. "This isn't our fault."

I nodded. She was right. But it still felt wrong. I should have known. If I hadn't been so wrapped up in all the bullshit of Buckhead, I would have realized that I was married to the worst kind of criminal. I could have saved these women. I could have stopped this.

"This isn't our fault," she repeated, squeezing my hand a

little tighter. I placed my other hand on hers and looked at her and nodded. I closed my eyes tightly. Then I reopened them, realizing what I had done wrong, what I could have done to stop this. I shifted in my seat, facing her.

"This is my fault," I said.

Crystal held her hand up to try to stop me, but I needed her to know something, the secret of hers I had been keeping.

"No, you don't understand. When Bryce left me, I hired a private investigator. I was consumed with sadness and jealousy, and I wanted to know who the woman was that stole him away," I confessed.

"You had me followed by a private investigator?" Crystal furrowed her brow, leaning away from me slightly.

"Yes." I nodded. "And if I'd had Bryce investigated instead of you, I would have known what he was up to, and I could have stopped this." I hung my head in shame.

"You know, don't you?" Crystal's eyes widened.

I raised my head back up. "I know. I know your real name is Savannah Hall, and you changed it to Crystal Redding a few years back."

"Did you tell anyone?" Crystal shifted uncomfortably.

"No. I couldn't. I wouldn't."

"Not even Bryce?" Her eyes searched mine.

"No. After I saw the police records, I decided to keep it to myself. Even though I despised you, you had been through enough." I placed my hand on her shoulder for comfort.

Crystal's eyes shifted left to right. "I didn't mean to kill him," she said, shaking her head.

"I know, honey. I know." I pulled her in for a hug and rubbed her back. "It was self-defense."

"The gun just went off," she cried into my shoulder.

I had known about Crystal's past for months. After reading

all the police reports and statements provided by the private investigator, I decided to keep her secret, a secret she didn't even know I had. That girl had been through hell and back with an abusive ex-boyfriend. There was more after the case closed, after it was deemed self-defense. There were restraining orders against his friends and family. They harassed her, tried to retaliate against her, tried to make her pay for killing her abuser. The police reports were hard to read, but the one thing I learned from her past was that Crystal was strong. She was a fighter, and I would never use another woman's strength against her.

She pulled away from me, looking into my eyes. "Thank you."

I grabbed a Kleenex from the coffee table and handed it to her. "Of course."

Crystal wiped her eyes dry, looked at the laptop and then back at me. "What do we do now?"

"We do what women do: we handle it."

"There's more," Crystal said, looking down at her hands and then back again.

"More? What is it?" My eyes searched hers.

How could there be more than this?

"It's about Jenny."

My eyes went wide and my heart sank.

66
OLIVIA

I strolled into Bryce's office building and walked right past the secretary. She attempted to stop me, but she was no match for me. I flung open the door with force and found Bryce standing, facing his floor-to-ceiling windows. He was dressed in a custom suit, perfectly pulled together as usual.

"I'll take care of it." He ended the call and slid his phone into his pocket.

He turned toward me. "Olivia, to what do I owe the pleasure?" Bryce pulled out his chair and took a seat.

I plopped my bag on the desk and sat across from him, folding my arms to my chest. "We need to talk."

"Do we?" He cocked his head and began shuffling papers on his desk, practically dismissing me. He had no idea who he was dealing with. I was not one to be trifled with. I was Olivia fucking Petrov.

I grabbed my cell phone and pulled up the video. Turning the screen toward him, I pushed Play. His face tensed up. His shoulders slumped. A vein in the center of his forehead became very prominent. Pulled-together Bryce wasn't so pulled together anymore. I smirked.

After Bryce made the comment about my body ending up in the pile and laughed, I stopped the video and put the phone back in my purse.

"Where did you get that?" His eyes darted all over as if he were looking for an answer to this little problem he now had. I'm sure he was thinking about what object in the room he could bludgeon me with, but I wasn't scared of Bryce. I had all the power, and power makes you fearless.

"It doesn't matter where I got it. It matters what I'm going to do with it." I raised an eyebrow.

He took a deep breath and refocused his eyes on me, staring intently. "And what are you going to do with it?" He clenched his jaw.

"That's up to you." I pulled out a tube of lip gloss from my purse and applied it without a care in the world, slowly and with precision.

Bryce leaned back in his chair and swiveled it slightly, contemplating what to say next. He was finally taking me seriously. Women had to do drastic things to be taken seriously these days.

"What do you want, Olivia?"

"I want in," I said, returning the tube of gloss to my purse.

"Interesting." He brought his hands in front of him, placing the tips of his fingers together.

"And I want money."

"Of course you do. Women are so shortsighted." He chuckled.

I stood from my seat and threw my bag over my shoulder. I was not about to be laughed at. I had all the power. I knew that. He just needed to be reminded of it. Just as I was turning for the door, he stood from his seat. "Hold on, wait," Bryce said putting his hands up.

I smiled and turned back toward him.

"How much?"

"Five hundred thousand dollars," I said without missing a beat.

"And you give me the video." He jutted up his chin.

"Not a chance. I'll hold on to the video as a life insurance policy. But I'd like in. As long as you treat me like a fair partner, this video will never see the light of day," I said, putting a hand on my hip. "We can work out the exact terms of our partnership later, but I want the money by tomorrow night."

He pretended to be considering the offer, but he knew he had no other choice, and I knew it too.

"If you go to the police, you and your husband will be done as well," he said confidently. Oh, silly boy, still thinking he had the upper hand.

"Without money, we're already done," I spat back.

He walked to my side of the desk and stood in front of me, less than a step between us. He was so close I could feel his breath on me. I wasn't backing down. I looked him right in the eye.

"I hope you know what you're doing, little girl."

I took one small step toward him, closing the distance between us. I reached my hand out, grabbing his dick with force—just hard enough to hurt in a pleasurable way. He jolted a tiny bit, but he didn't resist. He smiled and raised an eyebrow, the tightness in his eyes disappeared.

I bit my lower lip. "You have no idea what I can do."

67

JENNY

"You ready for this?" I asked as I straightened up the refreshment table in the middle of the salon.

Keisha finished wiping down her station. "Can we cancel?" she said with a laugh.

"I wish."

I looked around the salon to make sure everything was in place. We had a few contract SFX makeup artists and manicurists set up as Keisha and I wouldn't be able to handle it all by ourselves. We had already finished nearly all our full-time clients this morning, and we only had Olivia, Crystal, Karen, and surprisingly, Shannon—who made a last-minute appointment with us—left. I wasn't keen on seeing Olivia, but she had phoned earlier, explaining her behavior the other night. She said Dean had an emergency and that she would reimburse us for the night out and clear up her membership fees. I had a feeling she was full of shit, and I was tired of her excuses, but Keisha and I were also attending the party, so I figured I had better play nice . . . at least for tonight.

"You're right, Keisha."

She gave me a look that said, *Who, me?* "I'm not sure what you're referring to, but I won't argue with that." She laughed as she set out glasses for wine and cocktails.

"I mean, you were right about me hiring another person and taking time for myself. I'm going to do just that. After this party, I'm only working forty hours a week, fifty tops."

"What made you decide that?" Keisha raised an eyebrow.

I shrugged my shoulders. "Life's just too short. For all I know, I could die tonight, and I don't want my legacy to be an upscale salon for catty middle-aged women. When I die, I hope I leave behind people that truly loved and cared for me."

Keisha walked over to me. "You have me. But I know what you mean." She smiled, pulling me in for a hug. "I'm going to hold you to that," she whispered.

"I wouldn't expect anything less."

The front door chimed, and Olivia emerged from behind the curtains like a bat flying out of hell.

"Converting another one, I see," Olivia said, pulling a pair of oversized sunglasses down her nose and off her face. We ignored her quip. Keisha patted my back and told me she was proud of me.

Olivia slid her glasses into her bag and took off her coat, tossing it at Mary without even looking. It landed right on Mary's face. Mary groaned, straightened herself out, and returned to the front, carrying Olivia's coat.

"Was that necessary?" Keisha asked.

Olivia ignored her. She probably hadn't even realized what she had done to Mary, but then again, knowing her, I'm sure she did.

"Let's get started. What are you dressing up as?" I asked, trying to get this over with as quickly as possible.

"Not so fast. I'll have a drink first, and I'd like to settle my debt." Olivia put up a finger, then dropped her hand into her oversized bag, pulling out a wad of cash. She held it out to me. "It's six thousand dollars. You can count it if you'd like."

"Not necessary." I walked to her and took the money. Keisha begrudgingly handed her a glass of champagne.

Olivia smiled and sipped her drink. "Perfect. Everything is settled. Now, I'm going as a sexy skeleton. I'd like big voluminous hair, sky-high eyelashes, and perfect skeleton makeup."

I nodded. "All right. Have a seat. One of the SFX artists will take care of the makeup, and I'll do your hair after."

Olivia plopped her skinny ass in a chair. Her head was held high as she clutched her drink, slowly bringing it to her lips. She was comfortable and at peace, almost like she knew everything was going to be just fine, like all the pieces in her life had fallen perfectly into place. She took another drink, emptying it, then tapped her long nails on the glass. Keisha rolled her eyes and refilled it, then filled a glass for herself and one for me. As she handed it over, she whispered, "You're going to need this." I smiled at her and took a drink. Keisha leaned against her station and fiddled with her phone.

"Where are the rest of the ladies?" Olivia glanced around.

"They should be here shortly. Shannon's coming too. She called me earlier." I raised an eyebrow.

"That's the saddest thing I've ever heard," Olivia said with an obnoxious laugh. "But it should make for some good entertainment."

"Yeah, you sure like to be entertained," I said just above a whisper as I pulled out several sets of curlers and cans of hairspray.

"What are you two going as?" Olivia took a sip of her drink. Just as I was about to answer, she interrupted, "The help?"

She let out a loud cackle. Keisha shook her head, biting back her anger.

"I'm just teasing, of course," she said through her deep throaty laugh.

"We're going as Cher and Dionne from *Clueless*." My voice was as patient and calm as it could be.

Olivia opened her mouth, ready for another rude remark, but closed her bloated lips just as the front door chimed.

68
KAREN

"Go on back," Mary said as I entered the salon.

"Thanks so much, Mary."

She smiled as I disappeared through the curtains. I found Olivia sitting in a chair, sipping a glass of champagne. Jenny was rearranging her station, even though everything was already in place. Keisha stood from her chair, and her face lit up when she noticed I was standing there. We exchanged pleased smiles. I was wearing loungewear. I would get dressed for the party back at the house with Mark.

"Nice to see you, Karen," Olivia said coyly.

I grabbed the small red Saint Laurent purse from inside my larger bag. I walked to Olivia and tossed it in her lap. "Here. You forgot your purse at my house." The purse was actually mine, but it was filled with the money I "owed" her.

"That was sweet of you to bring this to me. I so appreciate it. I was looking for this purse. It goes perfect with my outfit," she lied. I rolled my eyes and took a seat at Keisha's station.

Keisha handed me a glass of red wine. Our fingers touched for a moment, and it caused my lips to curve upward. She returned the smile and patted my shoulder.

"What are you dressing up as?" Keisha asked.

"A sexy skeleton."

"No way. That's what I'm going as, Karen. There can't be two of us," Olivia pouted. I looked at her in the mirror.

"Well, I already bought my costume. So, feel free to change." I smirked.

Olivia took another drink and let out a huff. "You knew I was going as that. I told you the other day."

"I must have forgotten."

She raised her chin at me. "It's fine. I'm sure I'll look better."

"You're right. I'm sure you'd look so much better as a skeleton." I twisted up my lips and rolled my eyes.

"What do you want to do with your hair?" Keisha asked.

"Nothing. I'm wearing a wig. For the makeup: whatever Olivia's having done, I'll have, but better." I laughed.

I didn't care anymore. I had had it with Olivia. I was no longer playing nice with her. She was dead to me.

The front door chimed.

"Hey, y'all," Crystal said as she entered the salon. Her voice was more twangy than usual. Jenny walked to her and gave her a hug.

"Hello, Crystal. Is Bryce ready for tonight?" Olivia asked.

"I'm sure he is." Crystal followed Jenny and took a seat at her station. Jenny wrapped a cape around her and then poured her a glass of champagne.

"How does the house look?" Jenny asked.

Crystal's eyes lit up. "It looks amazing. Everything came together perfectly," she gushed.

"And everything's all set for tonight?" I asked.

"It is," Crystal said with a nod.

The makeup artist was outlining Olivia's lips with skeleton teeth, so fortunately for the rest of us, she couldn't talk.

"I can't wait to see it!" Jenny combed through Crystal's long blond locks.

"You're going as a cowgirl, right?" I confirmed, glancing over at Crystal while keeping an eye on Keisha. I could never take my eyes off her.

Crystal shook her head. "Nope. Changed my mind. I'm going as Sandy from *Grease*." She smiled at herself in the mirror.

"That's perfect," Jenny said. "I'll put in really tight curls."

"And I'll do a smoky eye and dark-red lips when Jenny's done with your hair," Keisha said.

Olivia tried to mumble something, but the makeup artist told her to stop moving. That was probably the toughest thing Olivia ever had to do . . . keep her mouth shut.

"What about you?" Crystal took a drink from her glass and looked at Jenny in the mirror.

"Keisha and I are going as Cher and Dionne from *Clueless*."

"Oh, that's amazing. I love it."

"And you, Karen?" Crystal glanced over at me.

"A sexy skeleton."

"What about you, Olivia?" Crystal asked, looking in the mirror at Olivia who was still getting makeup applied to her lips. She tried to answer, but it came out all mumbled.

"She's going as a sexy skeleton too," I answered for her. "She copied me."

Olivia groaned.

"You could always change . . . your costume." Crystal raised her eyebrow. Olivia rolled her eyes and moaned again.

"Yeah, there's still time to uncopy me," I said with a laugh.

"Okay, all done. But keep your mouth closed for five minutes while everything dries. Otherwise, I'll have to redo it," the makeup artist said to Olivia. She made a grunting sound and pulled out her phone, setting a timer for five minutes.

The front door chimed again.

69
SHANNON

I said hello to Mary and waltzed right to the back. The wives were already there, getting their hair and makeup done. I greeted them all, even Olivia. Olivia nodded and didn't say a word. Her face was done in full skeleton makeup. It looked quite striking and beautiful.

"Wow, Olivia. Death looks good on you." I chuckled as I made my way to the drink table. I poured myself a nice, tall glass of wine and set it down. I turned back to Olivia. "What? Nothing to say?"

"She can't talk until her makeup dries," Karen said.

Olivia held up her cell phone, facing the screen toward me. A timer was clicking down. Three minutes, twenty-three seconds.

"Then I best not take these next three minutes for granted." I grinned.

Jenny smiled while she curled small sections of Crystal's hair into tiny tight ringlets. "What are you going as?" I asked Crystal.

She looked in the mirror at me. "Sandy from *Grease*."

I nodded and gave her a warm smile, "Wonderful."

I grabbed the bottle of red wine and champagne and walked around the room refilling everyone's drinks. "Let's get this party started, ladies."

"That's what I'm talking about," Keisha cheered.

I got to Olivia. She held out her glass to me like she expected me to serve her. Her wrist limp, while her skinny fingers held on to it. I tipped the bottle and poured until the red wine spilled onto her lap. "Sorry."

She scrambled, trying to wipe it off. One of the makeup artists handed her a towel. She dabbed herself dry, keeping composure in her face to ensure her makeup wouldn't be ruined, but her eyes were like daggers. She wanted to hurt me. That much was obvious. She held up her phone. The timer read one minute. Was she trying to threaten me? I wasn't scared of Olivia.

"What about you?" Crystal asked. "What are you dressing up as?"

"Corpse bride." I spun around, facing the other women.

The timer went off. Olivia took a big breath.

"How fitting!" she said. "Heck. You don't even need to dress up, Shannon. You're already a single, alone, forgotten nothing—just like a corpse. The only difference is you're not married . . . anymore." Olivia cackled.

Everyone else looked around awkwardly. All that venom Olivia held inside of her for five minutes had erupted. She took a drink and swallowed hard, realizing she may have gone too far . . . even for her. "I'm just kidding," she added. "I'm sure you'll look nice, Shannon." She took another drink.

"Anyway," Keisha said, changing the subject. "Is Mark coming tonight?"

Karen nodded and didn't say a word.

"Why? Do you have something to tell him?" Olivia asked.

Why was she being snarky to Keisha? Keisha never did a damn thing to her. Then again, none of us had. She was always toying with people. She thought she was the goddamn puppet master, just pulling the strings. Little did she know, she was the master of nothing.

"Oh, Olivia. Would it kill you to be nice?" I scowled at her as I threw up my arms. I walked over to the station next to hers and took a seat.

Olivia paused, then looked to me. "Yes, yes it would." She curled her lip.

"I figured as much."

"You would know, Shannon. You're the queen of mean," she quipped.

I gave her an odd look. I knew she was holding on to something, and if I didn't find out now, I never would.

"Is there a problem, Olivia?" I asked. Honestly, I didn't care what her issues with me were. But closure is powerful.

"One word: Nemo," she said. Her constricted eyes paired with her skeleton makeup made Olivia look truly terrifying.

"Nemo?" Karen asked. "Like the Pixar movie?"

I thought for a moment and then it clicked. I knew what Olivia was pissed at me for.

"No, Karen. Not like the movie. Nemo. New money." Olivia spat.

"That's why you have it in for me? A stupid nickname from years ago. Are you kidding me?" I was nearly laughing at the ridiculousness of it all.

"Among other things," she said, dismissing me.

I took a drink of my wine. "Well, I'm sorry for that, Olivia. I hadn't realized how much I had hurt you. But I'm not that person anymore."

She opened her mouth, then closed it. Her eyes searched mine, then they went dark. "It's too late for apologies, Shannon. A line has been drawn." She raised her chin at me.

I rolled my eyes and took another sip of wine, feeling perfectly okay with that closure, even if Olivia wasn't okay with hers.

Olivia got up from her seat and refilled her drink. She sipped it, while surveying the room, probably determining who her next target would be. She was one of those women who had issues with every other woman, most likely due to her own insecurities. Her eyes bounced around the room and, finally, they settled on Crystal. Hadn't she been through enough?

"So, Bryce will be at the party tonight?" Olivia raised an eyebrow.

"Yes. Obviously, it's his house," Crystal said curtly. Jenny continued to curl her hair, paying close attention to Olivia and Crystal's exchange.

"Good. We have things to discuss." Olivia smirked.

Crystal pulled out her phone and busied herself with it.

"It seems you always have things to discuss with married men," Karen cut in.

"It would appear someone is on a horse too high for their own morals." Olivia eyed her up and down.

Keisha finished Karen's makeup and helped her out of the chair. "It's beautiful," Karen said, admiring her freshly painted face. She walked over to the drink table where Olivia was standing. They stood only a foot apart, staring at one another, both wearing full skeleton makeup.

"I'd be careful with your accusations." Olivia narrowed her eyes.

Karen took a step closer to Olivia. "Or what?" She jutted her chin up.

"Or that makeup might become a little more permanent." Olivia's teeth gritted together.

"Now, now, ladies. This isn't the time. Can we have one night where we can all be civilized to one another?" I said.

Olivia stuck her nose up and walked over to Keisha's station, taking a seat in the chair. She flipped her hair over her shoulder in a dramatic fashion and gave Keisha a commanding look. Keisha rolled her eyes but didn't say a word. She pulled out a comb and a curling iron and started in on Olivia's hair.

"I agree with Shannon," Jenny said. "We're ladies. We can act like ladies."

"Oh, Shannon, I forgot to ask. Did that guy who stood you up ever contact you again?" Olivia asked, attempting to keep a straight face.

I narrowed my eyes but then relaxed them. "No, he didn't."

"You must feel awful. I know I would." Olivia raised her brows.

"His loss," Jenny said with a smile.

It was nice to have some support. I still didn't love the idea of a party being thrown at my old house with my ex-husband, but then again, if everything went according to plan, it wouldn't be his house for much longer.

70

CRYSTAL

I arrived home less than an hour before the party was set to begin. I opted to stay at the salon as long as I possibly could just so I didn't have to spend any additional time alone with Bryce. I didn't know how to be around him. I tried to act like my normal self but knowing who he was, what he was capable of, and what he had done terrified and enraged me. I wanted to kill him. After Olivia finally left, Karen, Keisha, Shannon, Jenny, and I had a nice time sipping wine and chatting.

I walked in through the front door, passing by a man dressed in a tux and a mask like the Phantom of the Opera. He was lining trays with glasses of champagne. It would be a nice welcome for our party guests. The house was completely decorated just as I had envisioned it. The bartender was finishing up with prepping the bar. The caterers were putting out all the food. The DJ was getting his music set up out by the red pool. I was dressed in skintight black leather pants, a cropped off-the-shoulder top, and six-inch heels. My hair was big and curly. My eyes were extra smoky, and my lips were painted a deep-red color.

Bryce strolled down the stairs dressed in a cowboy costume. When he saw me, his eyes lit up, then his face sported a look of disappointment.

"I thought you were dressing up like a cowgirl. That's why I'm wearing this damn thing." He gestured to his own childish costume.

"I changed my mind." I looked away from him and pretended to straighten up some decorations.

"I'm disappointed, but not too much. You look incredible." He walked to me and wrapped his arms around my waist from behind, kissing my bare shoulder. I nearly shuddered. I wanted to crawl out of my own skin. I closed my eyes and took a small breath. *Act normal. Act normal.*

"Tell me about it, stud," I said in my best Sandy voice. Shannon advised me to act like Sandy would whenever I felt uncomfortable with Bryce. He pressed into me a little harder. I could feel his longing for me on my lower back.

"Maybe we have time for a quickie before the guests arrive." He whispered hot breath into my ear.

"No. I have a few more finishing touches, and I don't want to ruin my costume." I was matter-of-fact and stern with my answer. The last thing I wanted to do was have sex with my husband.

He nuzzled me a little more. "You're no fun." He playfully touched my hair, pulling a strand of it straight and then letting it spring back into a tight curl.

"Can I get a scotch on the rocks?" Bryce backed away from me and redirected his attention to the bartender. The bartender nodded and almost immediately had a drink in his hand.

"Anything for you, Mrs. Madison?" the bartender asked.

Before I could answer, Bryce cut in, "Oh no. She's much too busy for a drink."

"Actually, I'll have a vodka soda. Thank you."

Bryce took a big swig of his drink and looked me over. "When are the guests arriving?"

The bartender handed me a tall vodka soda. I took a long drink, trying to ready myself to even speak to this man. A few days ago, I knew him as my husband, my lover, my soulmate, and now I knew him only as a monster and a murderer. I wasn't sure if I was going to survive this night. I was positive Bryce had no idea I knew about him. But could I keep him in the dark long enough? Olivia must have been holding on to that secret, probably to use it later against me or Bryce.

I couldn't stand playing nice with him. If he found out that I knew, would he have me killed? Would he kill me himself? He wasn't the type of man to get his own hands dirty. Would he grovel and try to politic his way out of it? Shannon knew too. What would he do to her? I felt like I was standing in a zoo enclosure with a lion, a lion that didn't realize it was backed into a corner.

"Any minute now." I sipped my drink.

"Did you see Olivia today?"

I didn't look over at him.

"Yes. She was at the salon." I could feel his burning eyes on me. He was trying to read me, trying to determine if Olivia had told me. Little did he know, I was the one who told Olivia. It was clear that he had spoken to her now. Had they made an arrangement? Were they working together? It wouldn't surprise me.

"Did she say anything to you?" I heard him clink the ice in his drink as if he were having a casual everyday conversation. But there was nothing casual about this.

I walked over to the tables covered with food. I pretended to check them all over. "About what?" I feigned ignorance.

"Never mind." He leaned against the counter, sipping his scotch.

"Was she supposed to tell me something?" Two could play the question game. I had learned well from Bryce.

"Are the rest of the girls coming? Minus Shannon, of course . . ." He quickly changed the subject.

"Yes, and Shannon is coming." I picked my drink up and looked at him. His eyes widened.

"Really? She must be more desperate than I thought she was." Bryce laughed.

I took another drink, slowly sipping, deciding what to say to this man.

"You did invite her. What makes accepting an invite desperate? Perhaps you wanted her to come?" I raised an eyebrow.

"Jealous, aren't you? Is that why you're so tense? Don't like the ex-wife interfering with our new life?" He took another slow sip of his scotch.

"Yeah, that's it." I nodded. I would let him believe what he wanted to believe . . . for now.

My attention was diverted from Bryce when I heard a loud, commanding voice from the front door. I was relieved at the interruption.

"Of course, I'll have a glass of champagne. What a nice touch," Shannon said. She was early. I knew it took all the strength in the world for her to even come here tonight, and I admired and appreciated her for that. She held on to my secret, a secret that literally could have destroyed me. Shannon was a good woman—she was an angry woman, but decent to her core—and I was proud to call her my friend.

"Hello," I called out, my voice light and cheerful now.

Shannon found Bryce and me standing awkwardly in the kitchen. Her zombie makeup looked incredible. Somehow, she made it look elegant and sophisticated. Only Shannon could do that. The wedding dress was torn and short for a sexy look. It was designer, of course. She took a small sip of her champagne and looked at me with concern and then at Bryce with disgust.

"The place looks wonderful," she gushed.

"Thank you. I think it came together really well." I glanced around, admiring the decor.

"It's so nice being married to someone with talent for a change," Bryce quipped.

"Too bad Crystal and I never experienced that," Shannon smirked.

Bryce looked her up and down. Before the video, I'd assume he was trying to intimidate her or was checking her out, but now, I thought he was probably thinking of all the different ways he could kill her. His features used to be soft to me, his eyes warm, but now everything about him was cutting, dark, and cold.

"I love the dress. Where did you get it?" I asked, changing the subject. It wasn't the time for fighting. We had bigger fish to fry.

"It's actually the dress I wore when I married Bryce." She laughed, taking another sip. I almost laughed too. Shannon took *petty* to a whole other level.

"You tore up your wedding dress? I paid fifteen thousand dollars for it," Bryce seethed.

"It's not like I was going to wear it again." She waved her hand dismissively.

"You're right." He laughed. "I couldn't imagine anyone else taking that bullet." Bryce drained the rest of his drink.

I grabbed Shannon by her arm. "Let me show you out back," I said, pulling her outside. "Why don't you get yourself another drink and put the crime scene tape on the stairs?" I suggested to Bryce as I walked away.

Once outside, the DJ began to play music. Servers bustled around with trays of drinks and appetizers. I walked Shannon over to a red chaise longue on the other side of the pool. We both took a seat, and I made sure Bryce wasn't looking at us and that we were out of earshot.

"What's the plan then?" I took another drink, my eyes bouncing between Shannon and the patio door.

"Just keep Bryce away from his office. I'll get in there and get what we need," she said matter-of-factly.

"Then what?"

"We take him down." Shannon pursed her lips.

"Party's here," Keisha called from inside the house. Shannon and I quickly got up and walked back in, finding Keisha, Karen, and Jenny. Karen wore a skintight black spandex suit with skeleton bones on it, six-inch stilettos, a long brown wig, and a red Saint Laurent purse. She was also clearly wearing a major push-up bra. For a moment there, I thought she was Olivia. Keisha and Jenny were adorably dressed like Cher and Dionne from *Clueless*, in plaid blazers, miniskirts, and flawless makeup and hair.

"Are we the first to arrive?" Jenny asked.

Shannon and I nodded in unison. A server handed each of them drinks.

"Perfect." Karen raised her glass. "Cheers to the day of the dead."

71
JENNY

I pace back and forth in the small interrogation room. Detective Sanford had left to take a call, leaving me alone for a few minutes to collect my thoughts. This whole process is taking far longer than I had anticipated.

The door opens. "So, where were we?" Sanford asks, his voice entering the room before him. He walks in and takes a seat, his head never coming up from the pages of his notepad. I mirror his movements and sit back down across from him.

"Ah, yes. So, you're at the party?"

I nod. "That's right."

"Did you notice anything unusual at the party?" He rubs his chin.

"Not particularly."

"And Shannon was in attendance?"

I nod.

"Would you not deem that unusual, given the circumstances?"

"Yes and no. True, she hated Bryce with a passion, but she was warming up to Crystal." I pull the ponytail holder from my wrist and tie up my hair.

"Did any of them ever leave the party together?"

"Not that I saw."

"What about Karen? Did she leave the party?"

"Not that I saw."

"Keisha?"

"I don't think so."

"Olivia?"

I shook my head.

"Any of them leave?"

"I told you, not that I saw."

He lets out a huff and scribbles some notes down. He's worn out. His eyes heavier than they were hours before. His appearance has become more and more disheveled throughout the day. Buttons undone. Loose tie. Wrinkled shirt. He is unraveling right before my eyes. Buckhead made people crazy, but rarely this quickly.

"You're not asking the right questions," I finally say. My patience with Detective Sanford has worn thin.

He stops for a moment and then looks up at me. It's probably the first time since meeting him that he's actually properly looked at me. Not just in my direction while asking questions, not just in a professional, assessing manner . . . he is looking in my eyes. Curiosity, suspicion, doubt—I'm not sure why, but I finally have his attention.

"And what, may I ask, are the *right* questions?" He holds his gaze tightly fixed on me, a boxer waiting for their opponent to swing.

"Ask me about Bryce."

72
OLIVIA

Dean and I arrived at the party . . . late, of course. The more important you are, the later you arrive. It lets people know that your time is more valuable than theirs. I assumed the girls had arrived early. I laughed to myself as Dean helped me out of the limo. He was dressed in an orange jumpsuit as he had chosen to go as a prison inmate. He didn't see the irony in the costume. Oh, but I did. I hadn't told Dean about the video or my arrangement with Bryce. It was best to keep men of low intelligence in the dark. He was my husband, but he was also the one that got us into this mess in the first place. I certainly couldn't trust him to fix it.

"You look beautiful," Dean whispered into my ear. I was dressed in a skintight black bodysuit with skeleton bone graphics, six-inch stilettos, a red Saint Laurent bag, and perfectly blown-out hair.

I kissed him on the cheek, and he led me to the front door, where a man wearing a Phantom of the Opera mask was standing with a tray of champagne glasses. He welcomed us, and we each took a glass. We waltzed into the house. It was impeccably decorated and on theme. The house was lit with only crystal chandeliers, candles, and party lights, making it difficult to see others. There were spiderwebs and skeletons and red bead curtains throughout. All the servers were dressed liked dominatrices, clad with leather and chains. The music boomed throughout the house, and the place was crowded with most everyone who was anyone from Buckhead. Dean and I made our way to the pool area, where the decor continued.

"Bryce and Crystal went all out," Dean said into my ear.

"With our money," I said under my breath.

The music was turned down a couple of notches. I scanned the party and found Crystal chatting with Shannon on the far end of the pool. What were they talking about? Actually, why were they even talking to one another?

"Get us something to eat," I said to Dean as I walked away from him. As I got closer, Karen, Keisha, and Jenny joined the gathering.

"Hello, ladies," I said, surveying each of them. My eyes stopped on Karen. Oh, you have to be fucking kidding me. It was like looking in a goddamn mirror. She looked exactly like me, even down to the purse—the one she had given me today. Why the hell did she have two of the same red Saint Laurent purse?

"Wow, Karen, look at you. They do say that imitation is the sincerest form of flattery," I said, sipping my champagne. "Is this the only way you can get Mark into bed?"

Karen's eyes tightened. I thought for sure she would strangle me right then and there. I watched Keisha's hand slide behind Karen's back. She was rubbing it. Karen was clearly having her cake and carpet munching it too. I wondered if I could get more money out of her. It seemed she had no intention of telling Mark the truth, nor of breaking it off with him or Keisha.

"I think you both look great," Jenny said. Always the peace-keeper, never anything else. Such a bore of a person.

"This party really is wonderful, Crystal," Karen gushed.

"Yes. I was just going to say the same thing. It looks extravagant and expensive." I raised an eyebrow at Crystal. "And where is the host of the evening?" I wouldn't be able to enjoy myself until I had the money.

"He's around." Crystal looked away from me. "I have to check in with the caterers."

"Do you need any help?" Shannon asked. I hadn't even noticed her. She was nothing. Crystal nodded, and the two walked off. I didn't like that they were getting along, but it was something I'd take care of after my arrangement with Bryce was completed. Shannon's apology was too late. Seriously, if she would have apologized the night it happened, it would have still been too late. Her whole *I'm not the same person anymore* was a load of shit. People don't change. Crystal had her ex-husband, and I had her chairwoman position. There was nothing left in Buckhead for Shannon. I took another slow sip of my champagne, scanning the party.

My phone buzzed.

I pulled it out of my purse. It was a text from Bryce.

> Meet me in ten minutes in the guesthouse. Back door is unlocked.

I smiled and stowed my phone. Perfect. Everything was going according to plan. Karen gave me a peculiar look when she noticed I was smiling.

"What are you so happy about?" she snipped.

"I get to be me. Why wouldn't I be happy?"

73
SHANNON

"He's at the bar. You're good to go," Crystal said as she watched her husband chat with Dean and Mark. She handed me a key.

"Text me if he's coming."

She nodded. I walked into the kitchen and then stumbled into the foyer, acting as though I was tipsy. If anyone asked where I was going or what I was doing, I would pretend to be inebriated—not far-fetched, considering my recent history of overindulging at social events. But tonight I was sober. I crawled under the crime scene tape and made my way up the stairs undetected. Everyone was mostly outside, except for a few servers and workers. But the help never asked questions. I stood in front of Bryce's office door, key in hand. Crystal had taken it earlier, made a copy, and returned the original before Bryce noticed it was missing. This was it. We were going to take that monster down. I slid the key in the lock and turned it. It opened with ease. I tiptoed into the office and locked the door behind me.

I texted Crystal.

I'm in.

Powering up the computer, I took a seat at the large oak desk. A password screen popped up.

Password?

Good. He's still at the bar.
Bryce2024.

The text popped up on my phone. I rolled my eyes. This moron actually thinks he's running for president in 2024. I quickly typed it in, and the computer booted up. I browsed the desktop, searching for the folder Crystal mentioned. It wasn't there. I went to the search bar and typed in *Insurance Policy*. No results.

Shit. It's not here.
The folder isn't here.

I started clicking anything and everything. Each folder that opened wasn't what we were looking for. He must have deleted it. Must have gotten scared when Olivia went to him. We knew they had made some sort of deal.

The text lit up my screen.

He's coming. Get out of
there now.

Shit. I quickly closed out of everything and turned off the computer. I heard footsteps outside the office door. I glanced around the room frantically. There was no closet to hide in. I crouched down, crawled underneath the desk, and pulled the chair in as far as it would go. The key slid into the lock. The door opened. The lights flicked on. A phone rang.

"Bryce Madison," he said.

There was silence as he walked farther into his office.

"I'm taking care of it now."

He opened a desk drawer. I was barely out of sight. I held my breath. I had never been afraid of Bryce before, but knowing what he had done—what he was doing—I was terrified. People without morals were meant to be feared.

"It ends tonight," he said. He hit a button on his phone and slid it back into the pocket of his pants. He closed the desk drawer, and I heard a *click*, followed by a *click, click, click*.

> He has a gun.

I quickly texted Crystal without even looking at my phone.

I heard him rustle around a bit more. The sound of a zipper on a bag, things being tossed around, and the gun—the bullets sliding into the clip, the clip into the chamber, and the hammer being pulled back. He was going to use that gun tonight.

74
CRYSTAL

Shit. Are you okay?

I fired off the message. I didn't know what to do. I walked to the foyer, ready to charge up those stairs and do whatever I needed to. The crime scene tape was ripped down. Bryce had clearly been in a hurry. I kept staring at the phone, waiting for Shannon to text me back, to tell me everything was fine. Just as I was about to bolt up the stairs, Bryce came jogging down them.

"Party's down here," I said calmly. He was carrying a duffel bag and had a look of determination on his face.

"I have to run an errand. I'll be back in a bit," he said as he reached me.

"Now? But the party . . ." I pouted.

"I know, I know. It won't take long." He kissed me on the forehead.

"You're going to miss the fireworks show."

"I won't. I promise. I have to go." He walked out the front

door, closing it behind him. I took a deep breath and ran up the stairs as fast as I possibly could. Shannon hadn't texted back. Out of breath, I tried to open the office door, but it was locked. I pounded on it.

"Shannon," I cried out. "Open the door! Are you okay?"

I pressed my ear against the door, but I didn't hear anything. I jiggled the knob and pounded and kicked. Oh my God. What did he do? My eyes welled up with tears as I banged harder.

The door unlocked and opened. Even though Shannon was wearing heavy Halloween makeup, I could tell underneath she was pale as a ghost. I wrapped my arms around her and pulled her in for a tight hug. "Thank God you're okay!" I exclaimed, out of breath.

"Did you get my text?"

I released her, still holding her shoulders. "Yes. Where is he going with that gun?"

"I have no idea."

Guns didn't bother me. I had one—hell, everyone in Texas had one. But they didn't walk around with the sinister look that Bryce had on his face.

75

KAREN

"So, what are you going to do?" Keisha asked. Her eyebrow raised. Her lip quivered. She wanted an answer . . . an answer about us. We were standing off to the side of the pool between the DJ booth and the bar that was set up outside. The party was so crowded and loud, I could barely think.

Would I leave Mark for her? Would I tell him the truth? Or would I pretend none of this ever happened and go back to being an unhappy wife whose husband cheats on her? Yes, what I suspected was true. Mark was sleeping with Olivia. I found out just earlier in the day. The private investigator sent pictures of Mark entering Olivia's house last week and then leaving about an hour later. That was all the proof I needed. Mark was a plastic surgeon. He didn't do house calls. I knew the only thing he was doing was Olivia.

I swirled my vodka soda and took a long drink.

"Well?" Keisha put her hand on her hip.

I looked at her and then over at Mark. He was dressed in

a lab coat with a stethoscope around his neck—how original. He was drinking near the bar with Dean but kept glancing around the room. He was looking for someone, probably Olivia. I couldn't fucking believe she blackmailed me for sleeping with Keisha when *she* was sleeping with my husband the whole time.

Jenny walked back over to us with a fresh drink in hand. "Have you two seen Crystal or Shannon?" she asked.

"Not in a while," I said, glancing around the party. It was packed. The music was loud. People were dancing. The drinks were flowing. There were even people swimming in the pool.

"There they are." Keisha pointed to Crystal and Shannon as they came out of the house.

"Oh, and there's Olivia . . . flirting with my fucking husband."

Olivia walked over to Dean and whispered in his ear. She turned to Mark and stroked his arm. Then she disappeared inside.

"That's it. I'm confronting him," I declared.

"Don't. It's not the time," Keisha urged. She grabbed my arm, but I shrugged her off.

I turned back to her for a moment. "It's now or never," I said, and I strutted right toward Mark. Keisha tried to stop me again, but I was determined. I looked back and saw she was following behind, so I quickened my pace.

"We need to talk," I said forcefully to Mark.

He looked at me and then took another drink. "About what?" He was nonchalant in his answer.

"About you fucking Olivia," I nearly yelled.

Mark tried to quiet me as Dean was standing only a few feet away, chatting with a couple of guys. He hadn't heard, because if he would have, he would have killed Mark right then and there. Mark tried to pull me aside, but I didn't budge.

"Tell me the truth," I demanded.

"Lower your voice." He glanced around again, making sure no one was listening. "Nothing happened with Olivia."

"Don't lie to me, you asshole!"

"Did Olivia tell you this? Jesus Christ, and even after I fucking paid her."

I couldn't believe it. The irony of it all. A small chuckle worked its way out of me. And then more and more, until I was in full-on hysterical laughter, doubling over dramatically.

"What's so funny?" Mark asked.

"That evil bitch." I was struggling to speak in between laughing. "You paid her for sex. And I paid her to keep her mouth shut," I said, connecting the dots for him. She was playing both of us all along.

He hung his head in shame and then picked it back up, ready to explain. I raised my hand to stop him. "Don't bother. I'm leaving you."

"Don't do this. I promise I'll be better. I love you, Karen," he begged.

"I'm not in love with you. I'm in love with someone else, and I want a divorce." The words came out of me like butter, smooth and easy.

"What the hell!? With whom?" Anger took residence on his face. He turned red and his mouth tightened.

"With her." I pointed back at Keisha, who was standing a few feet behind me. "Goodbye, Mark."

I turned away from him and walked right up to Keisha, not stopping for a moment. I heard him rant about how I was embarrassing myself and him. I wrapped my arms around Keisha and kissed her. I kissed her hard. I could hear Mark scream and yell as he took off inside. Some people cheered. Some gasped. Others were audible with their feelings of disgust. None of it mattered. The only thing that mattered in this moment was Keisha and me.

Loud bangs echoed, almost like gunshots. We stopped kissing. Above us bright fireworks pierced the night sky. We laughed and kissed again. It was truly magical. A night we would never forget.

76
OLIVIA

Why we had to meet in the back of the guesthouse made no sense to me. The party was such a riot, no one was paying attention to anyone but themselves. Just like any good party should be. We could have done this in five seconds in some side room of the house, but of course, Bryce was always one with a flair for the dramatics.

The noise of the party began its decrescendo as I slipped off to the side and made my way around to the guesthouse. It sat quietly tucked in a far corner of the yard, all the lights off, no movement inside. For a Halloween party, it fit the bill of being creepy and scary better than any of the decorations did.

My heels sunk into the grass as I walked, making my steps slow and awkward. Thank God no one could see me. As I made my way around the back of the house, I caught a glimpse of myself in the reflection of an unlit windowpane. No wonder Karen tried to look like me; who wouldn't when you look like this?

The back door was unlocked as promised, and I walked in slowly. I was positive we would be the only two people in here, but no need to go screaming through the house if I didn't have to.

"Bryce," I whispered loudly. I tiptoed farther and came into the rec room, full of reclining chairs, a home theater setup, and a wet bar for cocktails. Why the fuck wouldn't he just be in the first room?

"Bryce. We aren't playing hide-and-go-seek, just come out. No one is here," I said, this time louder. Nothing.

The guesthouse was clearly unused. None of the carpeting was worn down. None of the furniture touched. It looked like a model home, sterile and fake, and it fit Bryce perfectly.

I heard a creak above me in the ceiling. The noise that is made when someone shifts their weight on a floorboard. "Bryce, are you up there?" I called out.

I began to make my way up the spiral staircase. I fucking hated these. They're so tacky and childish. Bryce probably thought it would make him look young and hip. I reached the top and found three unlit rooms. As I looked in from the hall, I realized it was a bathroom and two bedrooms. I skipped the bathroom and went to the larger of the two bedrooms first.

"Bryce. This doesn't have to be a big thing. Just get out here and give me my money so I can get back to the party. People will notice that I'm not there." I entered the bedroom and flicked on the light switch, but nothing happened. I tried several more times but nothing. I pulled my phone out and turned on the flashlight. Panning the room, I saw nothing. Just more unused furniture and bland decorations, like a grandmother's house.

The floor creaked again, this time in the room next door.

"Bryce. This isn't funny. You aren't tough, you're a fucking politician. Just get out here."

I exited the room and entered the smaller bedroom. There, on the bed, was a duffel bag, money clearly visible as the bag was open.

"Ah, there it is," I whispered. The money. I didn't need Bryce to be here, just the beautiful prize that lay before me. That chickenshit was probably too afraid to come out here himself and sent some servant to drop it off.

I stepped forward to grab the bag, and then it was gone. Everything was gone.

77
JENNY

PRESENT

"Tell me about Bryce Madison then, Jenny," Detective Sanford says. He stares me down. Waiting for the big reveal I'd built it up to be. Just as I am about to speak, a police officer bursts into the room.

"Sir! It's Bryce Madison," he says, out of breath. Detective Sanford rises quickly and excuses himself, closing the door behind him.

What did Bryce do now? We were finally getting somewhere. I stand from my seat and pace the room. Did he do something to one of the girls? If something had happened, this is the detective's fault. His questions were all over the place. He just doesn't get it. He doesn't understand Buckhead.

My patience wears thin. I go and knock on the door, then I bang on it.

Sanford opens the door. "What are you doing?"

"What did Bryce do?" I ask, completely ignoring his question.

"He didn't do anything. He's dead."

My mouth falls open. I take a deep breath. A sense of relief rushes through me. It's over. It's finally over. I slowly walk back to my chair and take a seat. My shoulders slump, and I just stare off at nothing.

Detective Sanford surveys me, looking me up and down. He rubs his chin again. His brow knits together. He still doesn't get it.

"What were you going to tell me about Bryce? Why did you ask me what he had done?" He takes a seat across from me, pulling his chair in as close to the table as possible.

"I'll just show you instead." I bring out my phone, open a video, and hand it to him.

"Push Play."

He does.

When the video finishes, Detective Sanford scratches the top of his head. His eyes widen.

"That was Dean Petrov in the video?"

I'm not sure if it's a question, but I nod anyway.

"And the voice off-screen?" he asks, but I think he already knows.

"Bryce Madison," I say.

"Why didn't you show me this earlier?"

"I didn't know if I could trust you. Bryce had police on his payroll. But now that he's dead . . . it doesn't matter." I fold my arms to my chest. "Who killed him?"

"Dean Petrov. He walked right into his office and shot him in the head. He was sitting across from Bryce's body with the weapon in hand when the police arrived." Detective Sanford stands from his chair. "He's in custody."

"I'm not surprised," I say.

"Bryce killed Olivia, didn't he?"

"Yes."

"Shit. This is bigger than I thought it was. I was convinced one of those housewives did it." He paces the room, tapping his fingertips against his chin, trying to put all the pieces together. "How did Olivia get wrapped up in all of this?"

"I think she blackmailed the wrong person."

"Bryce?"

I nod.

78
KAREN

It has been three weeks since Bryce was killed and Dean was arrested. Olivia's murder was solved, and Buckhead was finally getting back to normal—well, a new normal. Dressed in Lululemon yoga pants and a matching tank, I walk into Glow. Mary leads me to the back, where I find Shannon holding a glass of Chardonnay, with her feet dipped in a pedicure tub. Not much has changed. Crystal is sitting beside her in the same fashion. Well, actually, a lot has changed. The two of them look like mother and daughter. Shannon would kill me for thinking that. I walk over to Keisha and kiss her while she's sweeping up her station.

"Get a room," Shannon says playfully. Keisha and I smirk.

"Got time for a wax?" I whisper into her ear. She kisses me again with a laugh. I take a seat at her station, and she wraps a cape around me.

"How's Buckhead treating you?" Jenny asks. I look over, realizing she's cutting the hair of a woman I don't recognize. She's a brunette with high cheekbones and a pointy nose.

"Pretty well. I was just so glad to get on your client list."
Jenny nods.

"Hi, I'm Karen. I don't think we've met," I say to her while Keisha combs out my hair.

She looks over at me. "I'm Laura. I just moved to Buckhead with my husband." She gives a small wave of her hand.

"Nice to meet you," I say with a pleased smile.

"Did you all know the woman who was murdered?" Laura looks at me, then Keisha, and then in the mirror at Crystal and Shannon.

"Well enough." Shannon takes a sip of her wine.

"What about you? She was your client, wasn't she?" Laura glances at Jenny in the mirror.

79
JENNY

"I knew her a little too well," I finally answer. I don't know what to say when people ask about Olivia. It isn't something I like to talk about.

Laura nods and gives me a sad look. "I'm really sorry for your loss," she says with complete sincerity.

I thank her.

Shannon and Crystal chat about their plans for lunch and yoga. Shannon is back to being chairwoman, and Crystal won the vice-chairwoman position. They have become close. Trauma will do that to people.

Keisha and Karen are openly dating, and they're happy, truly happy. Karen filed for divorce two weeks prior, and she even introduced Keisha to her son, Riley.

As for me, I've stayed true to my promise to Keisha and I'm no longer working more than fifty hours a week. I'm even dating someone—Detective Sanford. It seems all that time spent in the interrogation room did some good after all. He called me last week, and at first, I thought it was for more questioning, like they had uncovered some new evidence. I was relieved to learn his call was solely to ask me out on a date. He said he was waiting for the case to be closed so it wouldn't seem too unprofessional.

"It's such a shame. I saw a picture of her. She was beautiful," Laura comments.

"On the outside. Yes, she was," Shannon says pointedly and takes another sip of her Chardonnay. I look back at Shannon, giving her a disapproving look. Crystal lets out an awkward cough.

I refocus my attention on Laura's hair, careful to add just the right number of layers to flatter her heart-shaped face.

"How could someone do that to another person?" Laura asks.

I shrug my shoulders and shake my head, my body language acting in complete opposition to my own thoughts. *Easily.*

80
CRYSTAL

My phone buzzed. I quickly opened the message. It was from Olivia.

> Fine. I'll be there in ten. No funny business.

My phone buzzed again. It was from Bryce.

> Meet me at my work office in twenty minutes.

I quickly texted Bryce back.

> Your wish is my command. No funny business.

I stowed my phone back in my spandex pants and glanced around the party. Bryce came running down the stairs with a duffel bag in tow.

"Party's down here," I said.

Bryce had a look of determination on his face. "I have to run an errand. I'll be back in a bit."

"Now? But the party . . ." I pretended to pout.

"I know, I know. It won't take long." He kissed me on the forehead.

"You're going to miss the fireworks show."

"I won't. I promise. I have to go." He walked out the front door, closing it behind him.

As soon as he was out the door, I quickly ran up the stairs to check on Shannon. I banged on the door, but she didn't answer right away.

"Shannon," I yelled. "Open the door! Are you okay?"

For a moment, I thought Bryce had found her. But just as my eyes became wet, the handle turned and the door opened. There stood Shannon with a Glock 19.

"You got it?" I asked.

She held it up as if she were one of Charlie's Angels. "Yes, ma'am. All the texts went through?"

I nodded. "Yes. Everything is documented just in case."

Bryce didn't have his gun with him. Our texts back and forth indicating Bryce was armed and dangerous were purely precautions in case something went wrong. We had planned this like a game of Clue—Bryce in his office with the handgun.

"Where is Olivia?" Shannon holstered Bryce's gun in the top of her thigh-high stockings.

"On her way to the guesthouse."

"And Bryce?" She situated her dress back in place, carefully smoothing it out.

"On his way to his office."

Shannon gave a pleased smile. Everything was going according to plan. At the salon earlier, I had reprogrammed Bryce's number in Olivia's phone to go to a burner cell, and when I returned home, I did the same to Bryce's phone, reprogramming Olivia's number to the same burner cell. I would be sure to change them back before the evening was over and dispose of the phone. But right now, they were both exactly where we wanted them, alone and vulnerable, with a sense of false confidence.

81
KAREN

THE NIGHT OF THE HOUSEWARMING PARTY

Keisha and I stood near the pool in the center of everything. The party was in full motion with strobe lights, loud music, bustling servers, and drinks endlessly flowing. Crystal had done a fabulous job of ensuring this party had the same vibe as a club—disorienting and overwhelming. It was imperative that people notice Keisha and me. We wanted to be seen. We watched Olivia disappear inside. We watched everyone drinking and having fun, completely unaware of what was really happening.

"I'm having a really hard time finding you attractive right now," Keisha snarked.

"Yeah, because I look like fucking Olivia," I huffed.

Keisha laughed and grabbed my hand. Her face turned serious. "It'll all be over soon."

I nodded. "Is it time?"

She looked at her watch. "Yes."

I took a deep breath and replayed the plan in my head. Keisha put her arm on me, and I shrugged it off dramatically, yelling, "It's now or never." Eyes were immediately on us. Perfect. I strutted over to Mark, "We need to talk!"

He looked at me and then took another drink. "About what?"

"About you fucking Olivia," I raised my voice even louder. More eyes on us.

His whole demeanor changed in an instant, and he was now on high alert. Mark tried to quiet me. But I would no longer be silenced. I was a woman with a voice, a powerful combination.

"Tell me the truth," I demanded even louder.

"Lower your voice." He glanced around again, making sure no one was listening. "Nothing happened with Olivia."

"Don't lie to me, you asshole!"

"Did Olivia tell you this? Jesus Christ, and even after I fucking paid her." Mark looked around the party, trying to find her.

He hung his head in shame and then picked it back up, ready to explain. I put my hand up to stop him. "Don't bother. I'm leaving you."

"Don't do this. I promise I'll be better. I love you, Karen," he begged like a dog.

"I'm not in love with you. I'm in love with someone else, and I want a divorce," the words came out of me with ease.

"What the fuck!? With whom?" He turned red. His eyes narrowed. His mouth tightened.

"With her." I pointed back at Keisha, who was standing a few feet behind me. "Goodbye, Mark."

I turned away from him, walked over to Keisha, and kissed her hard. People gasped. People cheered. I didn't care about what reaction they were having as long as the attention was on us. We were the distraction, the car accident you can't keep your eyes off.

"Is that Olivia kissing her?" a person from the crowd asked.

It was working. I was passing as Olivia.

"No, that's Karen," another person responded.

After this, I would separate from Keisha and make the rounds of the party. Round and round, until no one could tell the difference between Olivia and me. Was Olivia there until ten? Eleven? Midnight? Sure, sure she was. She was at the party all night long.

Loud explosions echoed throughout, and the sky was lit up with bright colorful fireworks, taking everyone's eyes off of Keisha and me.

"Are you okay?" she asked.

"I am now." I smiled at Keisha.

We looked up and took it in for a few seconds: the night sky, the fireworks, the feeling that maybe everything was going to be okay.

"Be careful," Keisha said, taking a step away from me.

"You too." I walked away from her, disappearing into a crowd of people.

82

CRYSTAL

THE NIGHT OF THE HOUSEWARMING PARTY

"Hello," Olivia called out. "Bryce, are you here? I told you no funny business."

I watched Olivia slink in through the sliding door, carefully closing it behind her. She stumbled a little, trying to find the light switch. Her hand touched it and she flicked it several times, but no light came on.

"Bryce." Her voice wasn't light or airy this time. It was apprehensive, almost fearful. She peered around the living room, but her eyes hadn't adjusted to the dark. I stood in the darkness, leaning over the railing, waiting for her to come upstairs. My breath was slow and controlled. My hands gripped the baseball bat, while the top of it leaned against my shoulder.

I moved slightly to make some noise upstairs.

"Bryce, is that you?" Her voice was light again. She began to slowly walk up the stairs, feeling around for furniture and anything else that might be in her way. She checked the main bedroom first, and then the second room. She finally saw the bait on the bed. She was only steps away from the spot where I needed her to be.

"Ah, there it is," Olivia said.

My eyes widened.

She was there.

I held the bat up high and swung as hard I could, cracking right into the back of Olivia's head. She fell to the ground like a sack of potatoes, hard and loud. I wasn't sure if her skull had cracked or the bat had.

A light flicked on behind me.

83
SHANNON

"Holy shit. Well, I'll be damned. You did it," I said, patting Crystal on the back and looking down at Olivia sprawled out on the floor. "Honestly, I didn't think you had it in you."

Crystal looked over the bat. She ran her fingers along the fresh crack at the end of it and then set it down. She took a deep breath and then another. Her face was flush. Her eyes were wide. I knew she was tough when she needed to be, when she needed to defend herself, but this was different—or maybe it wasn't so different after all.

"I didn't think so either," she said, letting her shoulders fall.

I pushed my heel into Olivia's side, gently moving her. She didn't stir.

"Now what?" Crystal asked.

"We have to move her. We can't leave her here."

"Is she dead?" Crystal bit her lower lip.

I bent down and placed my hand on the side of her neck. Her heartbeat was faint, but it was there. Olivia was like a

344

cockroach, a pest you could never truly stamp out. "No, she's still breathing."

"Shannon. Crystal," a voice whispered from downstairs. "Where are you guys?"

"Up here," I called out.

Footsteps ascended the stairs and in walked Keisha. She looked at us and then down at the floor where Olivia was lying. "She looks so much better like that," Keisha quipped.

"What, you mean . . . unconscious?" Crystal asked.

Keisha nodded and then bent down and picked up Olivia's legs. "Grab her top half. Hurry, we don't have much time."

84
JENNY

Olivia stirred as Keisha and I dragged her body toward a shipping container in an empty truck yard. There was a blue tarp underneath her to make it easier on us. Her body crunched over the gravel and dirt.

"How is she this heavy?" Keisha said, out of breath.

"Just keep pulling," I said, hurling myself backward while I yanked on the tarp.

She moaned a little as we heaved her into the shipping container. After we got her body against the back, Keisha went out to the car while I waited for her to wake up. It was fifteen minutes of sitting with my back to the wall of the cold metal before she finally woke, completely disoriented, unsure of where she was. She attempted to stand but fell back to the floor. She looked around, trying to figure out where she was. Then she finally saw me, and reality set in for the first time in Olivia's life.

"Jenny? What the fuck is going on? What happened?"

I just stared at the wall opposite me. Never acknowledging her. I was tired of answering to Olivia. We were all tired of her.

"Listen up. I know the other women eat out of the palm of your hand, but you're nothing but the fucking help. Now answer me when I talk to you . . . you insignificant piece of shit. What the fuck did you do to me!" she screamed, putting her hand on the gash at the back of her head that Crystal had left behind.

I sighed. And began to laugh. She just didn't get it.

"What the fuck is funny to you? You are going to start answering my questions or—"

"Or what?" I stood up, flashing Bryce's gun.

She gasped but closed her mouth.

"I know what you did."

She brought her bloodstained hand in front of her face and looked back at me.

"I'm sorry, Jenny. You weren't supposed to be at the salon. It was just to scare you, to remind you that I made you." I think it was the first time Olivia had ever been honest in her life.

I pointed the gun directly at her. "Do you still think you made me?"

She shook her head insistently.

I lowered the gun and took a step back. "Good."

Olivia breathed a sigh of relief and tried to stand again. I raised the gun and turned off the safety.

"What the hell are you doing?" Her eyes were wide.

"Putting us out of your misery." I aimed the gun at her.

She gasped, "Jenny, ple—" and before she could speak, before she could beg for her life, I fired off three shots. Two through her chest and one through her head. The bright-red splatters across her face and chest contrasted beautifully with the white skeleton bones of her costume. I gave Olivia her final touch-up, her beauty glow in her favorite shade one last time.

"Is it done?" Keisha called from outside.

I walked out of the shipping container and closed the door behind me. "It's done," I said.

"Did she say anything?"

"She's said enough." I handed the gun to Keisha.

She nodded. "How do you feel?" Keisha wrapped her arm around my shoulder.

"Relieved."

We made our way to the car.

"Now what?" Keisha looked to me.

"We go back to the party."

We hopped into Bryce's black Range Rover. It was one of his five cars, so he hadn't even known it was missing as he always left this vehicle parked by the guesthouse. Crystal said he only ever used it if he had to haul something, like bodies perhaps. We drove slowly, careful not to attract any attention. Keisha thoroughly wiped down the gun several times.

We pulled to the back of the guesthouse with the lights off. Shannon was standing there in the dark, waiting for us, with the baseball bat partially wrapped in a towel.

"How'd it go?" Shannon asked as we got out of the vehicle.

I carefully closed the door. "Just as we planned."

Shannon and Keisha exchanged their weapons. Keisha walked to the back of the vehicle, opened the hatch, and tossed the baseball bat in. We quickly wiped down the doors and the interior of the SUV with a couple of rags.

"And she's dead?" Shannon looked to me.

I nodded. "Olivia is dead."

She let out a sigh of relief.

Keisha returned to my side. "Where's Bryce?"

"Last I checked, Bryce was in the garden. Crystal is keeping an eye on him. I'll get this put back in his office." Shannon held the gun up.

We nodded. "Anyone notice we were gone?" I asked.

"No, just as you suspected."

I smiled at Keisha and she smiled back. We knew we didn't need to worry about people questioning whether we were at the party or not. The girls would vouch for us and everyone else would remember seeing us because we faded into the background. We were the help. We didn't demand attention. We were like air . . . People just always assumed we were there.

Out back, Bryce was right where Shannon had said he was, standing at the bar with a drink in hand. He looked confused but also content. He probably thought he was in the clear with Olivia. That maybe she had changed her mind. Dean was at the bar with him, completely inebriated, ignorant of the fact that his wife was dead in a shipping container like the poor women he had been trafficking for God knows how long.

The remainder of the night, we drank, we laughed, we danced, and we waited . . . for the rest of our plan to unfold.

85
JENNY

PRESENT

Olivia was like a cancer, and not one that could be treated. She needed to be cut out. You might be questioning whether we really needed to kill her. The answer is yes. We knew Bryce would slime his way out of it. A jury would go easy on Olivia, and Dean would have taken a plea deal. They were wealthy. And we all know what happens to wealthy people . . . Nothing.

We planned to take all three of them down. How? It was rather simple actually.

After Olivia was dead, we knew the rest of the plan would fall into place. Two days after Olivia disappeared, Dean filed a missing person's report. Four days after that, her body was found. I went to the police station the very next day and asked for the lead detective on the case. I told him I had information on Olivia Petrov's murder, and then I spent hours and hours and hours distracting him, waiting for Dean to finish what we started. We knew Dean would go after Bryce once Olivia's body was found. After all, Bryce had threatened her life, and Dean was a hothead who didn't think rationally. I went in to speak with Detective Sanford early in the morning, and by 8:00 p.m., Bryce was dead and Dean was in custody. Case closed. We were all free from it—free from Olivia, Bryce, and Dean. Buckhead was a better place without them. Some people can be saved. But not all of them.

"You should come to Manis and Mimosas," Crystal says. "It's on Sunday."

Laura smiles. "Oh, I would love that."

"Well, we would love to have you," I say as I continue to gently comb out her perfectly layered hair, glancing back and forth between her and myself in the mirror.

My mouth curves into a large Buckhead smile—pleased, that is.

It shouldn't be surprising, what we did.

What I did.

I just did what I always do.

I took care of my clients.

ACKNOWLEDGMENTS

Acknowledgments are always the hardest thing for me to write because "thank you" isn't enough, and I worry I'll forget to recognize every single person that helped make this book possible. There are a lot of you, and I'm grateful that I have so many to thank.

Thank you, first, to my literary agent, Sandy Lu. You gave me a chance when no one else would. Literally, you were the only one that said yes to this project. I am beyond proud to have you in my corner. Thank you for believing in me.

Thank you to my husband, Drew. Without your support and encouragement, I wouldn't have written any of my books. Like I always say, you are my Annie Wilkes (minus the busted ankles and all the violence).

Thank you to my film agent, Lucy Stille, for championing my work off the page.

Thank you to the extraordinary team at Blackstone, who have rallied around this book and worked tirelessly to get it out into the world. Especially: Rick Bleiweiss, Naomi Hynes, Sara O'Keefe, Samantha Benson, Jeffrey Yamaguchi, Zena Coffman, Josie Woodbridge, Megan Bixler, Kathryn Zentgraf, and Stephanie Koven.

Thank you to my Ithaca Critique Group for your years of encouragement and for workshopping my books, one chapter at a time. You've made me a better writer!

Thank you to Olivia Wachsberger for your support, your friendship, and for championing *The Perfect Marriage*. Olivia Petrov was given her name before you and I met, so I promise she's not named after you.

Thank you to my first readers. Your insight and feedback kept me going and pushed me to get this book out into the world. Whether you were reading a terrible first draft or a more polished draft, you're responsible for some part of this book. Thanks goes out to Bri Becker, Erin Fitzpatrick, Emily Lehman, Cristina Frost, Hollie White, Kapri Dace, Lauren Huolihan, Noel Scheid, Marissa Rice, Yas Angoe, Amanda Epping, Hannah Willetts, Austin Nerge, Andrea Willetts, Kent Willetts, Gabbie Cramer, and Jimmy Nerge.

Thank you to my beta reader, April Gooding (aka @ callmestory on Twitter). Every book you touch improves tenfold.

To the bookstagrammers, booktokers, bloggers, and reviewers, thank you for your support and your never-ending passion for reading. You make the book world go round!

And finally, thank you to my readers. You're the reason I get to do what I love. And I don't think I could ever say thank you enough!